Callow
By N. S. Scholl

Part one of the Ardenti Terra Series

This is a work of fiction. Names, characters, businesses, places, events, locales, and incidents are either the products of the author's imagination or used in a fictitious manner. Any resemblance to actual persons, living or dead, or actual events is purely coincidental.
Cover photo by Maya Seymour

Copyright © 2018 N.S. Scholl
All rights reserved.

All rights reserved. No part of this publication may be reproduced, distributed, or transmitted in any form or by any means, including photocopying, recording, or other electronic or mechanical methods, without the prior written permission of the publisher, except in the case of brief quotations embodied in critical reviews and certain other noncommercial uses permitted by copyright law

ISBN-13: 978-1718850835
ISBN-10: 1718850832

Thank you
N.Mc., and D.M.
For your support and encouragement.

Callow

July
Chapter One
America

In 1964, the song "Eve of Destruction" was written by nineteen-year-old P.F. Sloan. At the time, people believed that the lyrics were an attack on the system, but in truth, the song pleads for help and attention during a desperate time. The song tried to give a small glimmer of hope and suggested that society could still be saved.

Don't you understand, what I'm trying to say?
And can't you feel the fears I'm feeling today?
If the button is pushed, there's no running away,
There'll be no one to save with the world in a grave,
Take a look around you, boy, it's bound to scare you, boy,
And you tell me over and over and over again my friend,
Ah, you don't believe we're on the eve of destruction.

Over fifty years later, the song lyrics seemed truer than ever. Except that, shortly before he died, Sloan told the *Wall Street Journal* that the song "sounds naïve — especially in today's world, with ISIS, ongoing wars and all these terror attacks. I was coming from the point of view that we can fix this, really — if we put our attention to it. Talk about naïve." Two years after his death, Sloan's statement during the interview was even more true; it was clear how beyond repair the world had become.

The world had changed radically in just six months. The American people had wanted change from what they felt was an unfair and corrupt government, so they elected the candidate that was the farthest from a traditional politician they could find. In just the first few months after taking office, the new President had insulted America's closest allies, provoked America's enemies, and brought the country to the brink of a civil and international war. Their unconventional President was quickly looking less than ideal, and protests spread across the county and around the world. Terrorist groups took advantage of the political misalignment and started to build strength. North America and Europe were repeatedly put on heightened alters.

It was the beginning of the end to the way of life North America had become accustomed to. People were naïve to think that things could still be fixed.

September
Chapter Two
Matt

Matthew Bailey watched his mother as she obsessed over the morning news, he could see that the stories being reported were distressing her again. Matt ran his hands through his dark hair with concern as he watched his mother's expression; the story was on the escalating threats between North Korea and America, which meant she may turn into the paranoid, *the world is ending* mom at any time. It embarrassed him when she became paranoid, and it made him wonder if mental illness was an issue for their family. Based on the expression on her face now, Matt believed she wasn't far from falling into a rant about a pending war or insisting impeachment. Though Matt wouldn't classify her as completely batshit crazy, he sometimes wondered if they were just one news report away from seeing her go postal or insist that they all become hermits in the Rocky Mountains.

Matt had lived in the same modest house his entire life. His parents had chosen to move out to the suburbs shortly after they were married, and the Baileys quickly became the average middle-class, suburban family. They had their two kids, Matt age sixteen, and Grace age eight. Mark and Heather were a sickly cute couple, and even after eighteen years of marriage, they still looked at each other like newlyweds.

Matt's father, Mark, was head of security for the largest buildings in the city's financial district—not exactly the most glamorous job, but it paid the bills. His mother, Heather, was working her way up the corporate ladder at the Canadian branch of a large international bank. She had recently been promoted to management in transaction analytics (whatever that meant) and had been putting long hours in to impress her new boss.

Today, Heather was concerned with the reports of more riots in various cities in the U.S. including a large protest in Manhattan.

"Looks like your New York office might not be too productive again today," Mark, said as he gave his wife a kiss.

"Looks like," Heather said with a sigh. "So, you found your keys?"

"Right where I left them apparently, ready to go Gracie? I'll drop you at school today."

Grace pulled herself from her cereal bowl. "Do I have to go to school? It's so boring."

"The school year has just started, honey. You can't complain until at least December." Mark pulled on his uniform jacket and motioned for Grace to hurry.

Grace gave her mom a hug and followed her father out of the house.

Matt hazarded a glance at his mother while he finished his breakfast. She was at the kitchen table with her laptop open in front of her, but her emails were neglected as she concentrated on the next news story. In addition to the political issues south of the border, there were also increasing international threats by terrorist groups. Matt knew these news reports were a recipe for disaster, and he could see Heather was on the verge of yelling at the TV again. She clenched her jaw tightly and started to type angrily on her laptop as she drafted an email.

"You know Mom, you can always un-volunteer, for tomorrow, it's no big deal," Matt said, trying to distract her.

Heather stared her son down before replying. "Why would you want me to cancel?"

"I just know you're busy—I wouldn't want you to get behind at work."

"Well, I appreciate your concern, but I'm sure a half day volunteering at your school for Career Day won't put me that far behind." Heather sighed.

Matt was worried, not about her workload, but what she would say in front of his classmates. She was often very vocal on her opinions regarding American politics, which she shared to whomever was unfortunate to engage her. It was disconcerting to take her out in public sometimes. She was preparing for an apocalypse, making sure there was always bottled water in the cold cellar, filling her car up with gas as soon as it was a quarter empty, and keeping a large stock of canned food in the basement.

Matt had tried to discuss his concerns with his father once and suggested that they cancel the news channels from their cable subscription. His father had just laughed at him, but Matt couldn't help feeling his parents were holding something back. He hoped his mother would tone it down when she presented to his classmates. Besides, the school already had one teacher, Mr. Roland, scaring the hell out of everyone by claiming the world was on the brink of a nuclear war—Matt didn't need his mom adding to the crazy.

"Don't worry, I'll make sure that my presentation is interesting," she assured him.

"So, you're going to lie about what you do?" Matt smirked.

"I don't need to! Do you even understand what I do Matt?"

Matt rolled his eyes. "Does anyone?" He picked up his now-empty cereal bowl and placed it in the sink, gave his mom a quick kiss on the cheek and grabbed his school bag from the floor.

"Bye Mom, see you at dinner."

Matt's walk to school was a long one, but while the weather was nice, he preferred walking rather than taking the school bus. His daily route took him past his best friend's house, and this morning, like all other mornings, he found Liam Allens waiting for him on the front porch. Liam was a year ahead of Matt in school and would be graduating in the spring. They had been friends for over a decade, shared a love for baseball and had played on the same teams together for several years.

It was late September and the two friends were a month into their school year. Their school had only a few hundred students, which was a small population compared to the city schools that held a few thousand students. But the small school meant that everyone knew everyone and everyone else's business. It was very hard to keep things private there.

"Are you limping?" Matt asked as he noticed his friend favoring his right side as he joined him on the sidewalk.

"It's nothing, just slept funny," Liam replied.

"We still have a game left this season, you better be able to play next week."

"I'm fine. So, is your mom still on the agenda for tomorrow's Career Day?" Liam changed the subject.

"At this point yes," Matt sighed. "I think she may be looking forward to it, so I feel guilty trying to make her cancel."

"Why are you so worried about it anyway?" Liam criticized.

"I'm just worried she's going to embarrass herself—and me." Matt watched his feet as he walked. He was feeling guilty, but he wasn't sure he really wanted all his classmates to have so much insight into his personal life.

"What does she do, anyway? I know she works at a bank, but what does she do there? IT stuff?" Liam asked, ignoring the concern in Matt's voice.

"No, she's a manger in transaction analytics." Matt offered no more explanation.

"What does that mean?" Liam continued to inquire.

"Hell if I know," Matt shrugged. "Let's move it or we'll be late."

"How long until you get your driver's license?" Liam groaned.

"I only just passed my learner's permit test; I still have to book my lessons," Matt explained.

"Well could you hurry it up? I don't want to be doing this walk in the winter."

Matt's eyes were starting to get heavy in his history class. It was fourth period and the day was almost done, but the last class always seemed to be the longest. Although it was a *history* class, these days the lessons focused more on current events. Mr. Roland was discussing the threat of war between the U.S. and North Korea. North Korea had threatened the U.S. with a mini nuclear warhead that could fit into a missile and reach the U.S. homeland. The U.S. President had responded with harsh words and counter threats. Mr. Roland was using the current situation to recap the lessons on the

Cold War. Even though, according to Mr. Roland, they were "living history," Matt felt far removed from the conflict and any threat. These were concerns for the U.S., not Canada; he knew he was safe north of the border. Who would ever want to attack Canada anyway? The world loved Canada. He had tried to watch the news the night before, like Mr. Roland had requested, but the public interest story of a pink dolphin sighting in Louisiana was the only story he could remember (who knew dolphins could be pink!).

"The U.S. is making it clear that they do not want a regime change in North Korea; they only want to remove the weapons. But the U.S. has not really stated what they are willing to accept, nor have they clearly stated what they will do to stop North Korea," Mr. Roland was saying.

"Mr. Roland," a girl in the front row, Emily, raised her hand and continued without waiting to be called on. "The news I watched last night was telling people what they should do to survive a nuclear attack. The news lady said find a cave or hide in your basement. Would that make a difference?"

"It would depend where the bomb was dropped. Many people who survive the blast would quickly, or eventually, die of radiation, as we saw in Japan in World War II."

Although the U.S. news was advising Americans to be ready and hide in their basements (or caves) if a nuclear war starts, the Canadian news was a little more level headed (and airing stories about Pink Dolphins). Mr. Roland liked the American news channels and used them to terrify the students at the end of each day. Each lesson that week had left the class in a deep depression and in fear of a fast-approaching doomsday. Matt figured that eventually someone would have to report Mr. Roland to the guidance counsellor before the whole class needed to be prescribed Prozac.

Mr. Roland pulled up pictures of Hiroshima from his iPad and projected them to the smartboard. The class had heard a lot about Hiroshima that week already. Matt stared blankly at the black and white photo of the mushroom cloud on the screen. Then there was a picture of the destroyed city, again in black and white, and piles of rubble everywhere, except for the skeleton of one building. It looked like it may have been a church, standing in the middle of the rubble. There were more pictures, hurt people being treated, more aerial pictures of the rubble, more hurt people, and finally a picture of a small child holding a puppy. This picture stuck with Matt. Matt couldn't tell if the child was a boy or girl. In the background he could see the destroyed buildings, but the child's expression stayed with Matt. The child wasn't sad, scared or crying. It had a blank face, looking into the camera, telling the world, "I'm going to die."

The picture was there to remind the world of what they had allowed to happen, and now the world was threatening to do it again. *Do the leaders of North Korea and the U.S. not see the same pictures that Mr. Roland has?* Matt thought. *Do they not Google, like everyone else?* The idea of one person having the ability to inflict so much pain and death on a society disturbed, but also intrigued, Matt. Just as Matt was about to contemplate booking a meeting with the school's psychologist for his Prozac prescription, the bell rang to confirm the end of the school day. Thoroughly depressed, he grabbed his bag and rushed out the door to find Liam at his locker.

"Do you ever worry about a war starting?" Matt asked Liam as they walked out of the building.

"Shit! Is it Mr. Roland's class? He's getting to you again?" Liam forced concern into his voice.

"I guess a bit. It makes me wonder if we are taking it for granted that we feel so safe."

"We're safe, we're in Canada. When does anything bad ever happen in Canada?" Liam laughed.

"See, that's what I was thinking," Matt surrendered. "I guess it's just the class getting to me."

When Matt got home he found his little sister giggling in the living room with her babysitter, Amy Campbell. Like Liam, Amy was a year ahead of Matt in school. She drove, so she was able to pick Grace up from elementary school and take care of her until either Matt or one of his parents got home. Usually Matt would have a ball practice or a game after school, but when he didn't, he had personal motives to rush home, so he could spend some time with Amy. In Matt's eyes Amy was the perfect girl: smart, beautiful and not stuck up. He had been infatuated with her for years, and when his parents hired her as Grace's babysitter, he thought he had lucked out. But he never had the courage to take any initiative; their interactions were limited to subtle flirting. Even though he was a year younger than her, Amy never treated him badly and would sometimes even talk to him at school. Matt was certain that Amy had no clue about his true feelings, and he was positive there was no chance she would consider dating a younger guy. Matt therefore made sure his flirting was innocent and low key.

"Good evening ladies," he said as he walked into the living room. Amy and Grace were hovering over a board game pretending to argue over the rules. Amy would do this with

Grace, pretend not to understand simple rules of the games to make Grace laugh. Matt knew full well Amy was a top student who made honour roll every year. He was sure Amy could understand the rules for the game *Sorry*.

"Hi Matt," Grace gave a wave over her shoulder to him. Amy gave him a quick smile.

"Was grade three exciting today?" Matt ruffled Grace's hair as he walked past her and took a seat of the sofa.

"Nope," Grace responded as she moved her marker on the board game. Apparently, that was the winning move, because Grace jumped to her feet and started a victory dance.

"Well played," Amy said as she packed up the game. Matt knew that Amy would be leaving now that he was home; his opportunity to start a conversation with her was quickly disappearing.

"So, Amy are you taking history with Mr. Roland this term?" Matt asked.

"Oh yeah, it's been interesting." Amy rolled her eyes.

"I think the man has finally cracked up," Matt said, trying to sound casual and cool.

"Well if he hasn't he will after tonight," Amy said as she nodded her head toward the TV. Matt turned to see that the TV was on, but muted. The U.S. news channel was on and the *Breaking News* headline stated that North Korea had bombed Guam.

"What's Guam?" Matt asked forgetting to sound cool.

"It's a small island, it's a U.S. territory in the western Pacific Ocean," Amy answered, still watching TV. "There's a lot of U.S. military bases there, but it's really close to North Korea, at least it's the closest U.S. territory to North Korea."

Matt turned the sound on for the TV.

"It is unclear how many causalities there are at this time, but early reports are indicating that the military base has significant damage," the news lady was reporting. "Currently, only satellite phones are working. It seems that the whole island may have lost power. The U.S. government has confirmed that they have been in contact with some military personnel in Guam, but they are not releasing any specific details."

"What happened Matt?" Grace had turned her attention to the TV. Matt quickly hit mute on the remote again; he wasn't sure how to explain this to an eight-year-old.

"I'm not sure Grace, we will have to see what Mom and Dad can tell us when they get home. You know, if you have any homework, you better get that done now." Matt noticed Grace's expression indicated that she was not impressed about having to do her homework, but at least she was distracted for now.

"OK fine," Grace sighed, heading to her room with her school bag.

"Do you think they can bomb North America?" Amy said once they heard Grace's door close.

"They claimed that they could, didn't they?" Matt shrugged.

"This is kind of scary. I know they are still thousands and thousands of miles away, but it still feels too close to home, like everything Mr. Roland was saying is coming true." Amy shuddered. "I need to get home," Amy said suddenly, and she quickly headed towards the front door.

"Sure, are you going to be OK? I mean, are you OK to head home alone?" Matt was worried for her; she seemed a little stunned.

"I'll be fine. Thanks Matt, I'll see you tomorrow." Amy headed out the front door. Matt watched from the door as she got in her car.

Once he was alone, Matt turned back to the TV and searched through the channels. Every channel had interrupted their regular shows to air news coverage of the bombings. No new information was available, but some channels were airing "expert" panelists who were discussing why the bombing had happened. Apparently, the panelists were ready to lay blame on the President as much as North Korea. Eventually it was confirmed that the President would be making a statement at eight p.m. Matt checked the clock; it was six p.m. He had been watching the news for almost an hour; Mr. Roland would have been proud. Matt heard the front door open, and based on the footsteps, he knew it was his dad coming home.

"Hello?" Mark called from the hall way. "Where is everyone?"

"Daddy!" Grace yelled as she came running down the stairs to give her father a hug.

"Hi Princess, how are you?"

"I finished all my homework!" Grace gloated.

"Good girl!" Mark replied as he hugged her back a little longer than usual. "I have an idea!" Mark suddenly changed to a cheerful voice. "Let's order a pizza for dinner. Mom will be working late, and I don't feel like cooking today."

"Yeah! Pizza," Grace cheered. "I'll get the iPad."

Grace quickly returned with the iPad and scrolled through the menu, picking dinner through the pizza delivery app. Matt pulled his dad aside. "The President is making a statement at eight p.m. tonight."

"Yes, I heard, I'll have to explain this to Grace before then. There are a lot of scared people out there right now."

"Dad, do we need to be worried?" Matt asked, he had been engrossed by the news coverage. The death and pain were like nothing he had seen before, but it still felt distant; he thought nothing like that could ever happen to him.

"I'm not sure. Maybe ask me after we hear what the President says. Your mom's bank has asked everyone to stay late today. They have been told that the stock markets might be closed tomorrow, so they are preparing for that."

Matt wasn't sure what that meant and why his mother needed to stay late. Selfishly, he hoped that meant that she would be cancelling on Career Day.

"Matt, don't worry," Mark misread Matt's concerned look. "We will be fine. We are in Canada after all. Even if the U.S. goes to war, Canada will likely not be impacted directly."

Matt had a feeling that his dad meant "attacked" or "bombed," not "impacted," but he wasn't going to ask for clarification. Impacted sounded so much better.

"OK, I picked what I want," Grace said, waving the iPad at them. Mark took the iPad to review the order. "This looks perfect," he said. "I'll order everything you picked."

"OK, I'll go set the table." Grace ran off to the kitchen.

"Let's pretend it's a picnic," Mark called after her. "Use paper plates."

"You just don't want to do dishes." Matt laughed.

"Do you?" Mark winked back at him.

Matt and Mark tried to keep themselves busy as they waited for pizza, but more so for eight p.m. to arrive. Just before eight, they heard the front door open and Heather walk in.

"I didn't think you would be home so early," Mark said as he greeted his wife at the door with a hug.

"I promised that I would sign on at home and keep an eye on my emails," Heather said as she pulled her laptop out of her bag. "Has the President started speaking yet?"

"No not yet. We are just waiting for that. I sent Grace for a bath."

"I think it's starting," Matt called from the family room. They all gathered on the sofas to watch.

The TV was showing the White House press room with a small podium. Just next to the podium was the American flag. Instead of the President standing at the podium, there was a man Matt didn't recognize.

"Who is that?" he asked his parents.

"He is the secretary of defence," Heather answered.

"Thank you all for waiting," the man on the TV was saying. "At this time, we wanted to provide the American people and the world with an update on the situation in Guam." He paused as he seemed to wait for a teleprompter to progress. "We can confirm that six missiles hit Guam this morning. These missiles were launched by North Korea. Initially, a total of ten missiles were launched, but thanks to the quick actions of our allies in Japan, four of the ten missiles were destroyed before they reached their intended targets. At this time, we can't confirm the exact number of casualties. The residents had a fifteen-minute warning, which we received from our allies in that region, and a good number of the citizens in Guam were able to find safety. The island has lost power, but we hope to have this, and other essential services restored quickly. We also have relief and support personnel on their way to the island from America, and closer allied countries have already sent medical and humanitarian support, which is arriving this evening." The secretary of defence paused again and focused his gaze into the camera. "What North Korea did today was an act of war on America and all democratic countries. America will not tolerate any attack against our people. We will work with our allies to respond and neutralize North Korea so that no more Americans or citizens from other countries will be harmed. I'm sorry I will not be taking any questions, but I promise that we will provide updates as soon as we have further information to provide." With that, the secretary of defence walked off camera. Several reporters could be heard asking questions from behind the camera, but they were ignored.

"I don't understand." Matt turned to his parents. "What did all that mean? And why was the President not talking?"

"I don't think they trust the President to handle this situation," Heather responded with a smirk. "The secretary of defence was telling North Korea and the world that the President isn't the one calling the shots now."

"That's good?" Matt asked.

"Yes, I think so. They haven't outright said that the President is not in charge, but they made it clear that whatever happens next will be a global response."

"Won't that just start World War III?"

"No. No one wants that," Heather continued. "Once you have the reasonable people involved negotiating, then it will be with minimal military action. With enough global support behind the U.S., the leaders in North Korea will likely step down, or at least stop their attacks on the U.S."

"So, we don't need to activate our emergency exit plan?" Mark laughed.

"Not yet," Heather responded, but without the humour or sarcasm.

Matt heard his mom on the phone early the next morning. She had started her work day well before anyone else was awake and did not leave her home office, even to join the rest of the family for breakfast. She did yell down the stairs as Matt was leaving to confirm she would see him later in school for the Career Day presentations.

Later that morning, Matt found himself in the crowded auditorium, where the grade eleven and twelve students had gathered to hear the Career Day presentations. There were six parents volunteering, and everyone was asked to present a quick overview and then they would station themselves around the auditorium to take questions from students on a one-on-one basis. The parents selected came from very different industries and held various positions. Matt was only half listening; he hadn't decided what he wanted to do after school, but it would not be a desk job. He had been considering being a firefighter. Two years of school still seemed like a lifetime to Matt, and he wasn't sure that he wanted to go to college or university and spend another four years studying. He hadn't told his parents he was interested in becoming a firefighter, but he was sure his parents would tell him it was too dangerous and try to stop him; he felt they had raised him as a "bubble wrapped" child. Eventually Heather took the stage and started her presentation.

"Good morning everyone," Heather said confidently. "My name is Heather Bailey. I work in transaction analytics, specifically in the anti-money-laundering division for a bank. My role basically is to prevent terrorist or organized crime groups from laundering money through our bank. I have a quick video I want to show you."

Heather hit a couple of keys on her laptop, and a video projected on the smartboard. The video was from a government organization that was the analysis centre for the financial transaction reporting from all the banks and investment companies. They used examples of the cases they saw and how the reports from the bank helped them prevent crime and terrorist attacks.

"So, my role is to monitor all our transactions and report anything fishy to the reporting centres at the government," Heather said after the video was done. "Obviously, I can't give you too many specific details, but there have been some interesting cases I have worked on. I have found money coming from biker gangs, drug dealers, and even a Nigerian prince, and ladies I can tell you that he was no prince." The audience gave a small laugh to that. Overall, everyone seemed to still be listening to her. Heather finished by answering some of the scripted questions from the teachers that everyone had been given. What schooling was needed for her career? What are the best parts of her job and what are the worst? Once all the presentations were completed, the speakers headed to their designated spots for the one-on-one times. Students were encouraged to speak with the parents to have their specific questions answered. Matt looked around the auditorium but had no interest to speak to anyone directly. Suddenly he found Amy beside him.

"You know, your mom's job is pretty cool," Amy said to him.

"You're actually interested in that kind of stuff?" Matt was thrilled to be talking to Amy, even if the topic was his mom.

"Sure, I like the numbers aspect; it sounds like putting a massive puzzle together."

"So, are you going to talk to her more?" Matt asked.

"I think I might wait and talk to her one night after school. She has a big crowd around her, and I get to see her all the time anyway."

Matt turned to see his mom at the far end of the auditorium talking to a group of students. Even Liam was standing there.

"Geez, I never thought she would be so popular." Matt sighed.

"I don't think you give your mom enough credit," Amy said and walk away.

"Dude your mom has some really cool stories," Liam was saying as they were walking home after ball practice. "I think what she does would be awesome. You get paid to watch money all day; how cool is that? Do you ever worry that some of the bad guys would ever come after her? You know, like the mafia or biker gangs?"

Matt stopped walking, "*No!*" he said, horrified. "She's just my mom. She's not like the CIA or something. Besides, everything she does is anonymous; they shouldn't be able to track it back to her. Otherwise the system wouldn't work."

"Sorry, I didn't realize you were so protective." Liam threw his hands up in a mock surrender.

"It's just strange to think of my mom having a life outside of the family. I mean, I know a bit about her job, it's just that she normally doesn't talk about it, or she can't talk about it."

Matt didn't want to talk about his mother, especially with Liam. Matt purposely avoided conversations about family with Liam ever since Liam's mother had abandoned him and his brothers. Liam's sudden interest in Heather's job confused Matt. He never thought Liam to be the desk-job type, as he would likely go to university on a baseball scholarship.

"You know you need to be really good in math if you want to do a job like that," Matt said, hoping to discourage Liam.

"I do alright in math," Liam responded but offered nothing further. Matt never asked Liam about grades. Since he was a year ahead of Matt, they were never in the same classes, so Matt realized that he had no clue how well Liam did in his classes, but Matt always assumed Liam wasn't the academic type.

"So, are we still on for this weekend?" Liam asked, changing the subject.

"For the movie? Yeah of course," Matt replied.

"OK great, text me later," Liam called over his shoulder as he headed to his house.

When Matt got home, he found Amy taking care of Grace, even though his mother was home.

"Hey Amy, is everything alright?" Matt asked as he joined them in the kitchen. Amy was making Grace a sandwich.

"Oh yeah, everything is fine. Your mom just asked me to stick around until you got home. She had a lot of work to do and wanted to make sure Grace wouldn't disturb her. But now that you are home, I need to head out."

"Hot date tonight?" Matt meant to tease her, but realized it sounded creepy.

"Um, no, not a date." Amy blushed. "It sounds stupid, but I'm actually going to have movie night with my grandma. I try to do that once a month. You know she's getting old and I worry she is lonely."

"That's cool," Matt said. "What are you going to watch?"

"I have to take a DVD over; she doesn't like to leave the apartment much anymore, so I was thinking of getting her started on *Game of Thrones*."

"Seriously?" Matt asked, shocked.

"No!" Amy laughed. "That may give her a heart attack! She has a thing for Robert Redford, so it might be *Out of Africa* again."

"Or the second Capitan America movie," Matt suggested as she headed to leave.

"Oh, I'm sure she would *love* that. See you Monday Matt." Amy gave him one last smile before she left. Matt's heart skipped a beat—she had a great smile.

Matt headed upstairs to find his mom. He wanted to see if he should start dinner, but as he approached the office, the door was open slightly and he could hear his mom on the phone.

"Are you telling me that you were able to trace that money back to a bank in Russia?" Heather was saying.

"It was buried, but yes, eventually, I found it," the voice on the speaker phone answered. It was a male voice; he was talking softly like he didn't want to be overheard.

"But how do we know there is a connection to North Korea?" Heather asked.

"I'm not certain, but I believe that the account is held by a Russian company that was flagged on the OFAC list. This Russian company supports North Korea."

"How did we not see it earlier?"

"They layered it well. It took awhile to find the path."

"Kevin, if this is true, there is a chance that our bank helped to indirectly fund the...."

"Heather, we haven't confirmed anything yet," Kevin interrupted. "And the money has already moved, so we may never be able to confirm."

"But shouldn't we be reporting it now?"

"We still have a little time; let me do some more digging. I would hate to get this one wrong." Kevin was almost whispering in the phone.

"OK thanks. Give me a call when you know."

Matt heard Heather disconnect the call. He wasn't sure what he had just heard, but he knew that he shouldn't have heard it. He waited a moment and then made a point of walking heavily up and down the hall before knocking on the door.

"Hey Mom, do you want me to get dinner started?" he asked as he pushed the door open.

"Yes please," Heather answered, a little startled. "I didn't know you were home already." She looked distracted and stressed. She was reading spreadsheets on her screen.

"OK I'll let you know when it's ready," Matt said as he slowly backed out of the room, trying to see her screen.

"Thanks hon," Heather mumbled as she kept her eyes on the spreadsheets, but then suddenly she turned her attention to Matt. "Matt, hold on a minute."

"Yeah Mom?" Matt was worried that she would ask him about the conversation he had just heard.

"Do you think the Career Day went OK? I mean, I didn't embarrass you at all, did I?"

Matt let out a small laugh, maybe what he had overheard wasn't that serious if she was worried about Career Day. "You did fine, Mom. And it looked like a few kids were interested in finding out more. You got Liam's attention anyway."

"He's a good kid. You didn't seem very interested in anything though. I noticed that you didn't talk to anyone after, except Amy." Heather stared at her son, waiting for a response, even though she hadn't actually asked a question.

"None of those speakers were in the line of work that I'm considering." Ignoring the jab about Amy, he turned to leave again.

"So, what is it you are considering?" Heather asked before he could leave.

"OK Mom, if I tell you, please don't get mad." Matt pause for a second and then blurted out, "I want to be a fireman."

"Really?" Heather's response was more of a surprise than anger. "What made you start thinking about that?"

"I have been thinking about it for awhile. I was just worried about telling you guys; I didn't think you would support that choice since it's dangerous."

"If that's what you really want to do, we will support you Matt," Heather walked over to her son and gave him a hug. "Obviously I would never want you to be hurt, but I like that you have a direction and a plan. I'm surprised you were worried about telling us." She paused for a minute and then added, "how about we go for a drive after dinner and you can practice."

"Really? That would be great!"

"OK, let me finish up here and you start dinner. Your father will be home soon too."

It was hard to feel calm and cool with his mom in the passenger seat critiquing every move he made, but Matt tried to enjoy his time behind the wheel. He hadn't had many opportunities to drive yet, but he was feeling confident in his abilities. On the few occasions he'd had to drive he realized he really enjoyed it. There was something about being behind the wheel of a car that made him feel like he had power and control.

"You are doing well Matt. I'm sorry, I don't mean to be so hard on you," Heather apologized. "Do you want to try the highway?"

"Are you being serious?"

"If you think you are ready?"

"Yes," Matt blurted out before he really thought of his answer. He wanted to try a faster speed, but now a nervousness was turning in the pit of his stomach.

"OK, the highway ramp is coming up. Stay in the right lane."

Matt carefully signalled, checked all his blind spots and slowly eased the car to the right lane to merge onto the highway. Because it was evening, the rush hour traffic was over, and he had plenty of room on the road. He brought the car up to speed and merged safely. He was careful to keep the car right at the speed limit.

"You can go a little faster if you feel comfortable. No one drives right on the speed limit. And you need to learn how to handle a car at a higher speed."

Matt increased the speed by another five kilometres. His heart was racing; this was the fastest he had ever driven, but even at that speed the cars were flying past him. He pressed his foot on the gas a little more until he was doing one hundred ten kilometres an hour. He risked a quick glance at his mom, but she didn't protest.

"Push it a little more; traffic is going around one hundred twenty. Try it if you feel like you can," Heather said casually.

"OK," Matt said, he was focusing hard on the road. He pushed the gas pedal down more, to match the speed of the car in front of him. He looked at the odometer: one hundred twenty-three kilometres an hour. His heart was racing, and he could feel the adrenaline rushing through him; he was feeling excited and terrified at the same time.

"Remember Matt, that at this speed, everything happens faster, and your reactions need to be much faster. You will get use to this, but always make sure that you are paying attention. Take the next exit though; we will take the backroads home."

Matt realized that his hands were sweating as he signalled and merged into the exit lane. He also realized that he had been holding his breath for a good part of the ride. He took a deep breath as he stopped at the lights and waited to take his turn. His heart slowed, and he felt disappointed that the rush was over.

"You OK?" Heather asked.

"Yeah, just a bit of a rush going that fast."

"Well, the car can go much faster. I don't want you trying it. Be smart, you were going a bit too fast just now." Matt was about to apologize when his mother continued. "But I'm glad you did while I was with you, you handled it fine. I'm proud of you."

They drove in silence back to the house. Matt pulled up into the driveway, parked the car and handed the keys to his mom. He was about to get out of the car when she held his arm.

"If you needed to, you would know how to get to our cottage, right?" she asked.

"Yes, I think so," Matt said, aware that crazy mom was about to surface.

"Without GPS?" Heather was sounding urgent. Matt was worried this was another one of her paranoid moments.

"Sure, it's fairly easy."

"Listen to me Matt—this is important. If anything should happen, if there is ever a threat to the city or it's not safe here, you take your sister and head to the cottage. Take one of the cars and head up there. You will be safe."

"Geez Mom, what are you talking about?" Matt was getting tired of this.

"I just want to make sure you know what to do. You realize that if anything should happen, your father and I could be stuck in the city. Transportation would likely be shut down and we wouldn't have any easy way to get home."

"But why would we leave?" Matt demanded.

"Only if there is a threat." Heather calmed her tone. "There is a nuclear power plant between our home and the city. If there is a threat, it could be against the power plant, which means you need to leave immediately. The cottage is the best bet; you will be safe there." Heather noticed Matt rolling his eyes. "This is important," she pleaded. "There is a box in the garage. I have marked it 'cottage stuff,' but it has a few supplies you need to take with you: water purification tablets, iodine pills, first aid stuff, and medicine. I've wanted to take it up there before now but haven't had the chance. Make sure you take that with you OK? The items in there could save your life. You take your sister and go to the cottage and we will try to meet you there."

"Do you really think there is going to be a nuclear war, Mom?" Matt didn't mean to sound sarcastic.

Heather hesitated only for a moment and then replied, "No, I don't, but I just want to be prepared. It scares me that I may not be able to protect my children. I just want to make sure that you and your sister are safe. There are terrorist attacks all over the world these days, and I think Canada has just been lucky so far. And since we live by the biggest city in Canada, we need to be a little more vigilant. Look at the bombing that happened a few weeks ago in England. The terrorists bombed a concert that was mostly attended by teenage girls. There are new horrors in this world, not just this conflict with the U.S. and North Korea, and we would be silly not to take some protective measures."

"OK Mom, don't worry. Exit plan is to grab Grace and head to the cottage. Got it." Matt wanted to end of the conversation. When he looked over at his mom, she had tears in her eyes. "Mom, thanks." He changed his tone to calm her. "I appreciate the driving lesson, and don't worry, I will take care of Gracie if anything should happen."

That seemed to be what she wanted to hear. She gave him a nod and opened the car door. Matt sat only for a second longer and took a few breaths. It had been an interesting evening.

Matt's head was racing as he lay in bed that night. He had enjoyed driving on the highway. The speed had been exciting and had made him want to try again soon. But with his learner's permit, he had to drive with his parents until he passed his road tests. Matt wondered if his father would have allowed him to drive on the highway, let alone go almost twenty-five kilometres over the speed limit.

He was worried about his mother too. She was getting more paranoid by the day. There had been a lot in the news the last few days. The attack by North Korea was still the biggest concern. The allies were holding an emergency meeting, and the U.S. President and the Canadian Prime Minister were attending. Still, protests demanded the President's resignation in many U.S. cities, most turning into riots. The national guard had been called in to help in several states. The terrorists used this opportunity to increase their threats against the U.S. again. Whether there was actually a pending attack seemed unlikely, but the terrorists were taking full advantage of the chaos to scare people further.

Matt rolled over in bed and saw his alarm was showing half past midnight. He sighed; he wasn't falling asleep soon. He got up and get a glass of milk. Everyone else was asleep and the house was quiet. He looked in at Grace quickly and saw she was snoring softly, surrounded by her stuffed animals. He headed downstairs to the kitchen and opened the refrigerator. He reached for the milk and stopped. There were beers chilling in fridge. Matt stopped reaching for the milk and picked up one of the beers; the bottle was damp and looked inviting. He had never had a beer before, but he was tempted to try one. He wondered if his dad would notice one beer missing. Then he thought of his mother and how she had let him speed on the highway that evening. She had trusted him to be responsible, and suddenly he felt guilty that he was thinking of betraying that trust. He put the beer back on the shelf and picked up the milk instead.

As he headed back up to his room with his warm milk, he heard a car engine running outside. Matt peeked through the front window curtains and saw a black sedan parked in front of the house. It was too dark to see the driver, but the driver must have seen him. The car drove away almost immediately. Matt wondered if their house was being sized up for a robbery. He was hoping he had scared them away. *Or is it just a guest leaving the neighbours house?* Matt thought. *Geez, Mom is really getting in my head.* Matt headed upstairs to drink his milk and hope for better luck with sleep.

Chapter Three
Matt

Matt's cell phone buzzed with text messages early the next morning. Liam was sending movie times to him.

"Why do I have to be best friends with the only teenager in the world that doesn't sleep in on a Saturday?" Matt mumbled as he read through the messages. Liam was also asking Matt to meet him at the park to hit baseballs before the movie. Matt rolled out of bed and headed downstairs, where the rest of his family was already having breakfast.

"You're up early," Mark said as Matt walked in.

"Liam decided to be my alarm clock this morning," Matt said, waving his phone at his dad and yawning.

"So, what are you planning today?" Heather asked over her cup of coffee.

"He wants to hit some balls and then head to a movie, if that's OK?"

"Of course, sounds fine. Not much going on for us today. We may take Grace over to the playground since the weather is so warm still. Shall we all meet for dinner then?" Heather looked hopeful at Matt.

"That sounds good. I'll be home by six." Matt grabbed some toast. "I'm going to go meet Liam, I'll be back in a bit to shower before the movie." Matt gave them a quick wave with the toast and headed out to the garage, where he collected his ball equipment and headed to the ball diamond.

He found Liam already at the park running laps of the outfield. They both played for the high school varsity baseball team, and staying fit was a high priority for them, but Liam was a lot more motivated than Matt.

"Come on, Sleeping Beauty, get your ass out here," Liam called from right field as he circled for another lap.

Matt sprinted over to catch up with Liam. "Geez man, you do know it is Saturday, right?"

Liam laughed, "Yeah, and could you think of a better way to spend it?" he joked as he picked up his speed, forcing Matt to sprint hard to keep up with him.

"I've only had a piece of toast so far for breakfast," Matt complained.

"Oh, is that why you are running slower than my grandma?" Liam joked, speeding up even more.

"You know I can still beat your ass even though I'm half asleep," Matt challenged. "First one to the fence, go!" Both Matt and Liam sprinted at top speed to the third base line fence, but Matt was quickly ahead of Liam. Matt may not have been as built as Liam, but he was still tall and ridiculously fast. Matt reached the fence a full stride ahead of Liam, and they were both out of breath.

"You know Matt," Liam panted. "Maybe you could get a scholarship for university in the States if you worked a little harder at it."

"Geez, you sound like my dad," Matt scolded. "Besides, you know I want be a firefighter—no need for me to go to school in the States."

"Wouldn't you rather play in the major leagues?" Liam asked.

"I really don't think that's going to happen," Matt sighed. "I like playing, but I think I'm a long way from being good enough for the major leagues. Come on, let's hit."

They took turns hitting fly balls as the sun moved higher into the sky, and eventually they were hot and tired enough to call it quits.

"We have to see an earlier show; I promised my mom I would be home for dinner tonight," Matt told Liam as they were packing up.

"OK sure, just let me know when you are ready to go, and I'll come by," Liam said as he headed back to his house. "Make sure you have a good shower — you friggin' stink."

Matt shook his head as his friend walked away. As Matt approached the top of his street, he noticed the black Sedan parked in front of his house again. This time he could see a man sitting in the front seat, talking on a phone. The man had dark hair and was wearing dark sunglasses and looked agitated about something as he spoke. As Matt got closer, the man ended his phone conversation. He looked in Matt's direction, and then started his car and drove off. Matt wasn't certain that the man had looked at him directly, but he was certain that he didn't recognize the car as one from the neighbourhood. He wondered why it would be back again this morning and felt uneasy.

Matt came home to an empty house; his parents had made good on their promise to take Grace to the park. They would likely have taken a picnic and would be gone for a few hours. He headed upstairs and showered, picked out a clean shirt and jeans, ran a brush through his hair and contemplated if he needed a shave. He sent Liam a text to let him know that he was almost ready and then headed to the kitchen for a proper meal.

Liam was knocking on the door just as Matt was finishing his lunch: left over pizza, a side of shepherd pie, a Coke and an apple.

"Seriously guy, that could feed a village in Africa," Liam said, frowning at Matt's meal.

"I didn't get breakfast you know." Matt complained through a mouthful of pizza.

"You are disgusting. You eat like that with your mother around?"

"Like what?" Matt mumbled as he stuffed the last bites of crust into his mouth and purposely chewed with his mouth open. "By the way," he said once his mouth was empty. "My mom let me drive on the highway yesterday. I was going one twenty-three."

"Bullshit!" Liam responded. "Your mom was letting you speed on the highway?"

"I know it sounds strange, but she did."

"Why would she let you do that?" Liam exclaimed. "If you had been pulled over you would have lost your learners permit for six months and she would have gotten a ticket. I'll be walking to school forever!"

Matt raised his eyebrows, "You know you could try for your own license."

Liam frowned, "You know full well that's not an option for me."

"Sorry man, didn't mean anything by it," Matt apologized. He knew he had hit a sore spot for Liam. Although Liam would be seventeen next month, he still hadn't tried to get his learners' permit. Liam's father had always been a drunk, but when Liam's mother had walked out on them last year, things had gotten a lot worse. Liam lived alone with his father, who somehow held down a job, but when he wasn't at work he was either at some bar or passed out drunk in a chair in the family room. It was Liam's dark secret that only his closest friend knew. Matt respected Liam's privacy, and because of this, he tried to avoid family around Liam as much as possible. Every so often Liam would mention something about his personal life, like when one of his brothers had been in contact with him. Both of his brothers were older and had moved away. One was just traveling the world with no expected return date, while the other was planting trees on the west coast. Every few weeks Liam would get an email from one brother or the other with an update. Sometimes they would ask about their father, sometimes they would offer to send money to Liam, but Liam was pretty much on his own and preferred not to let anyone know about it.

    The theatre was busy for a Saturday afternoon. A few new movies had come out that weekend, which seemed to have attracted a crowd. Liam was eager to see the new action flick, with fast cars and hot chicks (as he put it). The movie was entertaining, but it certainly wasn't going to win an academy award for acting. As they were walking out of the theatre, raised voices caught Matt's attention. He heard an argument starting on the far side of the parking lot. It was a couple having a fight between some of the parked cars. They were still too far to see exactly what was happening, but Matt gave Liam a nudge and pointed in their direction.
    "Let's head that way," Matt said. Liam nodded in agreement. As they got closer, they could see that a guy was

holding his date tightly around the wrists while she was trying to push him away. He seemed to be trying to pull her into his car while the girl fought hard to avoid that.

"I don't owe you anything!" she yelled, and Matt realized that he recognized the voice.

"That's Amy," he said, and he quickly ran to towards the couple without waiting to be sure that Liam was following him. As he got closer, Matt saw Amy struggling hard against the guy's grip, which caused her to trip and fall between the cars. He saw the guy grab at her arms again, trying to pull her up and into the car.

"Leave her alone!" Matt yelled as he approached Amy and the guy. Then a few things happened almost all at once. Matt heard Amy yell his name and tell him to stay out of it, Matt shoved the guy hoping to get him to release his hold on Amy, which he did, but then he grabbed Matt by the shirt collar and landed two quick punches to Matt's face. Just as Matt felt himself fall to the pavement, he saw Liam throwing himself against the guy and holding him up against the car.

"You need to get the hell out of here buddy," Liam yelled as he delivered a quick punch to the guy's nose. Matt heard a crack and the guy yelled in pain, blood streaming from a surely broken nose. Matt could feel Amy pulling on his arm.

"Matt are you OK? Can you get up?" she was asking.

Dazed, he slowly got to his feet and saw Liam still holding the guy against the car. He threatened him with another punch, but then just shoved him down and went to help Matt. Matt let Amy and Liam guide him across the parking lot toward their neighbourhood.

"Matt, you OK?" Liam asked after they had walked a few minutes.

"Yeah, I think so," Matt replied as best he could, but he felt like his lip was dragging on the ground. It was then that he noticed Amy was still holding his arm.

"You're bleeding. Hold on, I have some tissues in my pursue," she said as she stopped. She was about to hand him the tissues and then seemed to think better of it and wiped the blood running from his lip. He was becoming painfully aware that the punches had landed on his lip and cheek. The whole left side of his face felt hard and swollen, like a bowling ball. He felt like a small child as Amy wiped his face.

"Who was that jerk?" Liam asked as Amy tried to clean up Matt.

"Oh, my lovely blind date," Amy said in a shaky sarcastic voice. "He thought that a movie and a bag of popcorn meant that I owed him a little more. Goddamn jerk wouldn't keep his hands off me during the movie, and we had just met!"

"Why on earth would someone as hot as you need to go on a blind date?" Liam said in his most charming voice, which annoyed Matt, since Liam could actually sound charming.

"I was doing a friend a favour. It had started out as a double date, but they snuck out on us halfway through the movie." She pulled more tissues out of her purse. "Thank you both so much for coming to my rescue," she said as she wiped Matt's lip again. "I'm so sorry you got hurt."

"I'm OK," Matt tried to say, but it sounded more like *Mm ODaym.*

"No, you really aren't," Amy said. "You need to get ice on this quickly. I live just over there. Come on to my place and I'll get you some ice."

Matt didn't protest as Amy led them to her place. She was still holding onto Matt's arm, but he realized this was likely because he couldn't walk in a straight line on his own. His head was pounding; his cheek was swelling, he was certain he would have a black eye and his split lip was making speech almost impossible. When they got to Amy's house, she led them to the living room, sat Matt down on the sofa and quickly returned with an ice.

"I really am sorry, Matt," Amy said again as she handed him the ice pack. She sat down next to him, and he could feel she was trembling. Matt looked down at her hands, which she was gripping tightly together, and noticed there was bruising around her wrists where she had been grabbed. He took the ice off his cheek and placed it on her wrist.

"You goof," she laughed, "you need this much more than I do." She put the pack back to Matt's face and held it there. Now she was partly leaning across him to hold the ice in place. Matt was very aware of her arm pressing gently against his chest and her leg ever so slightly touching his. Suddenly he felt his phone buzzing in his pocket; he pulled it out and saw there was a text message from his mom.

"My mom's expecting me home for dinner," Matt explained to Amy after he read the text.

"You may want to clean up a little better; she's going to have a fit when she sees you," Amy said as she stood up. "The bathroom is this way."

Amy showed Matt to the bathroom. When he finally looked at himself in the mirror, he was a little shocked at what he saw. He had a fair amount of dried blood down the front of his shirt. His lip was swollen, and his cheek was definitely bruising and turning into a black eye. He washed the dried blood off his face. He figured he would have no luck with his shirt and didn't bother trying to clean it. When he came back out of the bathroom, he found Liam and Amy standing in the living room waiting for him; they quickly stopped talking as he approached. He noticed that Amy was looking shy and embarrassed. He realized this situation must have been embarrassing for her too.

"I'll give you a ride home. That way I can apologize to your parents too," Amy explained.

They dropped Liam off first and then headed to Matt's house. Matt's head was aching terribly but having the extra time with Amy was helping him forget about that. Amy parked her car in the driveway and they walked to the house together.

"You know you don't need to come in and explain, I can handle this," Matt said before he opened the door.

"I think I better," Amy insisted. "I know how your mom can be; she's going to think the worst and jump to conclusions. She may not believe that you were saving me."

"OK, your choice. You know my mom will freak." Matt slowly opened the door. The smell of a roast beef greeted them first when they walked into the kitchen, quickly followed by Heather yelling, "Oh my god! What happened?" Heather's yell attracted Mark and Grace to the kitchen. There was a fair amount of commotion from his parents, and eventually Matt raised his voice to state he was fine but needed to sit and get some ice on his face.

As Matt settled into a chair with a new ice pack, Amy retold the story for Matt's parents. She made Matt's efforts sound a lot more heroic and downplayed Liam's role. She shared just enough details about her nightmare date to explain the situation, but again downplayed the danger. Matt noticed that Amy's story was very calculated. Heather went to give Amy a hug.

"Are your parents home tonight?" Heather asked when Amy was done telling her story.

"No, they both have night shifts," Amy replied. Her dad was a fireman and her mom a nurse and being an only child, she was left alone a fair bit.

"You have to stay for dinner and the night. I'm not letting you go home to an empty house after what you just went through."

"Thank you Mrs. Bailey that's kind. I would love to stay."

"And you," Heather turned her attention back to her son. "Do you think you may have a concussion?" She checked his eyes and fussed over him again.

"No Mom, I'm fine," Matt lied. But he didn't need to be babied, especially in front of Amy; he was sure he would live.

Heather fussed a moment longer while Matt tried to swat her hands away. "Fine, go get changed," she sighed in defeat.

When Matt came out of his room wearing a clean shirt, his father was waiting for him in the hall with a fresh ice pack.

"Keep this on your face," he said, but he didn't immediately allow him to go down for dinner. "Did things really unfold the way Amy said?" he asked.

"For the most part," Matt explained. "She left out the part that I went down like a rock after I got hit and Liam actually saved the day by breaking the dude's nose."

Mark seemed satisfied with that explanation. He pulled out his phone and quickly snapped a picture of him.

"What the hell Dad? You needed a memory of your son's first ass kicking?"

"Just in case the police get involved, I want your injuries documented. I already have pictures of Amy's wrists."

"You aren't going to call the police, are you?" Matt sounded panicked.

"Not if you don't want me to. But Amy may feel differently tomorrow. Or her date might, depends on how much Liam messed him up." Mark stared hard at his son. "Let me ask you something," he continued, his voice low, "What do you think would have happened if Liam wasn't there."

Matt didn't answer, but his mind had been asking the same question the whole ride home. He likely would have had his ass kicked a lot more and Amy wouldn't have been out of danger. The truth was Matt felt that he'd been completely useless in the fight. He'd let his emotions get the best of him and put himself in danger and didn't think things through.

"I'm not saying that you don't help a friend," Mark continued. "In fact, I'm proud that you tried." The way his dad said *tried* made Matt feel like he was ten years old. "But if you are going to play the hero, I think you need to learn how to fight."

Matt looked up at his father in surprise. "You are OK if I fight?"

"No, don't misunderstand me. I don't want you fighting. But I want you to be able to defend yourself, or a pretty girl, if needed. You need to learn to throw a punch. But you also need to learn to assess a situation, as you may not always need to throw punches. Don't you think that Amy's date would have just let her go if you and Liam had approached him together? Two against one are never good odds—even a jerk like that would have known it. And now you were also witnesses to what he was trying to do. You already had the advantage over him just by being there."

"Sorry Dad." Matt was feeling more ashamed of his injuries.

"No, don't feel bad for what you did," Mark quickly responded. "Don't ever feel bad for trying to help someone. I'm just using this as an opportunity to teach you that there could have been other ways of handling the situation."

"Can you teach me more?" Matt said shyly.

"Yes, I can, but for now your mother has a great pot roast waiting for us."

"Hey Dad." Matt stopped his father before he went back downstairs. "I don't think Amy is giving the full details about what happened to her either. I think she's holding back."

"I agree, and unfortunately that's what girls do in these cases. Your mom has already called Amy's mother. She explained what happened and they agreed Amy would stay with us tonight. Hopefully Amy will be more open with her own parents. But for now, it's best that we just support her and make her feel safe."

After dinner, Heather offered Amy to use the shower. Grace was having her own bath and getting ready for bed, and Matt headed to the family room to settle onto the sofa and watch TV. Amy found him there when she came out of the shower. She was wearing one of his mother's T-shirts and sweatpants, and her long dark hair was brushed straight down her back. Even with her makeup washed off she looked beautiful.

"Do you mind if I join you?" Amy asked, sitting down next to him.

"Not at all. Do you have any preference on what movie to watch?" Matt asked her as he scrolled through the selections menu.

"I feel like I need a comedy," Amy said, pulling her knees to her chest and holding them there.

Matt looked over at her and saw tears in her eyes. "Are you OK?" he said slowly, turning to face her.

"Yeah, sorry, I'm just shaken up a bit. I was thinking of what could have happened if you guys hadn't come by." She gave a shudder. "I just feel so gross—he kept trying to kiss me and make out with me in the theatre. He was being so aggressive, even though we were in a public place. He was grabbing me and touching me." She paused, her voice was cracking, and Matt could tell she was fighting back the tears. "I kept pushing him away, but I didn't want to make a big scene in the middle of the movie, so I told him I was going to use the bathroom—I was hoping to just sneak out. But he followed me, and when I tried to leave, he followed me out of the building. That's when he grabbed me and started leading me to his car. I don't know why I didn't just scream. I guess I was too embarrassed. And if anyone saw us in the theatre they would have thought we were a couple. I'm so glad that you guys found me."

"He doesn't know where you live, does he?" Matt asked softly.

"No, we had just met at the theatre. He doesn't even have my phone number." Amy took Matt's hand and gave it a squeeze. "Thank you," she whispered to him again.

Matt took a risk and put his arm around her shoulders to give her a hug. It wasn't the kind of hug he had always hoped to give her. It was the kind of hug he would have given Grace had she had a nightmare. At that moment he only wanted to protect Amy and make her feel safe.

"Is there a chance you may run into him by accident somewhere?" he asked as she rested her head on his shoulder.

"No, I don't think so. He's a student at the university; he lives in the city." She then pulled away slightly to look him in the eye. "Matt, what are you going to tell people at school about how you got hurt?"

Matt paused. He had no intention of telling people anything; if Amy wanted to keep this quiet, he would also. But she was right, people will ask how he got hurt. It was unlikely all the bruising would be gone by Monday. "I'll tell them that Liam beaned me with one of his terrible pitches."

Amy laughed, "I guess that's believable. I have seen him pitch."

"You have? When?" Matt couldn't think of any time she would have saw Liam pitch, since he never did during the games.

"I've watched some of your team practices at lunch. I eat outside, in the stands, usually with a few friends. I hate to admit it, but we watch you guys." Amy was giggling now, embarrassed.

Matt was shocked; he had no clue a bunch of girls had been watching their practices. He tried to recall all the lunchtime practices they'd had so far to remember if he had ever done anything embarrassing.

"We get a little silly — sometimes we rank you guys. We especially like it when the team changes their shirts on the field," she admired shyly.

"You rank us?" Matt was shocked.

"Well all the girls do, on a scale of one to ten, how hot you all are."

"Seriously?" Matt asked, slightly offended. "That's so sexist!"

"Oh, come on, don't tell me the guys don't do it?"

"Maybe some do, but I don't."

"Of course *you* don't." Amy sighed resting her head on his shoulder again. "But don't you want to know what we ranked you?"

Matt didn't answer right away. Yes, he wanted to know, but if he admitted that, then he was approving to the girls' ranking system.

"You are an eight point five," she told him without waiting for his answer.

"Really?" Matt felt impressed with himself. "Is that good?"

"It's good," she said, being shy again. "Each girl puts in her own ranking and then we just take the average."

"OK, so what was my range?"

"Six, to a nine point five."

"A six! Who ranked me a six?" Matt tried to sound like he was teasing, but he was slightly insulted and really wanted to know.

"Emily. She's in your history class. She thinks you're stuck up because you never talk to her."

Matt thought that was funny, since he purposely didn't talk to her because she always acted like a know it all.

"But she gave your friend Liam a ten. I think she definitely has a thing for him." Amy quickly pulled away from Matt and looked him in the eyes. "But you can't tell him that. Please don't tell anyone I told you about this. The girls will kill me."

Matt contemplated the leverage he now had on Amy. "OK," he said slowly. "I promise I won't tell anyone about this, under one condition." Matt took in Amy's pleading look. "You have to tell me who gave me the nine point five."

A pure look of horror passed across Amy's face. "I can't do that!"

"OK, well if that's your decision…." Matt pulled out his phone and pretended to be texting. "I could send a message right now to the whole ball team. No more shirt changing on the field for you girls," he teased.

"Oh, please don't make me say it!" Amy was laughing but still adamant not to release the name.

"All you have to do is tell me the name. I know it wasn't Emily, so was it Jessica? Rachel? Kiera?" Matt was trying to remember Amy's friends' names. Amy just shook her head as he named each girl. Matt typed on his phone again, showing Amy what he was typing. She was trying to grab for his phone, but Matt held it high above his head, so she couldn't reach it. She did one last failed swipe for it and sat back down in defeat.

"OK I'll tell you!" Amy said quickly. "It was me."

Matt sat back on the sofa in shock and Amy grabbed his phone and deleted the unsent message. He wasn't sure how to respond; he never would have thought that Amy would have been the one to rank him that high. He looked over at her and felt bad he had made her admit it, she was visibly embarrassed. After everything she had already been through that day, all she needed was a friend at that moment. He needed to break the tension and make her feel comfortable again.

"Only a nine point five? You know my mom tells me I'm a ten," Matt said with a smirk on his face.

"Seriously?" Amy laughed and hit him with a pillow. It was good to hear her laugh and relax again. He turned his attention to the movie options and quickly started a brainless comedy. Amy sat close to him on the sofa, but they weren't touching or holding hands anymore. The teasing was over, and they were back to just being two friends watching a movie.

Matt couldn't concentrate on the movie. Thoughts of the last few days were running through his head. Things seemed a bit unreal. North Korea had bombed the U.S. (well a U.S. territory), his mother had encouraged him to speed on the highway, his father would teach him how to fight and the girl of his dreams had told him she thought he was a nine point five. Unfortunately, he also had the painful reminder of his first real fight. He played back the fight in the parking lot in his mind; he remembered the fear in Amy's voice as she yelled, he could see her getting knocked down, and then Liam coming to everyone's rescue. Liam had known how to deliver a punch. One quick snap and the guy's nose had broken. Liam was stronger than Matt since he worked out a lot more (hence the perfect ten ranking), but Matt wasn't far behind, he thought. He added working out more to his *things to do* list. Maybe he would meet Liam in the morning again.

Amy was giggling at something happening in the movie and Matt realized he had no clue what the plot was; he had been too lost in his own thoughts. He suffered through the remainder of the movie, which was a small price to pay to spend more time with Amy.

"I'm going to head to bed," Amy said as the movie ended.

"Sure, me too," Matt said as he turned off the TV. His head was pounding again, and he wanted rest.

"Hey Amy," he called to her before she left the room. "I promise I won't tell anyone about today. I mean about the parking lot as well as what you told me about the girls and the rankings. You can trust me." Amy walked back and gave Matt a hug.

"Thanks Matt," she said. "It means a lot to me that I can trust someone." Then she gave him a quick kiss on the cheek. It was a very soft brush of her lips across his uninjured cheek, but it sent a warmth right through his body.

"Good night," she said and then headed upstairs to the spare bedroom. Matt exhaled deeply as he watched her head up the stairs. He waited until he heard the bedroom door close before he turned off the lights and headed to his own room.

Liam

Liam found the house empty when Amy dropped him off. He figured his father was at some bar, as usual, putting back a few beers before coming home, which meant he had a few hours before Peter would be home.

Liam put together some dinner with what he could find around the kitchen. He was impressed at his own cooking abilities. There was always minimal food in the house, and he challenged himself to create the best meal possible with what he could find. It was amazing what some extra spices could do to freezer-burned chicken and canned corn.

Liam cleaned up his dishes and then attempted to clean the rest of the house. The place was a disaster; his father never attempted house work and had no expectation that Liam would do it. But Liam tried to keep at least the areas he used clean: that included the kitchen, living room, his room and his bathroom. He avoided his father's room, which hadn't been cleaned since his mother left, except for throwing out all his mother's belongings she hadn't taken with her.

Liam picked up the empty beer cans that had piled up around the house. He tossed them all in the recycling, then wiped up the spilled beer from the table and countertops. He hated the smell of stale beer, and the house reeked of it. While he was cleaning, he found forty dollars stuffed in the sofa. It had likely fallen out of Peter's pocket after he had passed out there the night before. This was normal—and the main source of income for Liam. His father rarely offered him money; what money he had either came from his brothers, finding it in the sofa or stealing it from his father. Since his father seldom remembered how much he had spent on alcohol, it was easy to take cash Liam found lying around the house, if he was careful not to take too much. He used the money mostly for food, clothing or other necessities, such as school supplies, and saved what he could; he had a few hundred dollars hidden in his room.

After watching some TV, he headed to bed. A few weeks ago, Liam had installed a lock on his bedroom door. In his drunken stupors, Peter had started to stumble into Liam's room to slap him awake and tell Liam how worthless he was. It was never too severe, but it was becoming too frequent for Liam's liking. He locked the door carefully and headed to bed.

Liam heard his dad stumble in around two a.m. He could hear Peter tripping over the furniture and then cursing. Liam waited to hear his father head to bed, but instead, he continued to walk around the house, cursing loudly. Then

Liam heard Peter open the back door and walk out of the house. A moment later, Peter was in the backyard shed. Liam sighed and slowly got out of bed. It was one thing for Peter to stumble around drunk inside the house; it was another when he was doing it outside and waking up all the neighbours.

Liam found Peter in the shed with one of the kitchen chairs. He had the power saw and was chopping off the chair legs.

"What are you doing Dad?" Liam said gently in hopes of avoid a confrontation.

"The chair is broken," Peter replied, continuing to cut it up. As he moved the saw back and forth, Liam noticed that he was dangerously close to cutting off his own leg.

"You're going to wake the neighbours," Liam said cautiously. He didn't want to start a fight.

"Screw the neighbours." Peter now had a two by four and cut it into four pieces, presumably for new chair legs. Peter wasn't using the work bench; he had everything on a low countertop, and again he was an inch away from slicing into his own body as he clumsily cut through the wood. Liam quickly unplugged the saw just a second before it slipped from its intended target; the saw stopped just before it sliced into his father.

"You need to come inside, you're going to hurt yourself," he tried to explain to Peter.

"Who the hell do you think you are?" Peter yelled at Liam. Peter threw the saw into the corner of the shed, causing a loud crash. He picked up one of the two by four pieces he had just cut and took a swing at Liam. Liam ducked quickly, but his father advanced on him. It was a small shed, and Peter now stood between him and the door. Liam reached for one of the

larger pieces of the broken chair, hoping to have something to shield himself with, but his father was faster. Peter swung the piece of wood he was holding, bringing it down hard on Liam's left hand. Pain shot through Liam's hand as he stumbled backwards with a cry. He held his it to his chest; he was backed up against the wall of the shed with nowhere to go. Peter started another swing at Liam's head and then stopped.

"You chicken shit," Peter snarled. He tossed the wood to the floor and stumbled out of the shed.

Liam didn't move from the shed right away. He was out of breath and sweating; the pain in his hand was unbearable. He tried moving his fingers and a sharp stabbing feeling radiated through his hand and up his arm. He tried to control his breathing, taking in deep breaths and filling his lungs. He had learned awhile ago that through extra oxygen intake and focus, he could manage the pain better. After awhile, he carefully left the shed, making sure Peter wasn't waiting for him. He found Peter passed out on the sofa snoring, a newly opened beer in his hand about to tip and spill on him. Liam went to the kitchen and pulled an ice tray from the freezer. Awkwardly, with one hand, he pulled the ice out of the tray and wrapped it in a towel and placed it on his injury. Then he stood and stared at Peter. He hated him. He wanted to hurt him—he wished him dead. Liam contemplated what would happen to him if Peter choked to death on his own vomit. Where would he live? How would he be able to support himself? Would he have to drop out of school to work so he could afford an apartment? Liam looked around the family room and considered how easy it would be to just grab something, anything, and return the beating he had just received, but he knew it would be a cheap shot to hit a man passed out. He carefully reached forward and tapped the beer can Peter was holding. It slipped from Peter's weak grip and spilled into his lap, Peter mumbled but did not wake up.

"Asshole," Liam muttered as he headed to his room. He had his plan: stick it out until he graduated high school. Then, with a little luck, he would get into university or college somewhere far away.

Matt

The next morning Matt woke up to voices in the downstairs foyer. He opened his door and saw his mother at the front door with Amy and her mother. They were talking softly, but the voices still carried in the open foyer. Amy's mother was still in her nurse's uniform; she must have come straight from her night shift.

"Melissa, if you or Amy ever need anything, don't hesitate to ask," Heather was saying.

"Heather, you have been so kind. Thanks so much for taking care of Amy. I'm sorry that your son got hurt. And I'm very sorry you had to take on this burden," Melissa responded. But her voice sounded annoyed, more than grateful. "Come on now Amy, lets get home, and we can leave these poor people in peace."

"See you Monday Amy," Heather said as Melissa turned to leave.

"Thanks for everything Mrs. Bailey," Amy replied and then added, "See you Matt." She gave him a quick wave as she walked out the front door. Matt blushed. He hadn't realized she had seen him. He had literally had just rolled out of bed, his hair was a mess and he was only wearing the sweat pants he had slept in. He went back to his room and pulled on a shirt and grabbed his phone. It was seven thirty a.m.—way too early for a Sunday morning. He got a jump on Liam and sent him a text asking if he wanted to meet at the park. To Matt's surprise, a reply came almost instantly confirming a meeting in twenty minutes. Then he heard voices outside just below his window. His room overlooked the sidewalk and driveway, and he could see Amy and her mother arguing next to their cars.

"Really Mom? You think that this was my fault somehow?" Amy was saying.

"No dear," Melissa responded, sounding cross, "I'm saying you can take a little better care with who you go out with so that these types of things don't happen. Look at what happened to that poor boy. Now get in your car and get home. You are grounded until further notice."

Matt quickly stepped back from his window, so Amy couldn't see him as she drove away. He was shocked that Amy's mother wasn't being more understanding and supportive. It made him realize that Amy may never tell her mother the full story of what had almost happened to her.

He headed downstairs to grab a quick breakfast but was quickly confronted by his mother.

"What are your plans today?" she asked as he poured himself some juice.

"I was going to meet Liam to hit some balls—other than that, nothing."

"Is your head feeling OK?" she asked, checking him out up close.

"Yeah, I'm fine. Everything thing feels back to normal." His eye still felt swollen, but the lip was back to normal size and his head wasn't hurting anymore. He didn't want his mother fussing.

"OK," Heather backed away from Matt, satisfied there wasn't any permanent damage. "But if your head starts hurting, you come home, OK?"

"Yes Mom, I promise." Matt grabbed an apple and headed out the door.

When Matt arrived at the ball diamond, he found Liam running laps again. He jogged over to him and matched his speed.

"How are you feeling?" Liam asked, only slightly out of breath.

"Better," Matt replied. "The sleep and ice helped."

Liam waved a bruised left hand in front of Matt as they jogged. "Jesus Liam, how hard did you hit the guy?" Matt asked shocked at his friend's injured hand.

"Hard enough. Buddy's face was like a brick wall. I don't think I can bat for a couple of days. Coach is going to be pissed."

"Hey Liam," Matt said urgently. "I spoke with Amy last night and she doesn't want anyone knowing what happened."

"Really?" Liam stopped running and Matt came to his side.

"Yeah, she's embarrassed and doesn't want anyone to know," Matt explained. "You know what the school can be like. She told me a little more about what had happened. I think that guy would have hurt her bad if we hadn't been there."

Liam seemed to contemplate this for a moment. "OK, I won't tell anyone, but how are you explaining away your face? And what should I say about my hand? You know coach has a no fighting rule; he will grill us."

"Crap, I hadn't thought of that," Matt said. It was true they could be kicked off the team for fighting, even if it was outside of the school. Coach Andrews wanted discipline on his team and was serious to enforce it. "Maybe we can tell him I got jumped and you came to my rescue. My parents will support that story if I tell them Amy wants to keep her story private."

"Oh great, so now *you* are my damsel in distress? The story is so much better when someone hot like Amy is involved." Liam frowned. "Though I supposed that isn't far from the truth anyway. That guy just fed you."

"Sorry I'm not hot enough to make your effort worthwhile," Matt joked. "So, do you think you can throw a ball? Or are we calling it quits for today?"

"I better rest my hand. It still hurts. Coach will still have a fit, even though it was for the good cause, saving our *star* pitcher."

"You better be able to play this week. I need you behind the plate if I'm pitching." As well as being Matt's best friend, Liam was also the catcher on the team that Matt trusted the most. Liam had great ball sense and always called the right pitches for Matt. The two were a strong combination, something that was not lost to the coach.

"Alright then, lets hit the showers," Liam said, collecting his gear from the bench.

"Actually, I was wondering if you could do me a favour," Matt said as he grabbed his own gear. "Do you still have the gym set up in your garage?"

"Yeah of course, why?"

"Do you mind if I come and work out with you?"

A smiled spread across Liam's face. "It's about time you got serious about your health," he said. "Yeah come on over and I'll show you some stuff."

Liam had shown Matt several exercises. Although Liam couldn't do much with his hand hurt, he put Matt through a full workout. Matt was sore as he walked back to his home. When he got there, he found his dad in the garage pulling the lawnmower out.

"Hi Matt," Mark called to him. "You had another early morning."

"Yeah, I was just working out with Liam." Matt walked up to his dad in the garage. "Hey Dad, I need a favour."

"What is it bud?" Mark stopped with the lawnmower and turned to Matt.

"Liam had said that he thinks coach may kick us off the team for fighting," Matt explained. "But Amy doesn't want anyone to know what had happened to her. So, I was thinking, can you write a note to coach explaining I got jumped. Maybe say some kids were trying to steal my phone, and then Liam came in and knocked one out to save me." Matt felt embarrassed with his story, but he knew coach wouldn't kick them off the team if he was the victim.

"Yeah Matt, that sounds fair," Mark said walking over to his son. "You shouldn't be punished for trying to do the right thing. I'll give you a note you can give to Coach tomorrow at practice."

"Thanks Dad," Matt was about to head inside when he remembered about the sedan he had seen the day before. "Oh,

Dad there was something I wanted to tell you. But with everything else that went on I totally forgot." Matt explained about seeing the car Friday night and Saturday morning, and described the man as best he could.

"Probably nothing," Mark said when Matt was done. "But I'll ask the neighbourhood watch to keep an eye out. So, are you going to give me a hand with this lawn?"

Matt groaned but conceded to helping, and he quickly found a weedwhacker in his hands.

After an hour of yard work, and Liam's workout, Matt's arms felt like jelly. He headed upstairs for a long, hot shower. When he got back to his room, he saw he had several text messages waiting for his reply. Liam was looking for confirmation that his dad would support their story. He was worried; Liam had sent repeated messages asking for an update. Matt understood, since there was no way Liam could count on his own father for support. Matt sent back a quick note that all was good. Then he saw Amy had texted him. It was a short message just saying, *I hope you are having a better day.* He smiled, he wasn't sure how to reply, so he sent a thumbs up back to her, then quickly added, *BTW, official story is that I got jumped for my phone and Liam came to my rescue.* Matt waited only a few seconds as Amy replied, *Sorry,* followed by a sad face.

Chapter Four
Matt

As Liam and Matt had predicted, Coach Andrews was not happy about the fight. But Mark's note helped defuse the situation, and neither of them would be benched for the next game, assuming Liam was even able to play. He was considered "day to day" as his hand continued to heal. Liam had lied to the coach and said he'd had his hand checked by a doctor to confirm nothing was broken. Matt was certain Liam never went to the doctor. Coach handed out a punishment to make an example of them. They found themselves running "poles" the whole lunch hour practice while the rest of the team did drills.

As Matt jogged beside Liam, Liam was cursing the coach. "It's not like you can hit or catch right now anyway," Matt reminded him as they turned for another lap. He had lost count around twenty, and that felt like ages ago.

"I know, but what good is it to have us do poles," Liam complained again. "In fact, you should be doing my laps; all I did was save your melon."

"Yeah, and now the whole school knows it too," Matt complained. News spread quickly about Matt's "almost mugging," and Liam was quickly becoming a small-town hero.

"You ever notice those girls watching us," Liam asked, completely off topic. Matt looked up at the bleachers and saw Amy with her friends watching the practice. He almost tripped. He hadn't realized that they were there.

"No," Matt said as he stumbled. "What makes you think that they are watching us?"

"They don't seem to try to hide it. Look at them watching, then whispering to each other and giggling. I have seen them there a few times now. That's Amy, isn't it?'

Matt pretended to notice Amy for the first time, "Yeah, that's her. And Emily from my history class." Matt wanted to draw Liam's attention away from Amy.

"Yeah, she's cute too, but I had calculus with her last year; she's a pain in the ass, know it all." Liam and Matt turned to start another lap, which had them running in the direction that faced the bleachers. "So, is Amy a cool chick?" he asked.

"Yeah, why, what do you mean?" Matt was confused by the question.

"Well, it seems like we are going through a whole lot of trouble for her. You more than me, since the whole school thinks you're a wimp now. Just trying to figure out if she's worth it."

"Yeah, she's worth it," Matt replied.

"Aw crap," Liam laughed. "You *like* her, don't you?"

"Yeah." There was no point trying to hide it from Liam; Liam knew him too well.

"So, did you get it on? Saturday when she spent the night at your house?"

"No!" Matt was disgusted. "Seriously? After what had just happened to her, you think I would put a move on her?" Matt was angry.

"Sorry man. You're right, that wasn't cool." Liam threw his hands up in apology.

Just then coach blew his whistle to signal end of practice. Liam and Matt slowed to a walk and headed towards the school. It was a hot September day and they were both dripping with sweat from their long jog. Liam pulled his T-Shirt off and wiped the sweat from his forehead with it. Matt was about to do the same when he noticed Amy staring at him from the bleachers. He hesitated only for a second and then pulled his shirt off too and dried his face with it. When he looked back up at Amy, he noticed her blushing and pretending not to be watching, but he still caught her eye. He gave her a quick wink and jogged towards the school to change and get ready for the next class.

Fourth period, Matt was walking into history class and saw that Emily was sitting in the front row again. She was turned in her seat, talking to her friend beside her. Her sweater had slipped off the back of her chair and was laying on the floor. Matt went over, picked it up and placed in on the back of her chair. Startled, Emily turned to face him.

"Um you dropped your sweater," Matt explained.

"Thanks, Matt," Emily said, confused.

"No problem." Matt tried to give her his most charming smile, even with his bruised face, and then went to the back to take his seat. He noticed Emily still watching him from the front of the class; she had a slight smile on her lips.

"OK class, we have a lot to talk about today," Mr. Roland said as he walked in the door. "As you know, the United Nations has called an emergency meeting with the allied countries to discuss North Korea's actions. Does anyone know when and why the United Nations were formed?"

In the front row, Emily's hand was the only one raised to answer the question. Mr. Roland called on her to answer. "The

United Nations was formed after World War II to prevent further world wars."

"Good Emily. Someone has been keeping up with her reading."

Emily soaked in the praise, but Matt caught her glancing back his way and giving him a quick smile. Matt wasn't sure what that meant, since Amy had made it clear that Emily was interested in Liam.

"One of the first struggles the UN had was to preserve peace during the Cold War," Mr. Roland continued. "And this past weekend, they continued to keep world peace." Matt felt his eyes drifting again and losing focus on what Mr. Roland was saying. The end of day bell startled him awake and he realized he had fallen asleep in the class. He quickly gathered his books and school bag, but before he stood up, he heard a voice over his shoulder.

"You may want to wipe the drool from your chin," Emily said.

"Damn, you saw that eh?" Matt said.

"Don't worry, Mr. Roland was on his soap box; there was no stopping him. He was on a roll talking about the UN. Half the class was asleep, and he didn't notice."

"I may need to borrow your notes from today's class." Matt pulled his school bag over his shoulder and started for the door. Emily walked beside him, apparently still having something to say.

"So, you're friends with Liam, right?" she asked, but she didn't wait for an answer. "I was wondering if you could tell him something for me?"

"Yeah sure, no problem."

"Can you tell him to text me sometime?" She handed him a small piece of paper with her phone number written on it.

"Yeah, I will." Matt folded the paper and put it in his pocket.

"Thanks Matt, see you tomorrow." Emily skipped down the hall. Matt headed to his locker to find Liam waiting for him there.

"Here," Matt handed Liam the paper Emily had given him.

"What's this?" Liam asked, unfolding the paper.

"Emily's phone number. She wants you to text her."

"Aw man, another one?" Liam put the paper in his pocket.

"What do you mean 'another one'?"

"Well, since the story got out about me punching out *your* attacker, a bunch of girls have found me extra interesting."

"Really?"

"Yeah, I mean more than usual. But don't worry, I'm not saying anything about what happened. Our made-up story is full of holes once someone starts asking for details, so I'm just politely declining to comment. You know, out of respect for my friend's privacy."

"You are so considerate." Matt rolled his eyes. "So, Emily just gets added to the pile?"

"Yeah, I doubt she's even interested in me, she just likes that I'm in the spotlight right now."

Matt knew that wasn't the case. Based on what Amy had said, Emily had been interested in Liam well before now. "Maybe you should give her a chance?" Matt suggested.

"Why? You never liked her either?"

"I might have been wrong." Matt shrugged. "I talked to her today for the first time in a long time; she seemed cool. I think she just acts all nerdy for the teachers, but she's not really like that."

"Maybe I'll text her," Liam said with little commitment.

When Matt got home, he saw Amy's car in the driveway, but neither of his parents were home yet. He entered the house to find Grace and Amy playing another board game, this time *Monopoly*.

"Good afternoon ladies," Matt said as he dropped his bag in the hall.

"Hi Matt," Grace smiled at her brother.

"You are in trouble, *Mister Smooth*," Amy said in place of a greeting.

"What did I do?" Matt asked, confused.

"Emily has been texting me all afternoon. Apparently, you spoke with her today? Picked her sweater up off the floor! And offered to pass her number on to Liam for her?"

Matt laughed, "Yeah, maybe I'm trying to up my average, I wanted to show her I was more than a six."

"Well you may have accomplished that; that sounds like at least seven material." Amy smiled at him. "Emily is so excited, she can't stop going on about Liam. He better text her."

"Maybe she shouldn't hold her breath," Matt said, discouraged.

"What's that supposed to mean?" Amy's tone changed quickly to concern.

"I guess a few girls were smitten by Liam's heroism. Emily may have to wait in line."

"Oh Matt, you have to tell him to text her. She is *so* in love with him. She has been forever!"

Grace giggled. "You guys are funny," she said. They had forgotten she was listening to the conversation.

"Don't you have homework or a room to clean or something?" Matt teased her.

"Nope, I'm good listening to you guys talk," Grace responded.

"How about I let you have as much ice cream as you want, if you go to the kitchen right now and let Amy and I talk?"

"Really, you won't tell Mom?"

"Promise, go and enjoy, just don't puke."

Grace ran off to the kitchen and Amy stared at Matt with a raised eyebrow. "Really? It's a good thing you don't babysit full time."

"I saw you girls gawking at us at lunch today," Matt changed the subject.

"Did you tell Liam about what I said?" Amy demanded.

"Oh no, I didn't say anything. He saw you girls up there and figured that you all were watching us. I'm sure his little strip show was intentional."

"Oh, and *yours* wasn't," Amy accused him. He blushed and didn't respond. "You were running laps as a punishment, weren't you? Because of the fight? Because of me?"

"Yeah," Matt confirmed. "But don't worry, we didn't mind, and it looked like you girls didn't either."

"Emily *was* going a little nuts over Liam again." Amy came around to stand close to Matt, a lot closer than necessary. "Can you please get him to text her?" she said, looking into his eyes. "Please? It would make her day." She gently put her hand on his chest and gave him a pleading look. Matt was certain Amy was very aware of the effect she had on him at that moment.

Matt sighed. "I'll try. That's all I can promise. Liam has his own mind, and I don't control him."

Amy gave him a big smile. "Thanks Matt, you're the best." She then turned to grab her purse and headed to the door. "I'll see you tomorrow."

Once she was gone, Matt pulled out his phone and sent a text to Liam. *Dude, do me a solid and text Emily tonight.* Matt waited for Liam's response. *Why's it so important to you?* Matt only responded one word: *Amy.* Liam's response was a thumbs up. He was grateful to have a friend that understood him so well.

Mark came home with a bucket of chicken, fries and salads for dinner. "Mom's working late again," he said, setting the food down in the kitchen. "Matt, can you text Amy and see if she can babysit tonight? I know it's a school night, but I want you to come somewhere with me and we won't be out late."

"Sure Dad," Matt answered and sent the message to Amy. He then helped unpack the food and set the table. Amy responded just as they were sitting down to eat.

"She says she can do it," Matt told his dad. "What time do you want her here?"

"Thirty minutes if that works for her?"

Matt sent the note back and Amy quickly confirmed she would be there.

"So where are we going, Dad?"

Mark seemed like he was about to respond but then looked at Grace and said, "You'll see. I'm taking you to meet a friend of mine."

Matt took the hint and didn't ask for further questions.

Thirty minutes later Amy was back at their house and Matt was getting ready to leave with his dad. "By the way Matt," Amy said before she closed the door. "Thanks, I owe you one. Liam texted Emily. Apparently, they have been texting all night. I keep getting the play by play from her."

Matt smiled at her as she closed the door, and he got into the car next to his dad.

"What was that about?" Mark asked his son.

"Aw nothing, we are just trying to set Liam up with one of her friends."

"Really?" Mark looked at his son, "So nothing's going on between you two?"

Matt laughed, "Can't a guy and girl just be friends?"

"I hope so." Mark laughed.

"What's that supposed to mean?" Matt asked defensively.

"Well, if your mother had to choose between her firstborn, or her favourite babysitter, she may choose the babysitter," Mark joked.

"Ha ha, very funny," Matt sighed. "So where are you taking me Dad?"

"To a friend of mine. He teaches many of my new hires. He's an instructor for combat fighting and self defence."

"Really?" Matt asked excitedly. "You are taking me to someone who will teach me how to fight!"

"Yes, but remember what I said: this is self defence and a last resort."

"Is this something we need to keep from Mom?" Matt asked sheepishly.

"No! I would never keep anything from your mother." Mark sounded offended.

Now probably isn't a good time to mention she told me not to tell you about my driving lesson then, Matt thought.

"Your mother supports this; she doesn't want to see you come home beat up again."

They pulled into the parking lot of an industrial complex. The sign over the door read *Lance's Training Centre*. The building looked dark and run down, a bit sketchy in Matt's opinion. It was hard to imagine his dad being associated with a place that looked like it was run by a biker gang.

Matt followed Mark into the building. Inside, the warehouse was a converted to a large training gym. On one side of the room there were half a dozen large punching bags hanging from the ceiling. Then there was a row of free-standing ones. There was also an area with several weights and machines for body building. On the far side there was a training-size boxing ring. A group of customers by the punching bags were working with an instructor. He was showing them punches in slow motion and explaining the technique. Matt was too far away to hear the instructions, but he watched as the group got on their feet and tried the same maneuvers.

"Mr. Bailey!" a voice called from behind them. Mark turned and offered his hand to the approaching man.

"Lance, how are you? Long time man!" Mark said as the two men shook hands.

"It has been too long. I was happy to get your call today, though I'm sorry for the circumstances," Lance said, looking at Matt. "You must be Matt."

"Yes sir," Matt said, not sure how to address this very intimidating man. Lance stood well over six feet tall. His dark hair was peppered with some grey, but his bulging muscles were well defined under his t-shirt.

"Sir?" Lance looked over at Mark. "Good work Mark, you taught this kid some respect."

"At least he learned something from me," Mark sighed.

"Mark, why don't you let me talk to your son, and we'll catch up with you later. There is a lounge in the back where you can wait."

"Thanks Lance," Mark shook Lance's hand again and headed to the lounge.

"OK kid," Lance said when Mark was gone. "Your dad told me what you told him, but why don't you tell me the specifics."

Matt wasn't sure what to say. "I told my dad everything. There isn't much more to it."

"Yes, there is — you just might not know it." Lance walked them to the area of the gym with the punching bags.

"Did you happen to notice how tall the guy was?" Lance continued. "Did you happen to notice if the guy had any weapons? Are you sure he didn't have any buddies nearby that were going to jump in and outnumber you? Was there anything lying around that may have worked as a weapon for you?"

Matt's head was spinning. He had considered none of the things Lance was saying. "No sir," was all he could say, a little ashamed.

"Don't be so hard on yourself kid," Lance said, putting an arm around him. "Unless you are trained to think of these things, most people don't."

Lance turned Matt toward the punching bag. "For today though," he continued, "I'm going to show you some basics:

how to throw a proper punch to start. Now, I don't want you hitting the bag too hard; your dad won't forgive me if I ruin your pitching arm." Matt was surprised how much Lance knew about him.

"So, start with your knees slightly bent, feet staggered, chin down, and hands raised." Lance demonstrated the stance and Matt copied his instruction.

"Good, so this is the basic fighting position you want to start in before throwing any punch. Using your lead hand, snap that hand out quickly as you push off with your back foot." Lance snapped a quick punch to the punching bag and it swung. He grabbed hold of it to steady it again. "OK now you try." He nodded at Matt. Matt tried to copy what Lance had done. When his hand hit the bag, he hit it a lot harder than he had intended, but the bag barely moved, and his hand was stinging from the impact.

"Not bad." Lance tried to sound encouraging. "Try again, but make sure that the palm of your hand is down, and the knuckles are up. And imagine a straight line that your arm needs to follow to make the impact."

Matt tried again; this time the bag swayed ever so slightly.

"Good kid. Try a few more, switch hands too. But don't hurt yourself."

Matt threw a dozen more punches with each hand and was surprised that he was breaking a sweat.

"You have good technique and strong arms. But a lot of the strength in a punch comes from your whole body. That's why the starting position is so important." Lance explained. "So, if you are willing, your father has asked that I teach you for a few weeks—not just how to throw a punch but how to defend yourself properly. Does that sound like something you would be interested in?"

"Yes sir," Matt answered.

"OK, but you have to cut out this sir crap—just call me Lance." Lance slapped Matt on the back.

"I thought you liked it?" Matt asked, confused.

"Naw, I said it showed respect, but I don't want to be called sir—this ain't the bloody army. Just call me Lance."

"OK."

"Great, let's go get your dad and book you in for your sessions." Lance led him over the so-called lounge, which turned out to be a few rundown sofas shoved against the far wall.

"The kid shows promise," Lance said to Mark.

"Thanks Lance, I really appreciate you doing this. I was going to teach him myself, but I thought he may benefit from an expert."

"Don't sell yourself short. I have seen you in action; you definitely have something to teach people."

Matt looked at his dad with new respect. If someone like Lance was praising his abilities, there was more to his father than he knew. Maybe his job wasn't just boring security detail in the offices downtown.

They set times over the next few weeks for Matt to return for his sessions. Matt had to work around his baseball schedule, but eventually they found time slots for eight sessions over the next month, at the end of which Lance promised Matt would be a "mean lean fighting machine."

"I just don't want to get my ass kicked again," he told Lance with a laugh as they were leaving.

"Not on my watch son!" Lance yelled after them.

"Well that was interesting," Matt said as he and his father drove home. "What did Lance mean when he said that you have something to teach people?"

"Nothing, he was just trying to make a sale and flatter me." Mark tried to dismiss it, but Matt would not let it drop.

"I don't think so Dad," Matt said. "The sale was pretty much confirmed at that point; you already told him you wanted him to teach me this afternoon."

Mark laughed, "OK, I'll come clean. Lance and I use to do ultimate fighting when we were younger. We trained together."

"Are you serious?" Matt couldn't hide his surprise. "How do I not know that!"

"It was a long time ago."

"Were you any good?"

"I won my fair share of fights," Mark said modestly.

"That's really cool Dad. Wow! You use to fight, that's awesome!" Suddenly a thought crossed his mind. "But Dad, if you were any good, how come we aren't rich?"

Mark laughed out loud. "It was a long time ago. Before it was popular, and people were making the big pay checks you hear about now."

"Man, that's too bad." Matt shook his head in disappointment, which only made Mark laugh harder.

"And before you ask, I have no intention of coming out of retirement," Mark said.

Chapter Five,
Matt

Wednesday afternoon was the last ball game of the fall season, and if a team was lucky enough, the last chance for scouts to see the graduating players play before university offer letters would go out. Their team had done well, but not well enough to attract the scouts. The game started just after lunch, and students were encouraged to watch the game and support the school. There was a big crowd out for this one.

The players were taking the field, and the coach had told Matt to be ready. Matt would not be starting pitcher, but he would definitely be used as the closing pitcher. Liam was back catching. His hand, he claimed, had healed, and he insisted he was able to catch, no problem.

As the game started, Matt sat on the bench and watched the first few innings unfold. They were playing the top team from the city; the kids played aggressive and didn't hold back. The game was tight, and when Matt got called in for the eighth inning, they were down by one run. Matt took the mound and started his warm-up pitches. Though he had already warmed up in the bullpen, it was different having Liam behind the plate calling the pitches for him. Just as the batter was about to take the plate, Liam called for a timeout and approached the mound.

"What's wrong?" Matt asked confused, as Liam approached.

"Nothing, I just wanted to see if you noticed our fan club?" Liam said, nodding his head towards the bleachers. Matt scanned the crowd until he saw Amy and Emily sitting together watching the game.

"Well that sucks," Matt said

"What, you can't handle the pressure?" Liam laughed.

"Not that. I was going to borrow Emily's notes for today's history class, but apparently, she's missing class too. Now get your ass back behind that plate so we can finally play some ball."

"So glad you can make it out," Liam joked, referring to Matt's late addition to the game.

"Well if you guys hadn't screwed up the batting we wouldn't be in this mess."

"Alright hotshot, lets see what you got," Liam called over his shoulder as he walked back to his spot behind home plate.

Matt smiled to himself; it was a bit of ritual for Liam and Matt to insult the hell out of each other during the games, but it was all good fun "chirping." It kept the mood light and calmed the nerves. Liam gave Matt a signal for a fastball, and Matt gave him a quick nod. He threw his fastball perfectly straight down the middle; the batter flinched but did not swing—strike one. Liam seemed to wince a little as he caught the ball in his glove. He carefully removed the ball from his gloved hand and threw it back to Matt with a reassuring nod. Liam called for another fastball. Again, Matt threw right down the middle, and this time the batter swung, but a little late. His contact to the ball sent it flying foul and out of bounds—strike two. For the third pitch, Liam called for a slider, exactly what Matt was thinking. He threw the pitch and the batter took a reaching swing at the ball, missing—strike three, the batter was out. The crowd in the stands cheered loudly. The next two batters struck out and Matt had a no hitter going.

"Is the hand OK?" Matt asked Liam as they walked back to the dugout.

"It's a bit sore, but nothing I can't handle," Liam said as he tossed his catcher's glove on the bench and quickly pulled on his batting gloves. Their first batter for their team struck out and then the second. The team was getting anxious. With the two outs, Matt was up to bat and he was nervous now. Somehow, knowing that Amy was in the stands watching him was affecting his focus as he was taking his warm up swings. He stepped into the batter's box and the first pitch came flying by him as soon as he was set. Strike one, he didn't even have a chance to swing. Matt held up his hand as he stepped out of the batter's box and took a few extra practice swings and tried to focus. He stepped back in, ready this time as the next pitch came. He swung and felt the ball hit the bat, but it made contact low on the bat, just above his hands, and the ball skidded in the grass, dropping very short, half way to third base. Matt ran as fast as he could, and, by some miracle, he heard the umpire yell "Safe!" as his foot hit the first-base bag and a split second later he heard the first baseman make the catch.

"You're a fast little shit," the first baseman said as Matt took his spot.

Matt looked at home plate to see Liam at bat. He knew that Liam would not swing at the first pitch to give him a chance to steal second base.

"You can watch it again as I steal second," Matt said, and as soon as the pitcher threw the ball, Matt started to run full speed. He heard someone yell "Slide!" and he quickly dropped to a slide, grabbing hold of the base with his hand. He felt the second baseman land a tag on his shoulder, but the umpire yelled safe. The crowd in the stands cheered loudly as Matt got up and brushed the dirt from his pants.

"OK Liam, your turn to be the hero again," Matt said under his breath. He slowly inched off he bag towards third base as the pitcher threw his next pitch. Liam made contact, and the ball went high, flying to the outfield. Matt didn't wait to see where the hit ended up: with two outs on them, he had to run. As he approached third base, the coach was signaling him to run home. He could hear the cheering in the stands, and he made it home with no challenge. He turned to watch what was happening and saw that the ball had made it all the way to the fence. By now Liam was running towards third with no intention of stopping. The outfielder was making a throw but didn't have the arm to beat Liam home. Liam was safe, and they were now up by one run. The crowd continued to cheer as they walked back to the dugout and high-fived their teammates. Matt noticed that Liam would only fist bump with his right hand, and he was cradling his left protectively against his stomach.

"How are you going to catch?" Matt asked quietly as Liam started putting his catcher's gear back on.

"Don't worry about me, I can finish the game," Liam said without looking up. They heard more cheering, this time from the visiting team's fans, as they had gotten the third out.

"Alright then, lets shut this down," Matt said as he grabbed his glove. He looked down at Liam, who was struggling to buckle the last strap on his shin pad. Matt quickly bent down and snapped it on.

"What, I have to dress you now?" Matt complained. "Come on hero, don't keep your fans waiting."

"Good thing you're fast, since your skinny ass can't hit. I think my grandma could hit the ball further with her cane," Liam yelled back as they jogged onto the field.

The first batter took two strikes, but when the third pitch happened, Liam winced and dropped the ball, which meant that the batter could run and steal first. Liam scrambled to get the ball from his feet and made the throw to the first baseman just in time to get the batter out. Liam called time and approached the pitching mound.

"You can't catch, can you?" Matt whispered so no one would hear them.

"No, it hurts like hell. I'm sure it's broken. It happened when I hit."

"Then get out of the game!" Matt protested.

"No, I have a plan. Throw some off speed, if the batters connect, it will be easy outs."

Matt shook his head, "Or I end up walking everyone. You're putting a lot of faith in my pitching."

"If you two girls are done with your tea party, can we finish this game?" the short stop yelled. Liam handed the ball back to Matt and returned to home plate.

With the next batter, everything went just as Liam had planned: a high pop fly to left field. The outfielder made an easy catch for the second out. When the third batter came up, Matt wasn't able to get as much spin and he hung the ball up over the plate; he heard the crack of the bat as it hit the ball and sent it way into the outfield. The centre fielder turned and ran back, and with one last big step, dove and caught the ball. Matt sighed in relief. The game was over, and they had won by one run. The team came running to the pitcher's mound tossing their gloves in the air and high-fiving each other again.

Matt noticed Liam heading past the dugout, where he walked over to the trainer and showed him his hand. The trainer shook his head and immediately pulled an icepack out from the first aid kit. Matt then saw a man walk from the crowd and go over to speak to Liam. He had a clipboard with him and showed Liam something on it. Matt watched as they spoke; Liam kept nodding and smiling and eventually shook hands with the man.

"Who was that?" Matt asked when Liam returned to the bench.

"A scout," Liam smiled. "He was here watching one of the kids on the other team, but he wanted to talk to me. He says there may be room on his team for me next year. He wasn't overly impressed with my last inning, until he noticed that my hand was broken. He liked your pitching too by the way. He might be watching for you next year."

"Oh wow!" Matt exclaimed.

"Yeah, it might finally be my ticket out of my dad's house," Liam said.

"What school was he from?" Matt asked.

"Ottawa."

"Oh." Matt was disappointed. Ottawa was a great school, but he had no intention of being that far from home, and he hated the idea that Liam didn't think twice about leaving. The team trainer had put Liam's hand in a sling with an icepack and had told him to get to a doctor for x-rays. Matt was helping Liam with his equipment when Amy and Emily walked up to them.

"Good game you guys," Amy said.

"Oh my god, Liam, is your hand OK?" Emily said in an overly dramatic voice.

"Not sure. I should probably go for x-rays." Liam frowned. Matt could tell Liam didn't like to look weak, especially in front of the girls.

"Do you guys want a ride home?" Amy offered.

"Yeah that would be great, but don't you need to get my sister?"

"No, your mom sent me a text. I guess she was working from home today and was able to get her." They headed towards Amy's car and piled all the equipment into the trunk, which was barely big enough to fit everything. Emily quickly climbed into the back seat next to Liam, which left Matt taking the front seat next to Amy. Matt saw Emily moving closer to Liam in the back seat, trying to make small talk.

"You can drop us at my place," Matt told Amy as she drove out of the parking lot. "I'll take care of hero and make sure he gets his x-rays." Matt knew that Liam's father would likely not be in a state to drive him anywhere, especially a hospital.

"My moms on shift in the ER. I can take you, maybe we can get him in quicker," Amy suggested.

"That sounds like a great idea. You sure she won't mind?" Matt asked.

"It should be fine. I'll drop Emily off and we can go. Text your mom so she knows."

They drove Emily home, and she protested that she wanted to come along. Liam had to promise to text her as soon as he got home to finally have her agree to leave the car. Amy and Matt were barely suppressing their laughs as Emily walked through her front door.

"Shut up and get me to the hospital please, before I shoot myself," Liam complained.

"Bud, she has it bad for you." Matt was full-out laughing.

"And who are the ones who encouraged this?" Liam yelled at them.

Both Amy and Matt were in tears laughing.

"Amy, you have to talk to her," Liam pleaded. "I like her, but she is trying way too hard. She doesn't have to put on the act for me. I think she's cool, I just wish she would be herself and hang out, so I can get to know her."

"I'll talk to her, Liam," Amy promised. "She is a good person, you're right, she's being completely goofy around you. I think she is just nervous." Amy was heading towards the hospital now. Matt sent a text to his mother to explain what had happened and where they were going. Response was a quick *OK*. Followed with a *Keep me posted.*

When they arrived at the emergency room, there were several people waiting. Amy walked over to the registration desk and, after a brief conversation, they heard her mother's name being paged. They only waited a short time before Melissa came through the double doors to the waiting room.

"What are you doing here?" Melissa asked her daughter.

"My friend Liam," Amy quickly explained. "He was the one that helped me Saturday. He injured his hand, and we think he made it worse playing ball this afternoon."

Melissa sighed and walked over to Liam. She gently lifted his hand from the sling and Liam winced. "You will need some x-rays," Melissa confirmed. "Follow me."

They followed the signs to the x-ray department, and Melissa went in to talk to the technician.

"You are lucky there isn't a lineup," she said when she returned. "You can go in." She held the door for Liam.

"Where's his parents," Melissa asked once Liam was in the x-ray room.

"His mother left them last year," Matt explained.

"And his father?"

Matt shook his head. He didn't want to lie to Amy's mother, but he also didn't want to betray his friend.

"How old is he? Do I have to make a call to child services?" Melissa threatened.

"Mom no!" Amy cried.

"No, his dad's just working late and wasn't able to bring him. It's been hard since his mom left," Matt quickly explained.

"OK, then. I'll see if I can get a doctor to look at the x-rays as a favour," Melissa said.

"Thank you, Mom," Amy said quietly.

"You, young lady," Melissa said, turning her attention to her daughter, "are supposed to be grounded. What are you doing at a baseball game?"

"It was during school hours!" Amy protested.

"We will have to talk about it later," Melissa said as the doors to the x-ray room opened. Liam came out and the technician handed Melissa a folder. "The pictures are in the computer, but you can see on those prints that there are a couple of small fractures. He'll need a cast."

"Thanks," Melissa said, glancing at the file and shaking her head. "Alright, come on." She waved for them to follow her down another hallway, this time following the "Fracture Clinic" signs. Again, Melissa went into the room first and spoke with a doctor. This time it took a little longer, but somehow, she convinced the doctor to treat Liam.

"You two wait in the hall," Melissa instructed Amy and Matt as Liam went into the fracture clinic. They closed the door behind them and Amy and Matt were left alone.

"Your mom seems pretty mad at you," Matt said, leaning against the wall.

"She's always mad at me for something these days," Amy said, taking a place next to him. "I can't wait to graduate and get way."

"Where will you go?" This was the first time he had considered that Amy may be going away next fall. Of course, she was smart enough to get into any school she wanted.

"I don't know, I was thinking of maybe someplace on the west coast, or the east coast. But as far away as I can get."

"That would suck," Matt mumbled.

Amy glanced at him and leaned a little closer to him. "Really? Why?" she asked softly.

Matt's heart was racing, like it did every time she got close. But he wasn't ready to admit to her yet how he felt. "Just saying, I think it would suck, for me," Matt said a little louder. "I mean without your vote; my ranking would drop to what? A seven overall?"

Amy slapped him across the arm.

"What was that for?"

"I think you know full well what it was for!" she replied crossly.

They waited in silence until the fracture room door opened and Liam came out sporting a cast on his left hand, which was now wrapped protectively in a new sling.

"Remember what I said Liam, and I want to see you back here next week with your father," the doctor was saying as Liam walked out.

"Thanks, I will," Liam replied.

Melissa thanked the doctor one more time and then led them out of the hospital through the staff-only doors.

"You take them home and then you head right home yourself, do you understand me?" she said to Amy.

"Yes Mom. Sorry for the trouble."

"And Liam, you take care of yourself, OK? If you need anything you know where to find me."

"Thank you, Mrs. Campbell." Liam said overly polite.

They walked back to the car and drove in silence back to Liam's house.

"Thanks Amy, that was the fastest ER trip I ever had," Liam said before he got out. "Your mom was pretty cool helping like that, even though she was mad about it."

"She wanted to call children's services on you, you know," Amy said, apparently still angry.

"I know," Liam shrugged and then grinned, "but she didn't, I was able to convince her otherwise."

"Oh my god! Were you hitting on my mom?" Amy asked appalled.

"What? No!" Liam replied quickly. "I just turned on some charm, to make her like me a bit better. Hey, she convinced the doctor to help me, so that was cool. And I didn't have to bother my dickhead father to get off his ass and actually do something for once. Thanks again Amy, see you guys tomorrow." Liam got out of the car and walked into his house.

"I suppose, I shouldn't complain about my mom, I mean especially when Liam is around," Amy said sadly.

"No, you shouldn't," Matt agreed. "It was good of her to help like that. And Liam's dad really is an ass, you have nothing to complain about."

"You're right." Amy put the car in reverse and pulled out of Liam's driveway.

"Thanks for helping," Matt said. "If it wasn't for you I'm sure Liam would never have gone to the hospital."

"Well, it is my fault that his hand got broken in the first place. So, it's the least I can do."

"No Amy," Matt said urgently. "It's not your fault. Don't ever say that again. None of what happened was your fault."

Matt saw tears running down Amy's cheeks, and she sniffled to hold back a sob. He wondered if it was safe for her to drive a car in that state. But before he could ask, she signalled to pull the car over and she parked on the side of the road. Amy sat and cried for a minute saying nothing. Matt waited for her to finish crying; he gently took her hand in his and held it until she composed herself again.

"Why do you have to be such a nice guy?" she sobbed, trying to dry her tears. "I'm so sorry, that I got you into that mess. I mean, you have to lie to the teachers, coach, friends, doctors!" Amy continued to ramble, but Matt couldn't understand her through the sobs.

"Wait, slow down," Matt said as he turned to face her more directly. "I have no idea what you are saying."

Amy sucked in a deep breath and exhaled, trying to calm herself. "I just don't know why I always pick the wrong type of guy," she said when she was finally done crying.

"Amy, it's over. He can't hurt you anymore."

"I know, but it just keeps coming back to me. His face is always there in my mind when I close my eyes. It freaks me out. And seeing you and Liam still suffering from coming to my rescue! I just wish I could change everything, go back in time and never go on that date."

"I wouldn't want to change *everything*," Matt said quietly. "I wouldn't change that night when we watched the movie together, or you coming to my game, or even Emily and Liam finally talking to each other."

Amy stared at him for a long time and said nothing. Then she leaned over and kissed him. It was unexpected, and Matt didn't know how to react. He felt her lips on his and it took a brief moment for him to realize that he should be kissing her back. He slowly put his hand on her arm and gently kissed her. He felt her react, and her kiss became more passionate. The kissed lasted a few more seconds and then she pulled away. Amy gave him a shy smile and put the car back into drive. They drove back to his house without saying a word, and when they pulled into the driveway, Matt was still lost for words. He got out of the car and realized he should say something. "I'll see you at school tomorrow?" he said and regretted it immediately. *Dork,* he yelled at himself in his mind.

"Yeah, see you." She gave him another smile and he closed the door, so she could drive off. Dazed, he walked into his house.

At school the next day, Liam had become even more of a celebrity when students realized that he had played, and won, the baseball game with a broken hand. Coach had threatened to suspend him for spring ball as punishment for lying. Liam remained adamant that the injury had happened during the game and even credited Matt's fastball for the fractured bones.

Liam couldn't practice with a cast on, and coach couldn't even punish him with "poles". Instead Liam took up the role as official team heckler while his teammates sweated through a brutal practice.

Matt saw Amy for the first time that day at lunch while he was on the field running through the drills. She was sitting in her usual spot in the stands with her friends again, but she seemed to have purposely sat with her back to the field, so Matt couldn't catch her eye. At the end of practice (Matt had decided to keep his shirt on this time), he pulled out his phone and sent her a text. *You good?* A reply didn't come immediately, but she eventually replied *yes.* Matt shook his head; he wasn't sure how to handle older girls or what his next move needed to be. Liam was the expert with this type of thing. *We should talk?* Matt sent back. *Sure, I'll catch you later?* she replied. Matt sighed and tossed his phone in his school bag. Clearly, he had messed this up, but he had no clue what. It wasn't fair, he thought, *she* was older and more experienced in relationships; she shouldn't expect too much from him.

Matt became more annoyed with himself as the day moved on. He had sent a couple more texts to Amy when he had the chance, mostly emojis with varying degrees of happy to sad faces. When he got to history class, he was seriously thinking of skipping, but he wasn't that type of student. He also had his first full appointment with Lance that afternoon and didn't want to risk getting in trouble.

Matt sat in his usual spot in the back row, but a minute later Emily took the seat next to him.

"You're in trouble," she whispered to him.

"Why?'

"Amy's mad at you?"

"How do you know that?"

"Well, she's upset about something, and you were the last one to see her last night, weren't you?" Emily said sympathetically. "What did you do?"

"I have no idea," Matt answered honestly.

"Well you better fix it fast."

"Why do you care?" Matt was confused.

"Liam and I are going out Saturday. He suggested it be a double date; he thought you and Amy could join us?"

"Really?" Matt asked, confused. "Have you told Amy this?"

"Yeah, but she said to ask you?" Emily looked at him with pleading eyes. "Promise you will fix whatever you did and come on this date? I'm not sure Liam will still go if you aren't there?"

"I'll see what I can do." Matt laughed to himself, it was bad enough he messed up any relationship he had with Amy before it even started. Now the fate of Liam and Emily's relationship also rested on him.

"You're the best," Emily whispered quietly as Mr. Roland started his lesson.

"Thanks, maybe you can tell that to Amy," he said, leaning a little closer to her so they wouldn't be overheard. "So, she really didn't say why she was mad?"

"Not really, she just said she had a really bad night and didn't want to talk about it. Did something happen at the hospital?"

"A really bad night? You sure that's what she said?"

"Yeah what happened?"

"Well, we kissed, but I didn't think it was that bad," Matt whispered.

Emily covered her mouth with her hands. Her body was shaking as she worked hard to hold in the laugh.

"I'm so glad I amuse you," Matt said sarcastically.

"I'm sorry," Emily eventually said, wiping tears from her eyes. "Have you tried texting her?"

"Yeah, all she said was we will talk later. She hasn't responded all afternoon."

"Look Matt, I'm not sure what you did, but I doubt it was the kiss. No one can be *that* bad at kissing, not even you."

Because you think I'm a six, Matt thought.

"So, whatever it is, just apologize and make sure you guys can join us Saturday."

Suddenly Emily shot her hand up in the air and Mr. Roland called on her.

"In 1989 when Gorbachev met with George Bush Sr.," Emily said.

"That is correct, Emily, well done," Mr. Roland replied.

Matt just stared at Emily, confused.

"He asked when and how the Cold War ended, weren't you listening?" Emily explained.

"No, I guess I'll have to borrow your notes again." Matt leaned back in his chair and tried to focus on the class, but he could only think of Amy.

Lance was waiting for Matt by the front door.

"Ready to get started?" Lance said as he saw Matt.

"Absolutely!"

Lance took him through a few basic hitting and kicking drills. He had Matt with the punching bag again, but this time

Matt wasn't worried about hitting too hard. Ball season wouldn't start again for months; he didn't need to worry about any injuries. By the end of the lesson, Matt was impressed to see that his punches moved the bag a fair bit more.

"That's good work today," Lance praised him. "You may even be as good as your dad one day."

"Was he good?" Matt asked. "My dad said he did alright, but I'm not sure he was being honest."

"He was one of the best at that time."

"So, what happened? Why did he stop?"

"He met your mom," Lance said matter of factly. "At first she didn't mind him fighting; she was actually really into it. Then he had one fight where he got hurt bad. She said that she wasn't going to spend her life taking care of him if something serious happened, so she made him pick. Either he quit, or she would leave."

"So, he just quit?"

"Yeah, but I doubt your father regrets it. Back then there wasn't much money or fame in fighting. Quitting was the right thing to do and look what he got for it: a great wife and family."

Matt considered this for a moment. Would he ever consider quitting something he loved for a girl? He knew that he wouldn't give up baseball for anyone, even Amy, but then baseball wasn't nearly as dangerous as ultimate fighting.

"So, I'll see you Saturday?" Lance was saying.

"Yeah, thanks. I'll see you then."

When Matt headed out to the street, he realized he had just missed the bus. It was a long walk home, but it would be longer to wait for the next bus. He considered calling one of his parents but decided to walk. He wanted time to think about how to manage the Amy situation. He checked his phone and she hadn't texted back to him. Then suddenly his phone rang. It was Amy.

"Hi," he answered.

"Hi, where are you?" she asked. It sounded like she was driving.

"I'm just walking home. I had a session at this new gym my dad got me in," Matt explained.

"Well I was waiting for you at your house, but then your parents got home, and there were only so many excuses I could think of to stick around and not make it obvious that I was waiting for you."

"Why were you waiting for me?" Matt was confused by Amy's tone. She was talking like nothing was wrong.

"I said we would chat later. Look, I need to explain. I'm sorry I haven't been able to reply to your texts, but my mom is monitoring everything I do now. She takes my phone as soon as I get home. Reads any texts I get. And she even has a GPS tracking me to make sure I go straight home after babysitting."

Matt started laughing; he was laughing so hard that he had to stop walking.

"Why are you laughing at me?" Amy yelled at him. "This isn't funny! My mother is stalking me!"

"I thought you were mad at me!" Matt gasped into the phone when he could catch his breath again.

"Why would I be mad at you?" Amy said back, confused.

"Never mind, it's stupid. I'm stupid. And your friend Emily wasn't helping things. She said you were mad at me too."

"Oh my god! I was mad, but not at you. I'm just getting tired of being treated like a child by my mother. I was still upset today, and I guess I wasn't very friendly with the girls, but I wasn't mad at you. And I didn't want to send too many texts since my mom is monitoring it all."

"Well I guess we will have to be old school and talk to each other." Matt grinned into the phone.

"That's not the worst thing in the world I guess," Amy replied.

"So, did you hear about Saturday?" Matt remembered Emily's request.

"What's Saturday?"

"Emily and Liam want us to double date with them." There was a pause as Matt waited for Amy to reply. "You still there?"

"Yeah, so are you asking me out on a date?"

"Well, I think they kind of already did it for me. But I guess if you want formality…." Matt took a deep breath. "Amy, would you do me the honour of accompanying me on a date this Saturday night?"

Now Amy was laughing. "Oh wow, that was definitely a formal invitation. Yes, Matt it would be my pleasure to accompany you on a date this Saturday, assuming I can get ungrounded by then."

"Oh crap, I forgot about that." Matt's spirits dropped.

"Don't worry. My mom likes you. I think she will let me go when she hears it's you; she will like the idea that I'm dating a younger man for a change. Besides it's good for my on-going employment."

"So that's your angle! You are only dating me to make sure you can keep babysitting my sister?"

"Oh Matt, you worked it out, babysitting is very competitive and cutthroat, and a girl's gotta eat."

Matt was smiling again. "I'm sorry we didn't see each other today," he said softly into the phone.

"Me too." Her voice was getting quieter too. "If you don't have practice tomorrow, maybe we could have lunch together."

"Sure, that sounds good. There's no practice. Where do you want to meet?"

"Bleachers?"

"Sounds good. I'll see you there."

"Bye Matt." Amy disconnected the call.

Matt continued to walk home, but now he felt like he was on cloud nine. He also realized he was an idiot for thinking that Amy was mad at him. Matt finally reached his street and was only a few houses away from his house when he noticed the black car parked on the road not far from his home. It was already dark out, and Matt couldn't see if anyone was siting in the car. Matt stayed in the shadows, so he wouldn't be so easily seen. When he was right across the street from the car, he saw there was a man sitting in the driver's seat. He had dark hair, was wearing a suit, and was typing something on his phone. Suddenly he looked up and saw Matt staring at him. He seemed shocked, then started the car and slowly to drove away, but he gave Matt a small wave when he passed him. Matt watch the car drive up the street and turn out of the neighbourhood. Everything seemed normal, except that the car had no license plates.

Matt stepped into the house and went to find his dad. He was in the office paying bills online.

"Hey Dad, that car was in front of the house again," Matt said as soon as he saw him.

"Really? What happened?"

Matt recounted what had just happened; he described the man to Mark, including the wave and that the car had no licence plates. Mark considered the information and didn't speak for a few moments.

"Thanks for telling me Matt," Mark said slowly.

"Aren't you going to do something?" Matt was a little shocked by his father's reaction.

"I'm not sure what we can do. His actions are definitely suspicious, but he hasn't committed a crime. But if something does happen he would be the prime suspect. I'll let the neighbourhood watch know that you saw that car again. So how was your session with Lance?" Mark changed the subject.

"It was good—really good actually."

"So, you want to keep with it?"

"Absolutely," Matt responded enthusiastically.

"Good," Mark smiled, "I'm glad to hear you are enjoying it. So, you're going back there Saturday?"

"Yeah, Saturday morning."

"OK I can give you a ride; it's a long walk."

"Thanks Dad." Matt turned to leave, and then added, "By the way I'm going out with Amy Saturday night. It's a double date with Liam and Emily."

"Really?" Mark raised his eyebrow at his son. "Does your mother know?"

"No, why?"

"Well I imagine she will have something to say about it."

"Why?" Matt asked, puzzled. "I have been on plenty of dates before."

"True, but not with her favourite babysitter. Seriously, don't mess it up. Your mother will never forgive you if Amy quits on us."

"Thanks for the confidence Dad," Matt pouted.

"Mark, can you come down here?" Heather yelled from the family room.

Matt followed Mark downstairs to find Heather sitting on the sofa, her laptop resting on her crossed legs, the TV turned on to the news.

"What's going on?" Mark asked as he entered the room.

"Peace talks with North Korea have failed!" Heather explained. "They are refusing to meet any of the UN's demands. They won't even consider coming to the table to discuss things, and they have several countries supporting them. The news is saying war is imminent."

"Who would support them?" Matt said, taking a seat to watch the TV.

"Russia, Iraq, Iran, basically any country that has had an issue with America over the last couple of decades." She started looking for something. "Damn, I can't find my phone. Matt can you go check to see if I left it upstairs in my office?"

"Sure, no problem." Matt headed upstairs.

Matt searched Heather's desk for her phone. The desk was a mess with papers all over it. He carefully lifted the piles of paper, so he wouldn't mix items up. The phone was buried under one of the piles. As he was placing everything back to it's original place, he noticed the papers that were in his hand.

He knew he shouldn't read it, but a phrase on the page caught is attention: *possible funding to North Korea*. Matt read through the page that seemed to be the last page of a longer letter*:*

The money was moved on August 28th to the external financial institution. Calls with investigators at that institution confirmed that the account belongs to T Chenko's Industries, a company known for it's support of North Korea's military efforts. Investigators also confirmed that the money was moved two days later.

Based on the transaction evidence provided in the attached files, it is the author's suspicion that our customer's account may have participated in funding North Korea's military efforts. We are therefor fully disclosing all our records to cooperate with any pending investigations. Should you have any questions, please contact the undersigned.

Heather's signature and office contact information were at the bottom of the page. Matt put the page carefully down onto the table where he had found it. He didn't understand what he had read, but he knew it was serious, and he knew he shouldn't have read it. If what the report suspected was true, his mother's company could be in a lot of trouble. But then again, is seemed that his mother was doing what she was supposed to do by filing the report to the appropriate government agencies. So, if she was just doing her job, then everything should be fine. Matt tried to convince himself that it was all business as usual, but with the fact that war with North Korea was "imminent," he wasn't feeling very confident in his conclusions. He quickly headed downstairs with Heather's cell phone.

"I guess it's just wait and see then," Mark was saying when Matt returned to the family room.

"I guess. It seems strange that we have a lingering threat of war, and we all just get up and go to work tomorrow." Heather sighed. "Reminds me of the eighties."

"You are barely old enough to remember the eighties," Mark said, putting his arms around his wife.

"True, but I remember being a kid and watching the news and being afraid Russia was going to nuke us." Heather smiled at Mark and gave him a quick kiss. "Thank you for saying I'm not old enough to remember the eighties"

"Here you go Mom." Matt handed her the phone, purposely interrupting before things got too mushy. His mother wasn't behaving any differently than usual. Maybe what he had read was just business as usual for her, or maybe it wasn't even accurate, and that's why it was on her desk, piled there to be shredded later.

"Thanks Hon," she said and checked her messages right away. "I have to go and make a phone call," she said, quickly leaving the room.

"Dad?" Matt asked when his mother had left the room. "Do we need to be worried?"

"I hope not," he responded slowly. "I don't think things will get that out of hand. I hope we are safe."

"Mom doesn't think we are, does she?"

"Probably not. You know she has the exit plan all worked out, right? Any threat on our area and we head to the cottage?"

"Yeah, she told me," Matt sighed.

"So, I must admit, I had thought she was being paranoid, but now I'm thinking she may have been right about all of it," Mark explained. "She's actually stocked the cottage with months worth of supplies. There are mountains of canned food, water, powdered milk and supplements up there now. I thought she was going nuts, but I wonder now if she knows something." Mark looked at Matt and quickly said, "Don't tell her I said I thought she was nuts!"

"I thought you didn't keep secrets from Mom!" Matt threw back.

"Alright smartass, go do your homework." Mark scolded Matt.

Matt headed to his room, and on the way past his mother's office, he could hear Heather on the phone. He could only hear her side of the conversation; she was speaking quietly, and she was not on speakerphone this time.

"No Kevin, I didn't file the report, but I think we still need to. If the situation keeps escalating, the information we know could be valuable." She paused as she listened to the response from the other end of the call. "But it's our obligation," she argued. "OK fine, let's talk tomorrow morning. I'll be in by eight." She hung up the phone and Matt quietly headed to his room, so she wouldn't know he had heard anything. When he got to his room, he checked his phone and noticed Amy had sent him a text earlier. *Are you watching the news?* He sent a reply, *yeah sorry, didn't have my phone on me. Crazy stuff.* She sent a reply: *I guess Mr. Roland's class will be interesting tomorrow.* Matt smiled and sent back, *Personally, I'm looking forward to lunch.* Then he pulled out his homework and copied Emily's history notes.

The next morning, Matt took his usual path to school, which included the stop at Liam's house. This morning Liam wasn't waiting on the porch as normal. Matt slowly approached the door, contemplating if he should knock. He hadn't been in Liam's house since before Liam's mother had left. When he got to the porch he heard yelling inside.

"You ungrateful little shit, get the hell out then!" Liam's father yelled. Matt then heard the distinct sound of a slap.

"I'm not going to move out," Liam responded with a loud but much calmer voice. "As much as you hate it, you are still stuck with me for a few more months." With that Liam opened the front door and almost knocked Matt over.

"Sorry man," Matt quickly apologized, embarrassed for overhearing the fight.

"How much did you hear?" Liam said angrily, pulling his bag over his shoulder and walking to the sidewalk.

"Just the last bit. What was that about?"

"I told him we needed to go back to the hospital next week to see the doctor," Liam explained. "I guess he can't take the time off work. I made the mistake of bringing up my mother, and it set him off." Matt noticed a red mark across Liam's check. "I kind of had that coming," Liam said as Matt was staring at him. "Is it bad?"

"No, you can barely see anything," Matt answered honestly.

"The bastard is getting weak in his old age," Liam joked, but Matt didn't laugh. "Don't look at me like that man. You're supposed to be my friend."

"Look at you like what?"

"Like you feel sorry for me! I'm fine. I'll graduate school in the spring and I'll be done with him forever."

"Maybe you can come stay at my place?" Matt suggested.

"Matt, don't. I know that your parents would probably be cool with that, but don't say anything to anyone."

"OK, but the offer is there."

"Alright, let's stop talking like chicks and get going."

They reached school just as the bell was ringing, so they needed to hurry to make it to their homerooms on time. The morning seemed to drag, and Matt felt like the lunch hour would never arrive. Since Amy was a grade older, he usually did not see her during the school day, as their classes did not allow for their paths to intersect. When it was finally lunch hour, Matt headed to the ball diamond to meet Amy at the bleachers. She was there alone waiting for him.

"Hi," Matt said shyly. Suddenly he was nervous to be alone with her. "Where are the rest of the girls?"

"They have no interest coming out here if you guys aren't practicing," she said as she climbed the stairs to the top row of the stands. Matt followed obediently. Amy sat down on the bench, and Matt took his place next to her. He sat with his legs on either side of the bench, so he could face her better. She smiled and turned sideways as well, with her legs crossed so she could face him directly, their knees gently touching.

"So, I should warn you that Mr. Roland is on a roll," Amy said. She had her grade twelve history class in the mornings. "According to him, World War III is about to start."

"He might be right," Matt said, though he had no interest in discussing Mr. Roland's conspiracy theories. He looked at Amy and took in how beautiful she was: her straight dark hair was pulled into a low pony tail, and her green eyes seemed to shimmer in the sunlight. She was wearing a sweatshirt and jeans for the cooler fall weather, but it suited her and made her look elegant instead of casual.

"You're staring at me," she whispered.

"I'm sorry, I can't help it." Matt smiled but continued to stare at her. "I just want to make sure that I remember how great you look right now."

"You certainly have the charm turned on today," she teased.

"I'm not trying to be charming," he replied. "I'm just being honest." He took her hand in his and slowly traced his thumb across the back of her hand. "So, do you have any ideas of what you may want to do Saturday night?"

"Not really, do you?"

"Starting to, but I wanted to make sure you had no expectations first."

"So, you are setting the bar low?"

"Extremely. I hope you don't mind." Matt started to lean forward with the intention of kissing her, but then suddenly his phone rang in his pocket. He pulled it out quickly to check the call display; it was his father calling. There would be no reason for Mark to be calling in the middle of the day unless it was urgent. Matt gave Amy a concerned look and answered the call.

"Dad?"

"Matt, I need you to pick up your sister and head back to the house right now. Something's happened to your mother."

"OK, sure, but what happened?"

"She's gone missing. She never made it to work this morning. I just need you to get your sister and then call me when you are both home safe, OK? I called her school already to tell them you were coming."

"OK Dad, I'll call you in a few." Matt hung up the phone and stared at Amy, not sure what to say.

"What happened?" Amy demanded.

"He says my mom is missing," Matt said, completely in shock. "He wants me to go pick up Grace and call him from home."

"I'll drive you," Amy said, getting up and gathering her stuff.

Matt picked up his bag and followed her to the parking lot. "Did he give you any other details?" Amy asked while they walked.

"No, he just said she had gone missing and never made it to work." Matt felt like the world was trying to tip him over. He wasn't even sure how he stayed standing while he walked to Amy's car. They drove to the school and found Grace waiting outside with a teacher. The teacher came to Matt's side of the car, while Amy helped Grace with her seatbelt. Matt recognized the teacher but couldn't remember her name. He stepped out of the car to talk to her.

"Your father asked us not to tell her anything," the teacher said quietly. "Matt I'm so sorry, we are all praying that your mom returns quickly and safely."

"Thanks," Matt mumbled and got back in the car.

When they got home, Matt immediately dialed back his father's number.

"Hi Matt." Mark sounded exhausted. "Let me talk to you and Grace both and then I'll talk to you after."

"OK Dad." Matt switched the phone to speaker and waved Grace over. "Amy is here too, she drove me over to get Grace," Matt explained.

"OK, thanks Amy for helping out. Listen, Grace, I need to tell you something and it's very upsetting." Mark paused. It sounded like he my not be able to go on. "Your mom went missing this morning; she never showed up at work. Some police are going to come by the house in a little while. They want to look around to see if there are any clues to help find her. I need to stay with the police here in the city a little longer, but I will be home really soon, OK?" Grace shook and sobbed. Amy took Grace into a hug and held her while Mark continued. "I promise, you are safe Grace, and we will do everything we can to get Mom home quickly."

"Where did she go Daddy?" Grace cried from Amy's arms.

"We don't know that yet baby. That's what we are trying to work out. Matt, can you take me off speakerphone now?"

Matt picked up the phone and switched off the speaker. "Yeah Dad."

"So, I wanted to give you all the details, but I don't want to scare Grace any more."

"OK Dad." The room was spinning, and he could barely focus.

"When she wasn't answering her phone this morning, I tracked it. Someone had ditched her purse and all its contents — wallet, phone — in a garbage at the train station. The Police watched the security footage and they saw her being led out a back door to an alley by two men. The police are trying to figure out who the men are, but once she was out of the station there was no more camera footage."

"Jesus," Matt whispered into the phone.

"Matt, I'm coming home as soon as I can, but I need you to let the police in and let them have whatever they want. They are here to help us. Time is critical right now, and we need to move fast. But most importantly please take care of Grace. I'm sorry, but I need to ask you to do this without me. I hate that I can't be there right now, but I'm trying to do everything I can to figure this out."

"Dad, don't worry. I'll take care of things here. You do what you have to do."

"I'm so sorry Matt. I'll be home as soon as I can. Call me if you need anything."

Just then the doorbell rang, "Dad I think the cops are here now," Matt said.

"OK, go get the door. We will talk more after."

Matt disconnected the call and went to answer the door. Amy and Grace waited in the family room. There were two officers waiting on the porch. Both were dressed in full uniform. One officer looked to be in his fifties while the other looked like a rookie, barely older than Matt.

"Are you Matt Bailey?" the older officer asked when Matt opened the door.

"Yes, come on in. My dad called to say you were coming."

"Thanks, my name is Officer Robert Carson, and this is Officer Jay Harris. Is there some place we can talk?"

"Yeah sure, we can go to the kitchen." Matt led them through the house. As he passed Amy and Grace—Grace still sobbing in Amy's arms—Amy said to Matt, "I'll take Grace upstairs, so you can have privacy."

"Thanks." As Matt passed Amy, she gently reached out and took his hand and held it for only a split second before guiding Grace upstairs.

"Ah, can I get you anything?" Matt wasn't sure if he should be making them coffee or something.

"Don't worry about us son, we just want to talk and see if there is anything that can help us find your mother," Officer Carson answered.

Matt sat down at the table. He was sure his legs wouldn't support him anymore. Officer Carson sat across from him, but Officer Harris stood by the door.

"Son, I know you are probably in shock right now, but I need you to try and focus. Tell me, is there anything you can think of, that might help us find your mom?"

Matt's head was spinning; he couldn't focus on anything. The only thing he could think of was the black sedan he had seen on the street. He explained how he had seen it a few times and gave the best description he could of the man he had seen driving the car. Officer Harris took extensive notes while Carson asked all the questions.

"Do you think he's the one that could have done this?" Matt asked.

"We aren't disqualifying anything at this point Matt. Everything you tell us is helpful," Carson encouraged him. "Can you think of anyone else that was acting suspicious, or that may have threatened your mother? Anyone in the neighbourhood that she may have had a falling out with?"

Matt shook his head. "No, nothing."

"What about you or your dad? Is there anyone that you can think of that might be angry at either of you and would take it out on her?"

"No, not that I can think of. I mean, my friend and I got in a fight with this guy at the theatre last weekend, but we didn't even know the guy." Matt noticed Harris giving Carson a funny look. "The guy was harassing a girl we know from school, so we stepped in," Matt explained quickly. "But that guy wouldn't know who I was or where I lived."

Harris took more notes.

"Your dad told us that your mom had a home office? Can you show us where that is?" Carson asked.

"Yeah sure, it's upstairs. I'll show you." Matt led them upstairs. He opened the office door to let them in and then suddenly stopped.

"Is something wrong Matt?" Carson asked from just behind him.

Matt looked at the desk pushed against the wall next to the window. It had been cleaned off, all the piles of paper that had been there the night before were gone.

"Everything is gone," Matt said slowly. "I was in here last night," he explained, "and the desk was a mess. It usually is. There were stacks of papers everywhere, but it's all gone now."

"OK Matt, can you step out of the room?" Carson instructed. "We will get a forensic unit here to get prints. Does anyone else have keys to the house?"

"Just Amy. She babysits my little sister."

"Jay, do we know if they found Mrs. Bailey's keys in her purse?" Carson asked his partner.

"I don't think they said anything about keys," Harris spoke for the first time. "I'll call in and ask." Harris picked up his phone and dialed.

"Matt, can I ask you and the girls to head back downstairs to the family room? I want to limit how much of the house gets disturbed before the forensics team gets here."

"Yeah sure, I'll go get them." Then he remembered about the page he had read. "Last night when I was in here, there was a page from a report that I saw. It was a report my mom was supposed to file. I only saw the one page, but it talked about money moving from her bank to another and then to

Russia and North Korea. Then later I heard her on the phone. She was talking to someone—they were arguing—she said she would be at work early and they could meet."

"Do you have any idea who she may have been talking to?"

"I think she called him Kevin."

"OK thanks. Matt, you did good, go check on your sister."

Harris hung up the phone and reported to Carson: "No keys Carson, and a team is on its way," he confirmed.

Carson just nodded as Harris took more notes. Matt found the girls in Grace's room. Amy was sitting on the bed, and Grace was lying next to her with her arms wrapped tightly around her.

"We need to go back downstairs. There are going to be some more people coming to help," Matt explained.

Grace quickly got up from the bed, ran over to Matt, and hugged him, sobbing again. Matt just held her tight and hugged her for a few minutes. He saw that Amy also had tears in her eyes. After a little longer, he gently guided Grace downstairs and sat on the sofa next to her. She buried her face into his chest and wouldn't look up or speak. Amy sat on the other side of him and took his hand.

"Can I get you anything?" Amy asked softly.

Matt shook his head no. He held Grace tight, as it was the only thing he could think of doing. He wasn't sure how much time passed, but eventually the doorbell rang again, and it was the forensic team arriving. Carson explained to Matt they would need to take their prints, so they could exclude them from any other evidence they found. Matt found it surreal when he, Grace and Amy were sitting in the kitchen getting fingerprinted by Officer Harris. At one point, Liam sent him text messages. School had ended, and Liam was wondering where Matt had disappeared to. Matt didn't know how to respond, so he didn't. Amy had stepped out for a few minutes to call her parents. When she returned, she said nothing but sat back down next to him.

Mark came home and found Matt, Grace and Amy still sitting together on the sofa. At some point Grace had exhausted herself with so much crying she had fallen asleep, but she was still clinging to Matt. Mark looked like he had aged ten years since that morning. He had an extremely sad look in his eyes that amplified when he saw his children in the state they were in. He sat down on the coffee table across from them.

"I need to talk with the police," he said softly. "Is there anything you need right now?"

Matt didn't respond but only shook his head no. Amy squeezed his hand, but he barely noticed what was going on around him. His father headed to the kitchen and Matt could hear mumbled voices, but not the conversation. He continued to watch as the forensic team and various police officers as they went through his house. At one point two detectives had shown up. Mark was now speaking with them, then he returned to the family room.

"There is going to be a news story tonight," Mark explained with a big sigh. "The quicker we get this story out there the better the chance is of finding Mom. It might also push her abductor to contact us and start negotiations."

"What, like ask for a ransom?" Matt asked, confused.

"Yeah. It just doesn't make sense that someone would want to harm your mother. One of the possibilities is that there could be a ransom request." Mark stressed *one*.

Grace stirred next to Matt, then noticed Mark and quickly threw her arms around her father's neck. Mark hugged her back tightly, with tears in his eyes. "Baby, I'm so sorry, I love you and so does Mommy. You know she wants to come back to you," he whispered in her ear.

Matt suddenly felt like the walls were closing in on him. He stood up quickly.

"Matt?" Amy called after him.

"I just need a minute," he called over his shoulder as he headed outside.

He wasn't ready for the scene outside: there were half a dozen police vehicles park along the street in front of his house. Several neighbours were standing on the street watching his house. They all were all staring at him now. Suddenly he felt like he would vomit. He could feel the wet acid in the back of his throat and the water accumulating in his mouth. He knew he had no time before he vomited in full view of the whole neighbourhood. He quickly headed between the houses towards his backyard. He had almost made it to the backyard gate when he puked. Eventually he was just dry heaving, and then he noticed he had started to sob.

He stayed between the house long after he had stopped crying. He didn't want to go back in. In a matter of a few hours, his entire life had been turned upside down. Suddenly his mind was working overtime, like it had woken up from the hibernation it had put itself in to cope with everything that was happening. But now he couldn't stop thinking about everything: the black sedan, the letter on his mother's desk, the phone calls he had overheard. Were they somehow connected to his mother's disappearance? Or was it a random attack: they saw a woman alone early in the morning and took advantage of the opportunity. Thoughts of his mother lying dead somewhere tried to punch to the front of his mind, but he quickly pushed them back. This was too much for his head to process; he didn't know how to handle this, and suddenly he felt his body going into shock. He felt a cold wave wash over him and then everything turned yellow before it turned dark.

When Matt woke up, he found himself on the sofa. A paramedic was hovering over him, taking his blood pressure, and his father stood next to him. He vaguely recalled being helped back into the house by Officer Harris.

"Blood pressure is coming back up to normal. I think he's going to be fine. It was shock and dehydration, so make sure he has lots of fluids," the paramedic explained. "I'll check back in on you in thirty minutes." He left Matt and Mark alone in the room.

"I'm sorry Dad." Matt felt ashamed for his reaction.

"Sorry? What the hell for? You have done nothing wrong, it's been an impossible day for all of us." Mark sat next to him. "You went into shock and your body shut down for a little bit. Don't worry; you will be fine."

"Dad, I don't know how I'll ever be fine unless Mom comes back," Matt said softly.

"I know, sorry, bad choice of words. We are working on that. The police in the city are being interviewed on the six o'clock news, which will be any minute," Mark said looking at his watch. "I don't think you or Grace should watch it. She and Amy are waiting in the kitchen. Grace was freaked out when Officer Harris was helping you back into the house like that. She will want to know you are OK. Should I let them in?"

"Yeah sure," Matt said, sitting up on the sofa.

Mark went to the hall and waved the girls in. Grace ran over to him and sat next to him on the sofa again, without saying a word.

"I'm going to watch the news in the kitchen. You guys stay here, but let me know if you need anything," Mark said, leaving the room.

"You OK?" Amy asked, her face showing concern.

"Yeah mostly," Matt sighed. "I'm sorry I worried you."

"Don't apologize," Amy said, sitting next to him.

They waited, and Mark returned after a short while and confirmed that the news story had run. Almost immediately, Matt's phone buzzed with messages. He glanced at it and saw that several the kids from his school were sending him messages and offering support. It comforted him to know that he had so many people he could rely on. One of the very first messages was from Liam: *Dude if you need anything call me.* Simple and to the point, just like Liam. Amy's phone was buzzing too. Most of her friends knew that she babysat for the Bailey family, and they were trying to get the inside scoop. Amy just ignored the messages and held Matt's hand.

At some point people left the house. Amy brought Matt and Grace sandwiches, which they nibbled at. Grace hadn't spoken for hours, and she refused to leave Matt's side. Eventually Amy said that she needed to go home. Matt figured it was well after midnight. She said she would call in the morning. He carried Grace to bed, but she refused to be alone. She slipped into his room and slept in his bed with him, clinging to him tightly as she had a restless sleep. He lay in bed next to her, drifting in and out of sleep.

Chapter Six
Liam

Liam was lying in bed, only partially sleeping, when he heard his father coming home at two a.m. It was always two a.m. when Peter would come stumbling in, just after the bars had last call. Liam glanced at his door to ensure that he had locked it. So far, the lock had worked. Usually, when Peter found the door locked, he just moved on.

Liam was not in a mood to deal with his father. The story of Heather's abduction had been headline news all weekend. Matt would barely respond to text messages. Liam was worried for his best friend, and it made him angry to think that a good family like theirs would have something so horrible done to them. He heard Peter's steps in the hall outside his room. Then his door knob turned, and Liam could hear Peter's body banging against the door, but the lock held. Peter slammed the door one last time and cursed but moved on. Liam had been holding his breath and slowly exhaled — he was safe for another night. Eventually he dozed off.

When his alarm went off, Liam felt like he hadn't slept. He dragged himself out of bed and went to shower. He quietly went passed his father's room; the door was wide open, and he saw Peter lying on his bed, still fully dressed. Liam shook his head, disgusted by Peter.

He didn't expect to find Matt waiting for him, so he headed to school on his own. He wasn't far along his walk when he heard a car honk at him.

"Hi Liam, want a ride?" Amy called from her car.

"Yeah thanks! So much better than walking," he said, getting into the car.

"No problem." Amy smiled at him. "So, have you talked to Matt at all?"

"No," Liam replied, shaking his head. "I was going to ask you if you had."

"I spoke to him on Saturday, but not at all yesterday. I want to respect their privacy," she said sadly.

"I know. I've texted him a few times—sometimes he responds. But I'm not sure what to say to him."

"I can't believe that this is happening to them. It's so unfair. How could anyone want to hurt Heather?" Amy said angrily.

"Are you going to go by there tonight?" Liam asked.

"I think so. My mom keeps getting me to bring them food. I guess that's what people do, they take food?"

"Sure." Liam shrugged. "We had some neighbours do that when my mom first left. I think the old lady next door felt sorry for me, so she kept bringing me pastas and casseroles. They were pretty good actually."

Amy glanced at him sadly.

"I guess you haven't had the easiest time either," she said.

"I'll survive." He wanted to change the subject. He didn't like people feeling sorry for him.

"Your dad's not the best parent either, is he?"

"He's definitely not getting the #1 *Dad* mug from me," Liam said sarcastically, hoping she would get the hint and stop asking about his family.

"I'm sorry. I'm being nosey," she apologized.

"It's alright. It's just that I don't like talking about my home life," Liam replied.

She gave him another sideways glance. She was going to say something else, then stopped herself. Liam tried not to stare at her, but he couldn't help noticing that she was beautiful. He could see why Matt was fanatical about her.

"What is it? You're staring at me. Is my make up smudged or something?" Amy asked, all paranoid.

"No," Liam stuttered, a little embarrassed. "I was just thinking that, um…Emily may be mad at me for not calling her. Our plans kind of fell through with everything that happened with Matt."

"She was a bit upset, but of course she understood," Amy said.

"I'll make it up to her," Liam promised.

They pulled into the school parking lot, and there was still plenty of time before classes.

"Well, thanks for the ride," Liam said, getting out of the car. "It's nice not to be late for a change."

"Any time." Amy gave him one of her super smiles. Liam gave her a smile back but reminded himself this was Matt's girl.

"Hi Amy," they heard a voice call from behind them. Liam turned to see Emily heading their way. "Oh, hi Liam," Emily said, staring at them a little confused.

"Emily!" Amy said overly cheerful. "Liam was just telling me he was going to make it up to you for missing your date this weekend." With that Amy waved goodbye and headed into the school.

"Really?" Emily asked suspiciously. "And what were you thinking?" She took his hand and they walked towards the school together. Liam felt a little awkward holding her hand.

They hadn't officially been on a date yet, but Emily seemed to have committed herself completely to him.

"I hadn't thought that far," Liam confessed. "Only that I thought we should do something this week."

"Well, my parents are at a work thing tonight. They won't be home until late. Do you want to come to my place?" Emily suggested.

"Sure," Liam wasn't sure how he felt about a first date being in an empty house alone with her, but he had no excuse to get out of it.

"Great! Meet me in front of the school after classes, we can walk over together." She headed towards her locker, giving him a wave.

Classes moved a lot quicker than Liam would have preferred. He was able to avoid Emily at lunch by hanging out with some of the guys from the ball team. Most were asking about Matt and pressing Liam for details. Of course, Liam's knowledge was limited to what had been reported on the TV, so he mainly sat quietly while everyone else speculated. His classes after lunch flew by just as quickly, and once the dismissal bell rang, he found himself heading outside to meet Emily. She was waiting excitedly for him just outside the front door.

"Ready to go?" Emily asked.

"Absolutely." Liam gave her a quick smile.

She slipped her hand into his again and guided him toward her house.

"So, do you want to order a pizza?" she asked as they walked. Liam considered this for a moment. Being the first date, he wanted to make it a little more special than just hanging out and having pizza.

"How about I make you dinner?" Liam offered.

"You can cook?" Emily asked, surprised.

"I'm actually a pretty good cook. I bet I can make you a gourmet meal out of anything you have in your kitchen," Liam challenged.

"OK, I would like to see that, because my mom definitely can't make a gourmet meal out of anything," Emily laughed.

They made small talk as they walked to Emily's house. Liam was glad she didn't ask about Matt or even bring up the subject of Heather's abduction.

When they arrived at the house, Emily guided him to the kitchen.

"OK, work your magic," she said, opening the fridge doors. Liam looked at what he had to work with. There wasn't much in the fridge. He looked through the cupboards and took a mental inventory of the spices and canned sauces he saw.

"OK," he said, turning to Emily. "I have an idea, but you are going to have to help me on the account of my broken hand."

"OK chef, what do you need me to do?"

"Grab four eggs and crack them into a bowl," Liam instructed.

"Sounds easy." She went to get a bowl as Liam pulled out the chicken and eggs from the fridge. Liam pulled bread crumbs and seasoning from the cupboard as well as a box of pasta. Emily started to crack the eggs and almost immediately laughed and said a loud, "Oops."

"What did you do?" Liam asked, coming over to her to investigate the bowl. There was shell all over the place and her hands were covered in egg.

"Seriously?" Liam laughed as he reached around her to take the shells out of her hand and bowl. She started giggling, backing up closer to him until she was pressed against him.

"I guess I get my cooking skills from my mother," she giggled as Liam reached around her and helped clean her hands with a towel. Still reaching around her, he picked up the other eggs one by one, and using only one hand, cracked them into the bowl with no shells falling in.

"Very impressive," she said, looking up at him over her shoulder.

"OK, you take the chicken and just drop it into the bowl with the eggs, get it all covered in egg," Liam said as he mixed the spices and bread crumbs. He had also turned on the oven and set a pot on the stove to boil water. Emily handed him the bowl with the chicken. He seasoned the chicken and placed it in the oven, then focused on making a sauce for the pasta. Emily worked around him, mostly cleaning up after him or doing small jobs he couldn't because of his cast. Liam noticed that she took every opportunity to touch him, either on the arm or back, and not so subtly brushing against him when ever she could.

His final meal included the breaded chicken, pasta with a rosé sauce, and a side of glazed carrots. Emily had set the table with candles and dimmed the lights.

"Wow Liam, this is really good," Emily said as they ate. "I have to admit, I am impressed."

"Thanks. I like to cook, it's a bit of a hobby of mine. You should see what I can do when I actually buy the ingredients."

"I may have to take you up on that offer." She smiled at him.

"So, does this make up for missing our date on the weekend?" Liam grinned. He was enjoying his time with her.

Emily stood up and reached across him to take his empty plate. She took it to the sink, then she walked back, took him by the hand and pulled him up from his seat.

"Not yet," she whispered. She led him to the family room and sat on the sofa. He sat next to her, expecting her to turn on the TV. Instead she leaned towards him and kissed him softly. She pulled back slowly and looked at him for a moment. The room was dark; she hadn't turned on any lights, and the sun had set awhile ago. Her pale skin looked almost porcelain in the dark, her bright blue eyes looked at him longingly. She kissed him again, and this time Liam slipped his hand softly behind her head and returned the kiss. She lay down on the sofa, gently pulling him down so he was lying next to her. She traced her fingers over his chest and then along his arms, then kissed him more yearningly. She pulled him close, pressing her body to his and wrapping her arms around his neck. Then she slowly pulled his shirt off and kissed his neck and chest.

"Emily," Liam said breathless. "We need to slow down."

"No, we don't," she said, pulling something out of her pocket and slipping it into his hand. He knew from the feel of the package that she had just handed him a condom.

"Have you done this before?" he said, gently pulling back from her. He ran his hand slowly up and down her arm.

"No," she said, embarrassed.

"We barely know each other," Liam said. "How do you know you want to do this with me?"

"Have you? Before?" she asked starting to kiss his chest again.

"Well yes, but that's different," Liam said, trying to focus. "I don't want you to regret anything." She ran her hand along his thigh. He was finding it difficult to resist.

"I've had a crush on you since sixth grade," she whispered in his ear and then kissed his neck. She alternated between biting softly and kissing his neck and chest. His heartbeat started to race; he was forcing himself not to give in to his urges and react. She gently ran her hands down his side and kissed his abdomen. Liam's mind was screaming at him to get out of there. He knew if he didn't stop this they would both be regretting it quickly. It took all his will, but he sat up and gently pulled her to a sitting position.

"We shouldn't do this," he said, softly trying to catch his breath.

"Don't you want to?" she said, looking at him hurt.

"Believe me, I want to, but that doesn't mean we should." Liam took her hand. "Emily, I really like you. But we barely know each other. I don't want you to regret anything tomorrow."

She lowered her head, ashamed. "I already do," she whispered.

"No don't, please." Liam tried to look her in the eyes. "I'm flattered, really, and I really do like you; that's why I think we should wait."

Emily nodded and looked back at him with sad eyes. Liam pulled her close and hugged her. She rested her head on his chest and they sat there for awhile in silence.

"Let's do something this weekend," Liam suggested after a little while, hoping to cheer her up. He gave her a gentle kiss on her forehead.

"I would like that," she said, still embarrassed.

"I should head home, but how about we have lunch together tomorrow?" Liam said. He didn't want it to seem like he was brushing her off. He got up slowly, getting up and pulling his shirt on.

"Yeah OK," Emily said, a little more cheerful.

Liam took her in his arms and gave her another kiss. "I had a really good time tonight," he said honestly to her.

"Me too. Thanks for a great dinner." She smiled back at him.

She had a great smile. *Almost as great as Amy's* he thought but quickly pushed that to the back of his mind, disgusted with himself. Why would he be thinking of Amy, especially now?

She walked him to the door and gave him another passionate kiss.

"You really aren't making this easy for me," Liam said. Her face was very close to his, he brushed some of her hair from her eyes.

"I have no intention to." She grinned as he left.

Liam was grateful to be out in the cold fall air. When he was only a few houses away from hers, he saw a car turn the corner onto the street and into Emily's driveway. Her parents seemed to have come home early. Liam sighed in relief; they would have been caught by her parents if he hadn't had left when he did.

Chapter Seven
America

    The South Korean Intelligence Agency advised the world they believed that North Korea was mobilizing long-range missiles. North Korea publicly and proudly mocked the USA, claiming that they would bomb mainland America.

    In response, the U.S. and Canadian military mobilized. Emergency services were advised to be ready to implement their emergency response plans and possible mass evacuations for major cities. The world was preparing for war.

Matt

    The next few days were a blur. Mark never asked the kids to go to school, and Matt had no intention of going back there until his mom came home safe. He didn't leave the house for days. Other than Amy visiting and responding to Liam's occasional text, Matt had no interaction with the outside world. Neighbours brought food by, which Mark politely accepted, but most of it remained uneaten. Grace stopped clinging to Matt for every second of every day, but she seldom left his side and she still hadn't spoken. Mark was lost on what he could do to help her and eventually called a child therapist for her. Mark had also not gone back to work. He stayed home most of the time, usually on calls with the police trying to get updates on the investigation. But there was nothing new. There were no reliable leads and there was never a ransom request. With each passing day hope lessened that Heather would be found alive.

"I think you should go see Lance," Mark said one morning while he was making coffee.

"Why?" Matt snorted, a little horrified that he could think of doing anything for himself.

"He can help find a positive release for your anger," Mark explained. "I talked to him last night, he said you can go by anytime today."

Matt tried to think of an excuse not to go, "What about Grace?"

"Don't worry, I'll take care of her," Mark injected quickly. "I'm not really asking. Go once, for me. If you don't agree that it helped, I won't bother you again."

"Fine, I'll go." Matt didn't have the energy to argue.

Matt headed over to Lance's gym later that morning. He walked since he needed fresh air and daylight. Lance was waiting for him when he arrived. Since it was the middle of the workday, the gym was empty.

"It's good to see you Matt," Lance said. "I'm glad you came by."

"My father kind of made me," Matt admitted.

"I figured as much," Lance replied. "But I think this will help you. Listen, we don't need to talk about anything that's going on; I'm not a god damn therapist, but I have a feeling you have a bunch of anger you want to vent, and I can use that to teach you a few things."

"OK," Matt nodded.

"Great, let's start over here." Lance led him into the gym towards some of the equipment.

Lance started Matt with a basic workout and then had him do more work on the punching bag. Matt didn't hold back any of his anger; he punched the hell out of the bag until his hands were bruised. Lance never criticized him or told him to go easy. Instead, he showed him new moves and stances to help with balance. He showed him more kicks and defensive moves. After almost two hours, Matt was exhausted.

"You think you are done for today?" Lance asked.

"Yeah," Matt said, out of breath. "Thanks. You were right, I really needed that."

"Anytime, son," Lance said, smacking him on the back.

"Tomorrow?"

"Yes, if you like. I'll be here."

"Thanks," Matt said heading out the door.

As he walked home, the repercussions of his extreme workout became quickly apparent. His body was aching, his hands were bruised, and his legs felt heavy as he walked. Matt's head felt clear, and for the first time since Heather went missing, he noticed his surroundings. It was still a warm sunny day, although there was a crispness in the autumn air. Since it was a school day, no one else his age was out on the streets. People were going about their business, running errands, heading to work, or just enjoying the day. He was walking down one of the busier roads when the light changed, and he had to wait to cross at the intersection. Suddenly a car turned right in front of him, partly on the sidewalk, forcing him to jump back from the curb. He looked up quickly and noticed that it was the black sedan with no license plates. Matt started running after the car down the side street it had just turned onto. The car seemed to slow, almost allowing him to catch up. Then suddenly it drove faster, leaving Matt behind.

Matt quickly picked up a ball size rock from a garden next to the sidewalk. He pitched the rock at the car as hard as he could and a second later a loud bang echoed through the neighbourhood as the rock shattered the back window of the car. Matt kept running, but the car sped away quickly. Just then Matt heard a police siren blast behind him.

"Don't move! Put your hands on your head," the officer yelled, getting out of the car and running over to Matt.

"What are you doing, who was in that car?" the officer questioned Matt, but Matt was too stunned and angry to reply. He was certain that car had something to do with his mother's abduction.

"What's your name?"

Matt just stared at the officer and kept quiet. He wasn't sure how he could explain his actions, so he decided not to say anything.

"Why aren't you in school?"

Matt refused to respond.

"Fine, we'll take a trip to the station." Matt didn't resist as the officer pushed him against the car, handcuffed him and threw him into the back seat of the police cruiser.

Matt said nothing to the police officer as he continued to question him on his way to the station. The officer asked again why he wasn't in school, who the driver of the car was and how his hands has gotten so bruised, but Matt remained silent the whole time. When they arrived at the station, the officer pulled him out of the car and escorted him inside. He sat Matt at a desk, still handcuffed, and asked him for his name again.

"My name is Matt Bailey," Matt finally responded quietly. "Is Officer Carson here?"

"Matt Bailey?" the officer repeated like he was trying to place his name. "Your mother is Heather Bailey?"

Matt nodded. "Is Officer Carson here?" he repeated.

The officer left him at the desk and a minute later he heard Officer Carson's voice behind him.

"Get those cuffs off that kid," he bellowed, and someone quickly complied.

"Matt, what the hell happened?" Carson asked with concern, not anger.

"The car—it was the one that I told you about. He almost hit me when he turned the corner, so I chased him. When I got close enough, I threw the rock at him."

"Are you sure it was the same car?"

"Yeah, it was. The plates were missing. But it was almost like he was trying to lead me down that road. He made sure I saw him and then slowed so I could almost catch up to him."

"Carson," Harris said as he walked over to the desk. "I spoke with the officer. He was running his route when he saw the car almost hit Matt. He started following them, but when he turned onto the street they were on, the car started to speed away. That's when he saw Matt throwing the rock and smashing the back window of the car." Harris turned to Matt. "He said the car was at least eighty feet away when you threw that rock—you got quite an arm."

"Harris, get some guys out in cruisers and see if you can find any black cars with no plates and a smashed back window."

Harris left to organize the search.

"Matt, come on, I'll drive you home." Carson grabbed the keys from his desk while Matt followed him out of the station.

"So, am I allowed to ride in the front this time?" Matt asked sarcastically.

"Of course," Carson replied, unlocking the car. "Look Matt, you have to understand, the officer had to act based on what he saw. He didn't know who you were."

"I know," Matt said. "No hard feelings."

"I'm glad to hear that. Besides, any cop would have thought you were up to no good being out of school in the middle of the day with your fists are all bruised." Carson gave him an inquiring look.

Matt looked at his bruised and swollen hands. "I was at Lance's gym, he's training me."

"Really?" Carson was impressed. "I know Lance; I go to his gym, he's good. He knows what he's talking about. You must have been handing out quite a beating for your hands to be that bruised."

"I suppose, apparently I have a few feelings that I have been suppressing."

"No shit!" Carson agreed. "Sorry, I shouldn't swear in front of you."

"I don't care," Matt said matter of factly.

"Still, it's not professional on my part."

"Hey, you just saved me from being arrested; I'm not going to say anything to anyone if you drop a few curse words."

"Well, if you were right about that car, I doubt we will be getting a complaint."

"Do you think the driver of that car is involved with my mom's kidnapping?" Matt asked.

"Officially, I have to say that we are not excluding any leads right now." Carson looked over to Matt. "Personally, I think it's a strong lead, especially after what happened today. But you need to be careful."

"Me? Why?"

"If these people already have your mother, why are they still bothering you?" Carson explained. "I have a feeling there is something they still want, and they may try to get to you or you sister to get it."

"What could they possibly want with us?"

"I have no idea. Maybe just to use you for leverage, but I'm going to talk to your father about putting a police watch on your house. And you and your sister need to be careful when you go out. Your dad's a smart man. Thankfully, because of his job he's a little more sensitive to these things than most people."

They arrived at the house and Matt led Officer Carson inside. He explained to Mark what had happened. Mark's expression quickly changed to horror while Carson recommended the extra security measures.

"Of course, I agree. I want these kids to be safe. I'm just shocked that these people are continuing to threaten my family—and they have made no demands! What the hell are they after?"

"We are trying to figure that out," Carson said sympathetically.

"I know, I'm just feeling like I am losing my mind. I'm not sure how much more I can take," Mark said, rubbing his forehead.

"I promise we will do what we can to take care of your family and bring your wife home. Have you been talking to the social worker or therapist? It's not a sign of weakness to seek help to manage something, especially something like this."

Mark shook his head, "I'll be able to manage; the therapist is actually speaking with Grace right now in the other room."

"Any progress?" Carson inquired.

"No, she hasn't spoken since last Friday."

"I'm sorry Mark, for everything you are going through. I'm going to go back to my car and make some calls to arrange additional patrols to come around your place. I'll check back in on you in a little while."

Carson shook Mark's hand and then let himself out the front door.

Grace joined them in the kitchen with her therapist, Dr. Jane Woods. Grace slipped her hand into Matt's and stood quietly. She had gotten to a point where she could be left in a room by herself for a short time, but she still refused to talk or sleep by herself. Dr. Woods gave Mark a signal to follow her out of the room, so they could speak.

"Do you want some lunch?" Matt asked Grace when they were alone. "I'm starving, how about I make some mac and cheese for us?"

Grace just nodded in reply.

"You know," Matt said as he pulled out a pot and filled it with water. "Maybe we can watch a movie after?" Grace just shrugged. "What if I let you watch one of those girly high school singing movies? And I promise I'll stay awake for the whole thing!"

Grace gave him a half smile and a quick nod.

"Do you want the mac and cheese extra cheesy?"

Another smile and nod, but Grace still wouldn't talk. Matt continued cooking the pasta for them. Mark returned to the kitchen and gave Grave a hug. "That smells good," Mark said, inspecting Matt's cooking.

"Want some?" Matt offered as he scooped the pasta into the bowls.

"Yes thanks, I think I may have forgotten to eat today," Mark said. "Extra cheesy, just like your mom makes it," Mark said before he realized what he was saying. He looked at Grace, who looked like she was about to cry.

"Yeah, just like mom's," Matt said quickly. "Maybe when we eat this and think of her, she will feel it and it will give her strength to find her way home."

Grace sucked in one sob and then took her bowl of pasta. She hugged it tightly too her as she carried it to the table.

"Thanks," Mark whispered to Matt as they joined her at the table. "So how was your session with Lance?"

"It was good. You were right, it was just what I needed," Matt replied. "I would like to go back tomorrow."

Mark took a moment to consider this. "I'll drive you over then, I don't want you walking around the streets again."

"So, you'll drive me everywhere from now on? Dad, I can't be a hostage in my own home," Matt protested.

"I'm not going to let anything else happen to this family!!" Mark suddenly yelled. Grace cried immediately. "I'm so sorry," Mark said, going over quickly to hug her.

"Maybe we should all go?" Matt said quietly after a moment. Grace looked up at him with a confused look on her face. "I mean, today when I went I realized for the first time how angry I was. And you know what Grace? I beat the crap out of a punching bag and it felt really good." Grace gave a little giggle through her tears. "Do you want to come with me tomorrow? Maybe we can find a Grace-size punching bag you can beat the crap out of?" Grace nodded yes enthusiastically.

They sat down again and ate their pasta in silence. As Matt started with the dishes, there was a knock at the door. Mark went to answer it and a moment later Officer Carson entered the kitchen.

"Matt," Mark said. "Officer Carson needs to talk to us for a few minutes."

"Yeah sure," Matt said, drying his hands on a towel. They all looked at Grace, and Matt understood this wasn't something she was supposed to hear. "Hey Gracie, why don't you go pick out that movie I promised you. And I'll be there in a few minutes, OK?"

Grace nodded and slowly slid off her chair and headed to the family room. Matt, Mark and Carson sat around the table.

"We found the car," Carson explained. "It was abandoned behind a warehouse. It had been cleaned: there were no prints at all. When we ran the VIN, we found out that it had been stolen a couple of months ago. We found your rock in the back seat." Carson paused. "I know we have been over this a few times Matt, but I need you to tell me again about all the conversations you heard about your mom's work."

Matt told Carson what he had heard, first with the call on speakerphone and then the conversation the night before Heather had disappeared. Carson also asked about the letter Matt had read, and Matt tried to recall word for word what had been on the page.

"And you are certain the person she was talking to was named Kevin?" Carson asked

"Yeah pretty certain. Mom never talked much about work at home, but I'm pretty sure she called this guy Kevin a couple of times when she was talking to him."

"Are you thinking Heather's abduction has something to do with this Kevin guy and the report she was going to file?" Mark asked.

"Possibly," Carson sighed. "I'm going to tell you something, and I trust you won't repeat this to anyone, as it's only one theory we are looking into," he paused for a moment considering what he should tell them. "Heather's office hasn't been very cooperative with the investigation. They deny Heather had any coworkers named Kevin. They are also denying that any investigation Heather was working on matched what you told us Matt."

"Can you get a warrant?" Mark asked.

"No, I need more to go on. Unfortunately, Matt is the only witness to this, and a high-powered international bank executive seems to have a little more credibility than a high school kid."

"I'm not lying!" Matt said defensively.

"I believe you!" Carson threw his hands up. "The problem is there is nothing that supports it. The home office was cleaned out, either by your mother or someone else after she was taken, but we have no evidence that anyone outside of the family was in that room. We searched this house repeatedly to find those pages you saw, but we have found nothing. Matt, you are the only person right now who is admitting that report ever existed."

"Do you think that's why they came after me?" Matt asked slowly.

"It would be a pretty big conspiracy theory if that's true, but if that car was connected to your mom's abduction, and now they are coming after you, they may think you know or have something."

"Do you think my mom's still alive?" Matt asked softly.

"I think that's still a possibility," Carson said confidently. "I think if this conspiracy theory against the bank is true, your mother hasn't given them what they want yet, and they are trying to find another way to get it."

"What can we do?" Mark asked.

"Stay safe. Maybe they will reach out to negotiate if they get desperate enough," Carson said. "Let the police handle it." He gave Mark a stern look when he said the last part.

Matt suffered through two high school singing movies and a modern-day Cinderella movie to keep Grace company. In the early evening, Amy came by with more of his homework, which he added to the pile on his desk of the other assignments she had been bringing him. Grace had followed them upstairs and was lying on his bed watching videos on her iPad with headphones on.

"How are you?" Amy asked, taking Matt's hand as he stood next to the desk. The warmth that used to radiate through him every time she was near had somehow extinguished. As much as Matt wanted to have those feelings for Amy, the events of the past week had made it impossible to feel anything other than anger and rage. When he felt nothing at all, he thought it was an improvement.

"Managing," he said. She came closer and hugged him. He still felt nothing, but he hugged her back because he knew that's what he was supposed to do.

"Everyone has been asking about you," Amy said.

"I imagine the gossip rings are having the time of their life with this," Matt said angrily.

"No Matt, don't think that," Amy said sadly. "Everyone cares and are truly concerned. People are shocked too—everyone liked your mom."

"Apparently not *everyone*," he snapped back. He wasn't sure why he was being so rude to her; she was just trying to help. Amy pulled away from him. "Maybe I should just go."

Matt's gut was telling him he should tell her to stay and apologize to her. But nothing in his heart was motivating him to stop her.

"Wait!" he said just as she had her hand on the door. "I'm sorry. I'm being a jerk, I just don't know how to handle this."

"I understand," she said sadly. "I'm here for you, whatever you need. If you want me to go, I'll go. If you want me to stay, I'll stay. I don't know how to help you; I just know I want to."

Matt nodded, and he sat on the edge of his desk, shoving his hands deep into his pockets and staring at the floor. Amy stayed at the door waiting for him to respond.

Matt pulled in a deep breath. "I'm not sure what to do with us," he explained. "It's something I can't even begin to think about right now. Barely a week ago, you were the only thing I could think about. But now I'm angry all the time, and I want to lash out at everyone around me. I can't just go on and live a normal life." Amy was about to say something, but Matt stopped her, "and I'm particularly tired of people telling me how sorry they are for me." Amy looked ashamed. "And if the anger isn't there, then I feel nothing. I slip into this void, and everything I feel like I should be caring about—school, friends, baseball, and especially you—I feel nothing. There is nothing at all left inside me for those things right now."

Amy nodded. "This doesn't have to be anything right now," she said. "It doesn't have to be anything at all, until you think it can be again. I just want you to know that I'm here for you, and I'll do anything to help."

"Thank you," Matt said. "I appreciate that you can understand."

"I'm guessing you haven't been watching the news at all?" Amy asked, changing the subject.

"No, I'm worried the story about my mom will air. I don't want Grace to see it."

"Every once in awhile there is an update on her, but nothing's been reported in the last couple of days. The war is escalating though. North Korea has been firing missiles, mostly at U.S. crafts in international water, but it's starting to get serious."

"The Cuban missile crisis all over again," Matt mumbled.

"Wow, you actually learned something in Mr. Roland's class?"

"No," Matt replied. "Emily just keeps good notes."

"Well I thought you should know that you may want to turn on the news occasionally, just in case nuclear war starts," she said sadly.

"The world is really going to hell isn't it?" Matt said, looking at Grace, who seemed glued to her tablet screen.

"Seems like it," Amy said. "I'm going to head out. But Matt, if you or your family ever need anything, call me." She came over, gave him a soft kiss on the cheek and then left. Matt almost felt relieved when she left. He wanted to feel those feelings again for her, and he felt guilty that he couldn't. He also wanted to tell her about the car that morning, about him almost getting arrested, and about his mom's company possibly covering things up. But telling her all of that would require a desire to be with her, and that was something he did not have. He had no desire to see anyone or do anything except to figure out where Heather was.

Chapter Eight
Canada

Notifications were sent to all the regional police stations, hospitals, fire stations and paramedics. Everyone was asked to be diligent of threats and be ready at any time to activate their emergency plans. There was a true and real threat on America and Canada, being America's closest ally politically and geographically.

Authorities were specifically concerned about attacks on the nuclear power plants around the country. Shared intelligence suggested these could be targets. In the event of a threat on the nuclear plant, the evacuation plan included anyone within a ten-kilometre radius. Although it didn't include the city, there were over half a million people living within that radius.

Matt

The next morning, Mark, Grace and Matt went to Lance's gym together. Matt showed Grace the punching bags and showed her how to throw a punch. She hit her little fists into the bag over and over again. At first, she did it with anger, but eventually she giggled when she realized that even with her hardest hit, the bag wouldn't move. Matt showed her some moves Lance had taught him the day before, and Grace seemed impressed.

Lance eventually came over and offered to train Matt. Grace watched for a bit more and then explored the rest of the gym, and Mark watched silently as Lance coached Matt. Lance encouraged Matt to take him down. He showed him defensive moves first, and Matt repeatedly tried to get Lance down to the ground, or get a good swing at him, but Lance always avoided it. Then Lance coached Matt on the offensive moves. Once everything was explained, Lance encouraged Matt to come at him again. This time Matt moved a lot more thoughtfully. There was strategy behind his advancement, and he was paying attention to Lance's body stance to predict his moves. Matt was learning quickly what Lance was teaching him.

"Well done," Lance said, slightly out of breath when they were done.

"Thanks," Matt replied, completely out of breath.

"He reminds me of you," Lance said to Mark.

"I hope not!" Mark exclaimed. "I'm hoping he will have better sense than I did at that age."

"I don't think that you need to worry about that—that's a given," Lance jeered. "Do you want to have a go? Maybe with some boxing gloves on?"

"Maybe some other time." Mark declined. "But I did want to ask you something. Do you still do any PI work?"

"Not much anymore, but I still have a lot of contacts. I was hoping you would ask."

"Ask what?" Mark tried to sound confused.

"I know what you want to ask; you want me to see if I can find anything out about Heather. Police aren't getting anywhere are they?"

"No, this may require some non-legal means," Mark said quietly. He glanced at Matt and continued, "Matt overheard and saw some stuff with regards to Heather's work. It seems she was working on an investigation that didn't look so well for the company, and they weren't too happy about. All the papers from her home office have gone missing. And they deny that anything Matt heard is true." Matt took the lead from his father and explained what he had heard during the phone calls and what he'd seen in the letter. He also told Lance about the car he had seen around their house and how he had encountered it the day before.

"The police have asked us not to do anything; they want to handle this investigation without private interference, but they can't even get a warrant to search the company, and by now it might be too late," Mark concluded.

Lance listened quietly for a moment, considering what they told him. "I may know a few people to call," he said slowly. "Let me see who I can trust with this."

"Thanks Lance, I appreciate it," Mark said, sounding very tired.

"Will you be back again tomorrow?" Lance asked Matt.

"Yeah, if that's OK?" Matt looked at his dad.

"We will figure it out," Mark replied. "I still don't want you walking around alone. Even though you can clearly kick some serious ass now."

"If you bring the kids by tomorrow, I might, and I stress might, be able to get you an update."

"Really, that quick?"

"Don't get your hopes up. Like I said, I might have some contacts I can reach out too."

"Thanks man, you are the best." Mark smacked Lance on the back.

Grace had been playing on the weight training machines and sliding back and forth on the rowing machines. She had also spent a good amount of time using the Bosu Balls as a bouncy toy. She looked exhausted and almost happy. Matt realized sadly this had been the first time Grace had left the house since Heather had gone missing. He felt bad he hadn't thought to take her to the park or playground. Matt called Grace over and they said their good byes to Lance.

Amy

Amy was relieved it was Friday morning. Even though she had no plans for the weekend, doing nothing was still better than school. She packed her school bag and headed out to her little Hyundai Accent. She loved her cheap little car. It wasn't anything fancy, but it meant freedom. She took a detour again and see if she could find Liam on his way to school. She was feeling conflicted about the way she and Matt last parted and she was hoping she could talk to Liam about it. Technically, she and Matt had never even started dating, but she knew that he had felt the same way about her as she did for him. It was horrible what had happened to his mother. Amy wanted to be there for the family, not only to help with Grace, but to support Matt. She knew any type of a romantic relationship was out of the question right now with him, but that didn't change the way she felt for him.

Sure, enough Liam was just starting down his street when she turned the corner. Emily had eventually spilled the beans to Amy about their date. Amy wasn't sure why Liam didn't give in to Emily; she had originally thought of him as a dumb jock with a reputation for sleeping around, but as she got to know him better, he was proving that she had misjudged him.

She drove up behind him and honked the horn. He jumped and then smiled and waved.

"Need a ride?" Amy asked through the passenger window.

"Sure thanks," Liam said, getting in.

"So, how are you?" Amy attempted small talk but couldn't hold back her laugh.

"I'm good." Liam grinned at her. "Emily told you about our date, didn't she?"

"Um, yes." Amy gave him a smile. "I'm proud of you."

"Gee, thanks Mom," Liam said sarcastically. "Did she also tell you her parents got home only seconds after I left?"

"What? No!" Amy was shocked.

"If I hadn't stopped it, we would have been caught, right there on the sofa. Me defiling their sweet girl of her innocents, in full view of her parents as they walked in from their nice evening out." Liam laughed at the thought.

"I guess she has a couple of reasons to be grateful to you." Amy giggled. "By the way, I'm fairly sure her father owns a shotgun."

"Something you could have told me Monday!" Liam complained with a laugh.

"Can I ask you something?" Amy's tone got serious.

"Sure, but I may choose not to answer," Liam responded cautiously.

Amy nodded. "Why did you stop with Emily? I mean, you have a bit of a reputation."

Liam sighed. At first Amy didn't think he would answer, she worried she had offended him, but then he replied.

"It's true, I may have had some *fun* before," he explained. "When my brother was still living at home last summer, he used to party a lot and I would join him. My mom had just left, and I was angry and reckless. He told the girls I was in college with him. I was tall enough even then; no one questioned it. Those girls were all older, and more experienced. They always initiated it, but I wasn't exactly protesting." He paused; he seemed to consider if he could trust her with the next part. "One girl fell for me hard. When she realized I wasn't up for anything more than the physical aspect, she was crushed. She tried to hurt herself and her parents pulled her out of school."

Amy could hear the regret in Liam's voice, and it seemed to upset him to talk about it.

"I learned from that," he continued. "I want to make sure I don't do that to anyone else, Emily included. She just seems so young and innocent."

"Sounds like you might actually care for her," Amy said.

"I respect her, and I don't want her to get hurt," Liam said quickly. "Unfortunately, that was my mistake with the others, I wasn't thinking of them at all." Liam looked Amy in the eyes. She could see he was struggling talking about this. "Look Amy, I'm not proud of it, and I'm not the bragging type. The only reason it got around the school was because one of the guys on the ball team. His older brother was at some of the same parties and told him I had been sleeping around with older girls. He started bragging for me, but really I was just embarrassed."

Amy glanced at him, then made the turn into the school parking lot.

"You keep surprising me Liam," she said as she parked the car. "I promise you can trust me. I won't tell Emily anything."

"Thanks, I appreciate it."

"How come we haven't spoken like this before Liam?" Amy asked. "We've been in classes together all through high school. I think we have spoken more to each other during this car ride than we have in the last three years."

"That's probably because you thought I was a man-whore womaniser," Liam said only half joking.

"Yeah, you're right, that was it. I'm so sorry for that," she said, not denying his allegation. "I'm glad I know you better now. Can I ask you a favour?"

"Sure."

"If you happen to be talking with Matt, can you just let me know how he's doing?"

Liam gave her a confused look. "I haven't been talking to him really. Did something happen between you two?"

"We had a bit of a falling out." She sighed. "I'm not sure that he actually wants me around. I was just trying to be helpful, but he's so withdrawn, I don't know what I can do."

"It's just a crazy time for him," Liam said. "Hang in there, I know he needs you."

"Thanks Liam." She gently touched his arm. Behind them, the school bell rang to announce the start of classes.

"We better run," Amy said as they got out of the car.

At the end of the day, Amy gathered her stuff and headed to her car. She saw Liam and Emily walking home together; they had been talking about their plans over lunch. Dinner and a movie. Liam made a point of picking very public places now when they were together. Amy drove home. She debated stopping to visit with Matt, but she knew both her parents would be home, so she went straight there.

"Hello," she yelled as she opened the door.

"Hi honey, we're in here." Melissa called from the kitchen.

Amy found her parents sitting around the kitchen table, both still in their uniforms from their shifts.

"What's up?" she asked, setting her school bag down.

"We actually need to talk to you," Steve said. "Have a seat."

"OK, this sounds serious." Amy slid into a chair across from them.

"It is," Melissa said. "Both of our works have given us emergency response plans if the war escalates or if there are threats to this area." She paused to ensure Amy was following. "If, and this is a big if, there is a threat, then both your father and I are part of the emergency response team. So, if something happens or there is an evacuation order, we would be some of the last to leave."

"We have been discussing what we want you to do," her father jumped in. "We need you to take your grandma and head up to your aunt's house in Orillia. OK?"

"Why there?" Amy asked.

"Because it's remote enough that we hope that the traffic wouldn't be so bad, and it's also far enough that if anything happened in the city, you would be safe," Melissa explained.

"You want me to leave you behind?" Amy asked, a little terrified.

"We would have to stay to work, but we would follow you there as soon as we can," Steve said. "Listen, we have a thousand dollars hidden in the safe. You take that; it will be enough to get you to Orillia. Your aunt's expecting you in the event of an emergency."

"Wow." Amy shook her head. "I can't believe that we are having this conversation." But she understood these were the times they lived in.

October
Chapter Nine
Matt

It quickly turned into a habit to attend Lance's gym after breakfast every day. Grace would play on various machines or take punches at the punching bags. Lance would spend at least an hour training Matt, then Mark and Lance would disappear to the lounge to discuss the progress of Lance's investigation, while Matt worked out by himself. This routine continued until the end of the week, and then the next week as well. It had been almost two weeks since Heather had gone missing. Along with going to the gym daily, Matt started to work on the school work he had fallen behind on. He also helped Grace with some of the work sent home for her. Mark never pushed them to go back to school—or even to do the homework—but Matt thought that bringing back some normality may help Grace. It also distracted him and kept his mind from dwelling on reality. He sent his assignments back to school with Liam, who had visited more regularly. Amy still came by, but when she did she mostly spent time with Grace and only spoke with Matt if he initiated a conversation, which wasn't often.

On Thursday, Liam came by the house. Matt answered the door when he heard the doorbell and found Liam sitting on the front porch.

Matt sat down next to him. "How's it going?" he asked.

"It's going," Liam answered. "What about you?"

Matt just shrugged in response, he didn't bother to lie to Liam with a socially acceptable, polite response.

Liam waved his left hand in the air. "Got my cast off." It was now wrapped in a tensor bandage.

"So, you're better?" Matt asked, confused. Liam was supposed to go back to the hospital sometime that week, Matt recalled.

"Not exactly. My father took it upon himself to remove the cast. He felt it was fine. Now he fancies himself a doctor."

"Geez, Liam."

"No man, don't you dare start saying you feel sorry for me. You of all people." Liam groaned.

"No, I was going to say he's an asshole. As far as having a crap week goes, I think I'm still winning."

"Agreed," Liam said, "but look at this." He pulled up his shirt to expose his right side. There was a deep blue bruise on his ribs.

"What the hell happened?" Matt exclaimed.

"He kicked my ass. I guess he wasn't as old as I thought," Liam muttered. "So instead of helping me get my hand fixed, I'm fairly certain he broke my ribs."

"What are you going to do?" Matt asked.

"I don't know," Liam said running his hands through his hair. "It's been getting worse over the last couple of months. I sleep with my door locked, because if I don't, he will stumble in there drunk and start smacking the hell out of me. Today, he found out that my mother had emailed me. I never even replied, but he lost it on me." He paused and looked at Matt. "Look, I didn't mean to come over here to dump more crap on you. I just wanted to let you know that if it happens that I take off one day, you would understand why, right?"

Matt nodded his head. "I would understand. You know, you can stay here?"

Liam shook his head. "You have enough problems of your own, I can't trouble you guys right now." Liam then smirked. "Though on the flip side, Emily is giving me some good incentive to stay," Liam laughed.

"So, things are heating up with you and her?"

"Yeah she's cool. She's stopped with her silly girl act and talks to me like a real person now." Liam adjusted his seating, groaned and held his side tight. "Son of a bitch," he said through clenched teeth. "So how are things with you and Amy?" he said once he could catch his breath.

"They're not," Matt replied. Liam looked at Matt with raised eyebrows, but Matt didn't want to talk about it.

"So, is coach still running practices?" Matt quickly tried to change the subject.

"Yeah, I have been able to skip them because of my hand. But I'm not sure how I'll be able to cover up broken ribs for too long."

"Would you consider telling him the truth?"

"I can't. He's obligated to report it. If the police or child services get involved and dear old dad ends up in jail or something, I wouldn't be able to support myself. I just want to graduate, then I'll figure stuff out."

As they sat on the porch, the afternoon quickly turned to twilight and the cool air of the fall night settled in. The traffic on the street got busy as the people who worked in the city came home. It would have been the same train Heather took home. Matt tried to push that thought back down to where it had escaped from. He looked up at the cars and tried to recognize each neighbour before they passed. Being home for the two weeks with not much to do, Matt had become very familiar with the comings and goings of the neighbourhood. He watched one car slowly turn down the street. He didn't recognize it and immediately became suspicious. Liam noticed him intently watching the car.

"What is it?" Liam asked, but Matt didn't reply.

The car slowed as it approached the house, and Matt could see the man driving. It was the same man who had been in the black sedan. He waved at Matt again and continued to drive. Matt quickly jumped off the porched and ran after the car. The car sped down the street. Liam got up too and started to run, then doubled over after only a few steps.

"Matt, come on, I can't run with a broken rib." He winced, trying to catch his breath, and jogged slowly after him.

Matt ran as fast as he could after the car, but it got out of reach quickly.

"*Come back here you chicken shit!*" he yelled as the car turned out of sight.

"What was that?" Liam asked, eventually catching up with Matt. He was holding his side, in pain.

"That guy has something to do with my mom's abduction."

"Why is he scoping you out?"

"I have no idea, but I would love to get my hands on him," Matt affirmed.

Liam

Liam stayed with Matt a little longer, mainly to let the pain from his ribs lessen, before he attempted the walk home. He hid from Matt how much he was hurt—just like he had hidden all the previous injuries: the broken hand, black eyes and a concussion. Matt had enough to worry about with his mother missing; Liam had no intentions to add to Matt's problems.

As usual, when Liam arrived home, his father was nowhere to be found. Liam grabbed an ice pack and the Tylenol and headed to his room. He pulled his shirt off and lay down on his bed, applying the ice pack to his ribs. He pulled out his phone. There were a dozen text messages from Emily. He hadn't texted her all day and she was worried since he had missed school. He sent her a text: *Sorry, got a really bad flu, been sleeping all day. Text you when I feel better.* She responded immediately: *I can come take care of you.* He quickly replied, *No, I'm too sick just need rest, maybe I'll see you tomorrow.* She sent a happy face back. Liam sighed. He couldn't understand why a girl would want to come over to see a guy who just confessed to having the flu. He checked the other texts. Amy was asking if he had seen Matt. Liam responded carefully, saying Matt was basically the same. He wanted to keep Amy happy; he didn't want her to worry even more.

He moved on to the other messages. There were a few good jokes from the guys from the ball team. Then he pulled up the email his mother had sent. The email that had caused his father to freak out. He re-read it and considered the offer. She apologized for leaving; she now had a good job and a place to live, big enough for him to move into, but she was on the other end of the province, so it would mean leaving his school, baseball and friends and starting over, halfway through his graduating year. Besides, she had left him behind.

She had left in the middle of the night, with no warning and no goodbyes. In her email she claimed that she had wanted to take him, and she wanted to make that up to him now. She hinted that she was worried that Peter's temper would be "re-directed" at him. Liam tossed his phone angrily on the floor. Had she known, or even suspected this is what she would be leaving him with, then he could never forgive her for leaving without him. Liam lay on his bed in the dark, the icepack slowly melting and leaking into his sheets. At some point he fell asleep.

Liam woke to the sound of his father stumbling through the house. At first his mind told him to just go back to sleep, but then he snapped awake in a panic. He had forgotten to lock his bedroom door. He tried to get up too quickly, and a grinding ripping feeling shot through his broken ribs. He fell back down onto his bed, out of breath and temporarily paralyzed by his injury. Peter came slamming through the door, stumbling into Liam's bedroom.

"You still here?" He growled at Liam. "You know your mother's the one who left you here. She doesn't love you; she only wants you to go to her because she thinks it will punish me more, she wants to ruin me."

Peter stumbled over to the bed. "That's what you guys are planning, isn't it?" Peter grabbed Liam by the shoulders and threw him on the floor. Liam was gasping for breath. Peter was still wearing his work boots, which were steel toed, and he started to kick Liam, who was completely defenceless, in the gut.

"Come on you wimp." Peter landed another kick, this time to Liam's back. Liam tried to stand but could only manage to get to his knees.

"You are a drunken…worthless…piece of shit," Liam wheezed. "And if I fought back you would be dead."

"Are you threatening me?" Peter screamed. "You think you can take me? Come on!"

Peter swung at Liam, landing a punch to his left eye. Liam was immediately knocked down again. Peter continued to kick him in the side and the gut.

"Oh yeah, you're a tough guy," Peter taunted as he continued his attack. Liam was winded, gasping for breath, he could feel himself losing consciousness. He saw Peter hovering over him, smirking, just before he passed out.

Liam woke to his phone buzzing somewhere not far from his head and the sun beaming in through the window. He was still lying on his floor in his room, and every inch of him was aching. He took in a deep breath, and his ribs ached as he filled his lungs with air. He slowly exhaled and tried to focus on the pain in his back and gut. He wondered if he could sit up. *Maybe in a few minutes*, he told himself. His left hand was also throbbing. He vaguely recalled getting kicked in the hand while he tried to cover his head. He continued to breath deeply, slowly focusing on each limb before he tried to move it. He could feel dried blood on his face, Peter's punch had split the skin by his eyebrow, and the cut had bled significantly while he was unconscious. He closed his eyes and concentrated. Nothing else felt broken. He sucked in another deep breath, trying to ignore the pain, then exhaled, pulling himself up into a sitting position at the same time. He yelled a few curse words as he forced himself to stand up. He steadied himself and headed to the shower. He turned the water on cold and then pulled out a bottle of Tylenol Three from the medicine cabinet. There were still several pills in it from when he'd had his wisdom teeth pulled a few months ago. He swallowed two, paused, then took two more. Between the extra long cold shower and a double dose of the Tylenol Three, Liam found the pain almost bearable.

 He headed back to his room and clumsily wrapped a tensor bandage around his injured hand. Then he picked up his phone to check the time and was shocked to see it was already after lunch. He had missed almost a whole day of school while he was passed out. There were several text messages from Emily again wishing him to feel better. There was also a text from Matt, asking him to come over. He confirmed he would and regretted it almost immediately. He wasn't sure how he would get over there, but if Matt was asking for him, something important must have happened. Liam sighed. It would be a long walk over. He dressed slowly and eventually got himself out the door.

Matt

 Matt knew it was wrong, but he didn't tell his father about the man in the car coming around again. He decided he would tell Officer Carson the first chance he had, but he didn't want to worry his father any more. He also didn't want to be put on house arrest "for his own safety."

 Mark had kept Matt informed on Lance's investigation updates. Lance had told him he had some contacts that worked at the same bank as Heather. He said he had one person specifically that he trusted and who may be able to help. He needed time, Lance had said. The bank employed tens of thousands of people around the world, so it would take his contact some time to access what he needed without raising suspicion. It was Friday, two weeks after Heather's abduction, that they finally had some real news. Lance met them at the door holding some papers and led Mark and Matt to the lounge right away while Grace headed to her usual spots in the gym.

"I finally have some information," he started. "There is definitely a Kevin working at the company that Heather would have known." He pulled a paper from the file he was holding and handed it to Mark. Matt looked at the page, it was a picture of a man. Kevin Jacobs was the name listed under the picture. The page listed his department and phone number which were for New York.

"He's in New York?" Matt asked.

"Was. He's been missing at least as long as your mother, except the company says he's on medical leave," Lance explained.

"I have seen him before," Matt said slowly. "He looks like the man that was outside our house in the car."

"That puts him in our area around when Heather went missing," Mark said to Lance.

"And my contact was able to confirm that there was a report Heather was working on that has been completely deleted from the system. The bank tracks everything an employee does while they are logged into the system. A few days before Heather was taken, she printed a file that was called *T Chenko's Industries Investigation Report.* She also copied a bunch of data to an external hard drive. Normally employees are restricted from copying data to external drives, but given your mother's role, she had higher security clearance. The strange thing is, everything she copied has since been deleted. Only the tracking record of her making the copy exists."

"I guess the conspiracy theory wasn't that far off," Mark said.

"No, it wasn't," Lance agreed.

"Could they have killed her to shut her up?" Mark asked bluntly.

"Possibly, Mark, I'm sorry to say it, but if they think she is the last link to this report, they would likely want to eliminate her."

Matt felt his heart beat increasing as he sat there processing what Lance was saying. His hands started to sweat, and he realized he was about to have another panic attack. He bit his tongue to stay focused.

"We need to go to the police with this," Mark said urgently.

"If you do, please don't tell them that you got this from me. My contact is terrified of what he found out. He covered his tracks well, but he is worried for his safety."

"Understood," Mark said.

"What happened to the report, and the stuff she downloaded," Matt asked suddenly.

"Likely they took it when they cleaned out her desk," Mark replied.

"Are you sure?"

"Fairly sure. The police have gone through the house with a fine-tooth comb too. I think they would have found it, if it were still there. And I have looked too," Mark admitted. "I have been hoping that she hid that report somewhere, in a spot that only I would think of. But I haven't found anything either," Mark said sadly. He covered his face with his hands.

"I'll get Grace," Matt offered. "We should head home."

Mark nodded, and Matt walked off to find his sister. Matt found Grace playing on a treadmill. He waved her over, then pulled his phone out of his pocket and sent a text to Liam. *Can you meet at my place after school?* Liam replied a moment later with a thumbs up. Grace came over and took his hand and they walked over to meet Mark at the door.

"Can you drive for me?" Mark, who was looking completely exhausted, handed the car keys over to Matt.

"Yeah sure." Matt was a little reluctant; he hadn't been behind the wheel for a few weeks now, but he enjoyed driving. It meant freedom.

When they got home, Mark excused himself. He said he would be calling the police to explain the information Lance had given him. Matt turned on the TV for Grace and handed her the remote. She gave him her look that clearly said she wanted him to stay with her. Matt sighed and flopped down next to her on the sofa. Grace had found another mind-torturing tweeny show about kids that ran a music store, or maybe it was a hotel? Who cared? He didn't realize he had dozed off until he woke to the sound of the doorbell ringing.

"I'll get it," he yelled as he jumped up from the sofa.

He found Liam at the door when he opened it.

"Schools not out yet?" Matt said as he let him in, and then he noticed Liam seemed even worse off than the day before. He was walking slowly; his left eye was swollen, and he was sweating like crazy.

"Yeah, I had to skip today," Liam said slowly, easing into a chair in the living room. He looked like he would pass out.

Before Matt could ask what happened, Mark walked into the room. "Was that Officer Carson?" he was saying, but then stopped when he saw Liam. Liam tried to sit straighter and put his head down, but Mark had seen the bruises.

"What's going on Liam?" Mark said slowly. When Liam didn't answer, Mark turned to Matt. "Is this something that happened at school?"

"No," Liam answered quickly.

"You are getting hurt at home?" Mark asked.

"Yes," Liam replied quietly.

"Your father did this," Mark confirmed, and Liam nodded.

Mark was silent as he considered the situation. He stared hard at Liam and after a long time said, "you'll stay with us."

"Mr. Bailey, I can't intrude on you, especially now," Liam protested.

"And I won't let you go back there, knowing this is what is happening. Besides, it's exactly what Heather would have done." Mark's mind was made up, Matt knew Liam would not win this argument.

"How long has this been going on?" Mark directed this at Matt.

"He didn't know," Liam came to Matt's defence. "I made sure no one knew." He paused and drew in a deep breath. "His temper started after my mom left. At first, as long as I stayed out of his way, I was fine. Occasionally, I would do something to irritate him and he would send something flying at my head, or it was a quick backhand if I mouthed off. Nothing I couldn't handle." Matt saw his dad wince when Liam said that. He was likely thinking the same thing as Matt: *No one should have to handle that.*

"But the last couple of months it's gotten worse," Liam continued. "Once he gets to a certain point of drunk he comes after me. But this week was different. My mom sent an email, asking me to come live with her. I never even responded, but he saw it on my phone and freaked. Yesterday he accused me of wanting to leave and beat the crap out me. Then when he got home this morning, he said I was conspiring with my mother to ruin him. He pulled me out of bed. He was yelling rubbish and kicked the hell out of me again. I was still hurt from the day before, so I couldn't get away." Liam retold the details of the beating with no emotion. Matt stared at his friend, horrified.

"And you never fought back?" Mark asked sadly.

"No. Ironically, I was afraid that he would throw me out, and I would have nowhere to go. I just wanted to stay long enough to graduate and then move away for university."

"Well, you will stay here, and you had better graduate. Let me take a look at you. Is there anything serious you noticed?" Mark asked, coming closer to inspect Liam's injuries.

"I'm not sure, is pissing blood bad?" Liam asked shyly as he stood up.

"Yes," Mark sighed. "You get kicked in the back?"

"Yeah."

"Likely a bruised kidney." Mark lifted Liam's shirt and saw the bruised ribs. "Broken ribs too?" he said shaking his head.

"Yeah, he did that the day before, but definitely added to it today." Liam sat back down slowly.

"The broken hand?" Mark asked, unwrapping the tensor bandage.

"That was my fault; it started with the guy who was harassing Amy, then Liam jumped in to save my ass." Matt explained, "and he made it worse playing ball."

Mark wrapped the hand up properly again with the tensor and stared hard at Liam. "You're right-handed, aren't you?" Mark asked. Liam nodded. "I know what a broken hand from a fight looks like Liam," Mark confirmed.

"I didn't break my hand punching that guy," Liam confessed, not making eye contact with either Matt or Mark. "This was a late-night encounter in the shed. He was swinging a two by four."

Matt shuddered thinking about Liam's hand getting smashed by his father. Mark continued to inspect Liam, and with every bruise he saw, his eyes got sadder, but he wasn't pushing Liam for any more details.

"Do you think you may have a concussion?" Mark asked, checking Liam's eyes.

"Not this time, I don't think. He only got me once in the head." That Liam said *this time*, struck Matt. He recalled Liam having a concussion earlier this summer; he had blamed it on a bike crash. Matt was trying hard to control his already fuming anger. He started to remember all the unexplained injuries Liam had had over the last few months. The realization they had all been caused by Liam's father was making Matt's head spin.

"We should be getting you to the hospital," Mark concluded.

"Please no," Liam said from his chair. He looked like he was only half conscious. Mark stared hard at Liam again as he considered what to do. Matt knew that his dad had advanced first aid and could assess Liam well.

"No fever, vomiting, dizziness?"

"No, none of that," Liam said. "Honest," he added.

"OK, here's how it's going to work," Mark ordered. "No hospital yet, I think you would benefit more from rest. But you need to be checking your temperature every two hours and showing me the results. If you get a fever, if you start throwing up, if you get even a little dizzy, we are taking you to the ER. It means there is internal bleeding." Mark paused so Liam could nod in agreement. "I want you to go lie down, Matt can you get Liam settled in the guest room?"

"Yeah sure, come on bud," Matt said.

"Thanks, Mr. Bailey," Liam said to Mark.

"I'm sorry it wasn't sooner Liam," Mark replied. "By the way, if you are going to live in this house, please call me Mark."

Liam lay down on the bed in the guest room and let out a painful moan.

"Jesus, Liam. I'm sorry, I should have made you stay here last night." Matt was angry with himself and Liam. He closed the bedroom door and confronted Liam. "Why did you even go back home?"

"Do you have any idea how humiliating that was for me?" Liam said, exhausted. "To admit that I can't take care of myself? That my old man beats the hell out of me every night and I don't do anything about it?"

"Why didn't you? You could have taken him. I saw you take down the guy in the parking lot with one punch!"

"Because," Liam said slowly. "I was worried that if I started to hit back, I wouldn't be able to stop until he was dead."

Matt stared at Liam, his anger slowly subsiding. He realized that Liam wasn't weak; he was probably one of the strongest persons he knew.

"I'm glad you finally said something," Matt said.

"I didn't have much choice, did I? The last thing I want to do is intrude on your family," Liam said quietly.

"Well, too late. My dad won't let you out of his sight now."

"Your dad's awesome. But why did you ask me over? I know it wasn't to adopt me. What happened today?"

Matt told Liam everything. He started with seeing Kevin and the black sedan around the neighbourhood, then told him about the phone calls, the letter, and him almost getting arrested when he was chasing Kevin. He told him about training with Lance, and how his dad had asked Lance to investigate for them. He also told him about what Lance had found and how they believed that his mother was likely killed to cover up the investigation she was working on.

Liam had stayed quiet while Matt was talking. When he was done, Liam exhaled and looked intently at his friend. "And what are *you* thinking of doing about it?" he asked.

"I'm not sure yet, but I want them to pay for it," Matt said quietly, but his rage was clear.

"You don't trust the police will figure this out?"

"No," Matt said bluntly. "If they had any ability to handle this they would have found out what Lance did a week ago. I don't trust them, and in the meantime, the company has been able to destroy all the evidence."

"So, let me ask you something," Liam started. "If you believe that they killed your mother, and that they have taken all the evidence, then why is this Kevin guy still lingering around? He's from New York, right? Why hasn't he left yet?"

"He must still be looking for something?" Matt said slowly.

"The report and data your mom copied?" Liam suggested.

"My dad thought the report I saw could have been in the house. But he, and the police, have searched our place a few times, they never found anything."

"Maybe it's not here, but that Kevin guy sure seems to think it is," Liam said matter of factly.

"Crap, you're right," Matt said in shock. How had he not realized that before? Could his father have guessed that? Matt hadn't told Mark or the police he had seen Kevin again yesterday.

"You're not going to tell the police about seeing Kevin again, are you?" Liam read Matt's expression.

"Not yet. I need to think about it."

Just then there was a knock at the door. Matt gave Liam a warning look, to tell him he needed to keep everything between them. Liam gave him a quick nod. When Matt opened the door, Officer Harris was standing there.

"Hi Matt," he said. "Do you mind if I come in?"

"Sure," Matt said, inviting him to enter. "Liam, this is Officer Harris. Officer Harris, Liam."

"Call me Jay," Harris said, offering his hand to Liam, who was trying to sit up. "And please don't get up."

"Thanks," Liam said as he lay back down.

"Mark told us what happened Liam," Jay started. When he saw Liam and Matt both get angry, he quickly added, "Don't blame him. He did the right thing. Let me explain a few things. Since you are over sixteen, the rules are a little different for you. You are almost considered an adult by law and can make your own decisions on some things, including where you live. Child services will only get involved if you don't have a safe place to live. I understand Mark invited you to live here. Do you intend to stay?"

Liam looked at Matt and then responded, "Yeah I do."

"In that case, I need to ask you: do you want to press charges against your father?"

"No," Liam responded quickly.

"That's what I figured," Jay sighed. "Personally, I think you should. Liam, he's fractured your hand, broken your ribs, bruised your kidney and left you with endless bruises. A couple of better-landed kicks and he could have killed you last night. Why on earth would you want to protect him?"

Liam shrugged. "I just want him out of my life," he said softly.

"Since you are over sixteen and won't cooperate with filing a formal complaint, then I can't really do much," Jay confirmed.

Liam nodded in understanding, but Matt suspected Liam already knew this.

"Is there anything at the house you need?" Jay asked. "I can drive you over and make sure you can get what you need without interference."

"That would be great. If we go now he likely won't be home yet." Liam got up awkwardly, each movement caused him pain.

"You're going to feel like crap for a few weeks," Jay said sympathetically. "Make sure you take something for the pain, or you will be crying like a baby every time you sneeze."

Jay drove the boys to Liam's house while Officer Carson and Mark continued to talk. When they arrived at the house, there were no car in the driveway, which meant that Liam's father was not home from work yet.

"Um, do you guys mind waiting here?" Liam asked before he opened the door.

"No problem, just give a shout if you need anything." Jay said.

Matt leaned against the wall and waited with Jay.

"How's your girlfriend?" Jay asked suddenly. Matt took a moment to realize he meant Amy.

"She's not—wasn't my girlfriend," Matt hesitated.

"Really?" Jay said, surprised. "She definitely looked like she cared for you." Jay turned to look at Matt directly. "I know what you are going through is tough, but can I give you some advice?" He didn't wait for an answer. "Let the people who care about you help you. During a time when nothing makes sense, you need some stability."

"I feel guilty doing anything that makes me happy. I just feel angry all the time," Matt admitted.

"I get that, and I'm sure she does too. I'm just saying, when I saw you two together, that first day, I was thinking you were going to be OK because you had someone like her to help you through this. Don't push her away."

"I already did," Matt said sadly.

"It's not too late, kid, I'm sure of it." Jay quickly looked up as a car turned into the driveway. "We have company. I'm guessing this is good old dad?"

"Yeah, that would be him," Matt said staring at the car.

"What's his name?" Jay asked quickly.

"Peter Allens," Matt replied.

"What the hell is going on?" Liam's father said as he got out of the car. "What are you doing on my porch?" Peter was a tall and built man. The manual labour jobs kept him strong, but he was developing a large belly from too much drinking.

"We are here to help Liam, Mr. Allens," Jay said, stepping in front of Peter to stop him from coming up the porch stairs. Peter had at least three inches and forty pounds on Jay.

"What the hell are you talking about," Peter growled at Jay. "I'll take care of my own son. I even came home early to check on him. School called, saying he skipped again today."

"Maybe that's because you almost killed him this morning. I think his reason for skipping was justified," Jay said calmly.

"What the hell do you know about it?" Peter challenged.

"We are waiting for Liam to gather his stuff and then he will be staying with the Bailey's," Jay explained, keeping his voice steady.

"Like hell he is," Peter said, shoving Jay to get past him. But before he could step onto the porch, Jay tackled him down and held him to the ground with his arms pinned behind him, Jay's knee digging into his back to hold him in place. Just at that moment, Liam walked out of the house, struggling to carry a duffle bag and his school backpack. A small smile crossed his lips when he saw his father being held on the ground by Jay.

"Listen asshole," Jay hissed into Peter's ear. "I can arrest you right now for drunk driving because I can smell the alcohol on your breath twenty feet away. But my priority is getting Liam someplace safe. I'm going to let you up in a minute, but you better understand that if I ever hear you have laid even a finger on this kid, I will throw your ass in jail." Jay released Peter and Peter slowly stood up.

"Give me your keys," Jay said, and Peter complied. Jay took the car key off the key chain and put it in his pocket, dropping the rest of the keys into the grass. "You can pick this up tomorrow at the station, when you are sober." Peter nodded slowly. "Come on guys, let's go," Jay said to Matt and Liam. Jay took the bags from Liam, since it was clear he couldn't manage them any further and headed to put them in the trunk of the car. As Liam passed his dad, Peter reached out and grabbed his arm.

"So, you are going to leave me just like your whore mother," he spat at Liam. Before Liam could consider reacting, Matt was at his side. Without thinking he took a swing at Peter and landed him square on the jaw. Peter cursed at Matt but was too bloody and dazed to retaliate.

"Good bye Mr. Allens," Matt said. Liam pulled his house keys from his pocket and dropped them at Peter's feet. He didn't say a word to his father as he got in the car and Jay drove away.

In the car, Liam started laughing. "That was awesome guys, thanks. Crap, I can't laugh—ribs hurt too much." He wheezed in pain but was still laughing.

"I suppose I'm going to be in trouble for punching him?" Matt said timidly.

"Punching who?" Jay replied. "Sorry, I didn't see anything, I was putting the bags in the trunk. Did something happen?" Jay gave Matt a wink, "Great punch by the way."

"That felt really good," Matt said quietly so Liam wouldn't hear.

"I imagine it did." Jay gave Matt an approving nod.

Matt carried Liam's stuff up to the guest bedroom and Liam returned to lying on the bed.

"Well that was fun," Matt said, sitting on the desk.

"Yeah, that was good," Liam was still grinning. "Jay seems cool."

"I suppose," he shrugged. Then he remembered what he had said about Amy. Matt pulled out his phone and debated what to say in a text to her. He settled on *miss you.*

"Who you are texting?" Liam asked.

"Amy, I think I should make amends."

"Good plan," Liam agreed.

"What do you know about it?" Matt was confused. He didn't think he had told Liam anything about his falling out with Amy.

"More than I want to," Liam sighed. "When you brushed her off she started hounding me for updates on you every hour. She's worried about you."

"Sorry."

"Don't apologize to me, apologize to her."

Matt nodded. "I am."

How are you? Amy replied. *Hanging in,* he responded, then added, *I'm sorry for pushing you away.* She wrote, *I understand, do you want me to come by tomorrow?* Matt quickly replied, *yes.* She sent a smiley emoji back.

"How did relationships survive before text?" Liam said drowsily.

There was a soft knock on the door and Grace entered. She was holding a glass of water and Tylenol, which she handed to Liam, along with a thermometer.

"Thanks nurse Gracie," Liam said as he swallowed the Tylenol and stuck the thermometer under his tongue. Grace waited for the thermometer to beep, confirming the reading, then she stuck her hand out, indicating that she was supposed to return with it to Mark. Liam looked at the reading and handed it over to Grace.

"It's all normal," he assured her with a smile. She just nodded and headed out of the room.

"So, what are you going to do about this Kevin guy?" Liam asked once they were alone again.

"I'm not sure," Matt said slowly. "Maybe if I can make him think I have what he wants, he'll come after me, and I'll be able to get him to admit what he did."

"Yeah, sounds like a solid plan," Liam said sarcastically, his eyes closed.

"It sounded better in my head," Matt admitted.

"Just don't do anything stupid," Liam requested. "And wait long enough that I'm at least back on my feet so I can have your back." Then he was snoring.

Liam

Liam woke late the next morning after sleeping for almost fifteen hours. He recalled Matt and Mark checking in on him throughout the night and morning, but each time they came by to fuss over him, he found he was too exhausted to get up. When he woke around eleven, he almost felt like a different person. He was also starving. He picked up his phone and headed downstairs. The house was empty, but Mark had left a note on the kitchen table.

Liam, we had to do some shopping, help yourself to anything you want in the fridge.

Liam checked his phone, expecting a hundred missed messages from Emily. But he was shocked to see his phone had been deactivated.

"Thanks Dad," he muttered sarcastically and tossed the phone on the counter. He then made good on Mark's offer and helped himself to a proper breakfast. Liam was just cleaning up when Mark and Grace returned.

"You're looking better," Mark said, carrying the shopping bags into the kitchen, Grace following him closely.

"I am feeling better. Not close to one hundred percent yet, but a noticeable improvement." Liam gave him a reassuring smile.

"Come have a seat. We should talk about a few things." Mark motioned him to a chair at the kitchen table.

Liam sat across from Mark at the table, and Grace slid onto the chair next to him. Mark had one of the shopping bags on the table next to him.

"First, let me see your left hand," Mark requested. Liam held his hand over the table and Mark pulled a box from the shopping bag.

"It's a splint," Mark explained as he unpacked the box. "You really should be in a cast, but this will do. You will likely have to wear it a couple of weeks still." He helped Liam slide his hand into the splint and tighten the straps.

"Thanks," Liam said, inspecting the splint.

"And this," Mark pulled another box from the shopping bag and handed it to Liam. It was a new phone.

"Mr. Bailey, this is too much," Liam protested when he saw the new phone.

"I thought I told you to call me Mark." Mark gave him a smile.

"Um, OK Mark. I can't accept this," Liam said.

"You have to," Mark said mater of factly. "It's for my peace of mind, as much as yours. You need a way to communicate, to check in with me, and in case I ever need to reach you. Also, I suspect your father will be disconnecting your current phone soon."

"He already has. I just don't want to be a burden on you," Liam said sadly.

"I would never think of you that way, Liam. I have known you since you were five years old. I watched you grow up along side Matt, and I am so sorry that, as an adult who does care about you, I didn't see what was happening to you." Mark paused for a moment and looked deep into Liam's eyes. "As of this moment, as far as I'm concerned, you are one of the family. But that also means you will be subject to my rules."

"Of course," Liam agreed.

"Number one priority for me is that you are all safe." Mark didn't elaborate, but he didn't have to; Liam understood. "Once you are feeling better, I'll expect you to help around the house, maybe take care of Grace every once in awhile."

Liam nodded in agreement, and Grace stared up at him. "That might be the best part," Liam said, giving Grace a wink. She giggled and hid her face in her arms.

"And when you are ready, back to school. It's been kind of optional in this house lately, but both Grace and Matt have been keeping up with the assignments at least. I would expect the same from you. I'll call the school on Monday and explain."

"I'll definitely go back when I can," Liam confirmed.

"But your priority is to get yourself better," Mark said sternly. "And that would be physically as well as mentally."

Liam was about to nod again but then thought about what Mark had just said. He had been on survival mode since his mother had left, and he had never even considered the mental impact. He realized that he had woken up for the first time in months not exhausted and terrified for what the day might bring.

"If you ever need to talk," Mark continued, "I'm here for you. You have been through so much in the last year, I know it wasn't easy."

"Mr. Ba—Mark, I can't believe that you are doing all of this for me, especially now. Thank you."

"I'm glad that I can. Anyway, your new phone number is on the back of the box, I imagine you'll want to let your friends know, especially your girlfriend."

Liam blushed, "Matt told you about Emily?"

"Apparently she's been texting Amy nonstop trying to find you. Amy finally reached out to Matt, and Matt told her you were staying here."

"Sorry for the hassle," Liam blushed.

"Oh, one last thing." Mark pulled out a bottle of Tylenol. "I imagine you'll want these, but please stick to the recommended dose. If you need something stronger, you'll have to let me take you to the doctors." Liam gave him a questioning look. "I found the Tylenol Threes in your jean pocket last night when I was checking on you. I was worried when I couldn't wake you, but that explained it. Based on the date on the bottle, it seems those were prescribed awhile ago? For something different? Please no self medicating."

"I don't. I promise, I just needed something to help get me over here," Liam said defensively.

"I believe you," Mark said calmly. "I know you're smarter than that, and you have been through a lot. Remember, you're not alone anymore. I know it's a bit of a foreign concept to you, but there are people in this house that care about you and will take care of you."

Mark got up from the table, "I have to pick up Matt. Do you mind staying with Grace?"

"Sure, no problem, where is Matt?"

"At the gym. He's been training with a friend of mine. I'm happy to get you in there too once you are feeling up to it."

"That would be great, thanks."

Mark headed out the door and Grace sat staring at Liam.

"OK kiddo, wanna help me set up my new phone?" Liam offered. Grace nodded at him. "Great. Let's get some shows on the TV and see if we can figure it out." Grace followed him into the TV room, sat next to him on the sofa and watched him unpack the phone.

"I hope you don't mind me living here, do you?" Liam said as he added the SIM card to the phone. Grace shook her head and gave him a big smile. "You really don't want to talk, do you?" Grace shook her head again and gave him an angry look. "That's OK with me," Liam said and gave her a smile.

"So, did your dad tell you why I'm going to be living with you?" Grace shrugged. "He didn't tell you how I got hurt?" Another shake of the head, no. Liam sighed. "I had a secret," Liam said quietly. "Someone was hurting me, bad, and I was afraid that if I told anyone it would get worse." Liam looked at Grace to see if she was following. Her brow was lowered in concern as she listened. "Your dad found out my secret, and he helped me, and I don't think that person is going to be able to hurt me again." Grace stared at Liam, and he took her hand gently. "My point is, if there is any secret you have, I want you to know that you can tell me. Maybe I can even help you, but I promise you can trust me." Grace's eyes filled with tears.

She looked like she wanted to speak, but she bit her tongue, tears streaming down her cheeks.

"No, please, don't cry," Liam said, a little panicked, he handed her a tissue from a nearby box and she dried her cheeks. "I just want you to know, I'm here for you, if you need me, like your dad said he was for me." Grace nodded, drying her tears.

"OK, so my phone is ready. Can I add you as my wallpaper?" Grace smiled, and he snapped a picture of her. He showed it to her and made it his screensaver and wallpaper. She laughed at that. Then he added his contacts from his old phone. Grace flipped through the TV channels.

"It's my fault," she whispered so quietly Liam almost didn't realize she had spoken. He put his phone down and looked at her.

"What is?" he said, just as quietly.

"That she's gone." Liam knew Grace meant Heather.

"How could that possibly be your fault?"

"The morning that she disappeared, I yelled at her and told her I wished she wasn't my mom." Grace sobbed. Liam was stunned. He wasn't sure how to manage a crying child, but he was painfully aware of the fact this was the first time she had spoken in over two weeks.

"Come here." He gave her a hug and held her until her sobs slowed.

"It's not your fault Grace," he said once she had calmed down. "Some really bad men took her, and I promise you, it had nothing to do with the fight you guys had. I know she would never leave you."

Grace pulled away from Liam. "Your mommy left you," she said angrily at him.

Liam sighed and leaned back on the sofa. "You're right, she did, but that was because the bad man that was hurting her lived in our house. I know your mom would never want to leave you or Matt or Mark. She loves you guys very much. Do you understand that?"

Grace nodded, "Was it your dad that hurt you and your mom?"

"Yes," Liam answered truthfully. "You are a smart girl. You must know that your mom didn't leave because of anything you did." Grace sat quietly again. "You also don't need to feel guilty," Liam continued. "And even if you were a little angry with her that day, she knows you love her."

"How do you know?"

"Because you are an amazing kid, and one little argument doesn't change that. This isn't like my house, Grace; no one was safe in my house. My house is a bad place, and that's why I left and why my mom left too. This is a good place, there is no reason for anyone to want to leave." Grace seemed satisfied with this explanation. She flipped through the TV channels again.

"So, are you back to talking? Or is this our secret?" Liam asked her. She shrugged and then smiled. "Maybe I'll try talking again," she said softly.

Liam continued to transfer his contacts to his new phone. When he got to Emily's number he sent her a quick text. *This is Liam, had an issue with my old phone, this is my number now, sorry it took so long to reply.* He hit send and immediately saw the little bubble indicating she was replying. *I have been so worried about you, I heard you were at Matt's house, are you that sick!* Liam's instinct was to continue the lie and say yes. Then he thought about what Mark had said, and that people cared for him. He needed to learn to trust people again. Maybe he could give that curtesy to Emily too. *Not exactly, maybe we can hang out later and I can explain,* he replied. *Sure, let me know when and where, I'm free today.* She ended it with a happy face.

Liam lay back on the sofa with his eyes closed. He was feeling exhausted already. Grace sat next to him watching her shows. When she noticed he was falling asleep, she turned the volume down and snuggled against him.

When Mark and Matt got home, she looked up at them and put a finger to her lips, "Shh, she whispered. "He's sleeping."

Mark and Matt froze in their spot, shocked.

Liam woke to Mark and Matt hovering over him. Mark was standing with his arms crossed and a grin on his face.

"What?" Liam asked groggily.

"How did you do it?" Mark asked, still smiling.

"Do what?" Liam asked, confused.

"Get Grace to finally talk again? You know how much I have spent on useless therapy on her? You are alone with her for less than an hour and she's better!"

"Well," Liam started. "I wouldn't say she's better, but yes, I believe she has chosen to talk again."

"Thank you," Mark said extremely grateful. "So how are you feeling?"

"I'm sorry I just crashed," Liam, sitting up, slowly realized he had neglected his duty to take care of Grace. "I was exhausted, and I haven't even done anything."

"Makes sense, your body is trying to heal," Mark stated.

"Sorry to interrupt," Matt said, looking up from a text message he was reading. "But Amy just sent me a text, she's asking if it's OK for Emily and her to come for a visit. I guess that they have something for us all?"

"Sure, if you guys are up to company, I'm fine with that," Mark offered.

Liam shrugged. "I already committed to Emily that I would try and talk to her today. I guess I can't hide from her forever."

Liam saw Matt and Mark exchange looks, but neither of them said anything further to him. Liam realized that he didn't sound too enthusiastic about his relationship.

"OK, I'll tell them it's OK then," Matt confirmed.

"I better get cleaned up," Liam said, standing slowly and heading for the shower.

When Liam got upstairs, he quickly sent a text to Emily. *Please don't be upset when you see me. I'll explain when you get here, but I haven't been sick. Its something else.* She replied immediately with a heart and *OK*. Liam was dreading having to tell her the truth, but there was no way he could hide it.

The doorbell rang an hour later. Grace ran to open the door and let Amy and Emily in. As soon as she had the door open, a loud "Hurray," was heard through the house, which caught Mark, Matt and Liam's attention. Grace led the girls to the kitchen, where they were quickly met by the guys.

"What's all this," Mark inquired as the girls placed boxes full of Tupperware and a roasting pan on the counter.

"Well, my parents figured you probably didn't have the time to cook a Thanksgiving meal," Amy explained. "They made this for you and thought that Emily and I should bring it over."

"It's Thanksgiving?" Matt looked at Liam, puzzled. Liam just shrugged. He hadn't celebrated holidays in his house since his mother had left.

"Yes," Amy confirmed. "Well, Thanksgiving weekend at least. Officially, Thanksgiving is Monday." Amy caught Liam's eye. He could see that sad sorry look that Matt and Mark had been giving him since he'd showed up at the house yesterday. Liam assumed that Matt had given her some of the back story.

"I completely forgot," Mark said sadly. "This is really kind of you. Thanks so much."

Amy smiled, "Well, let me get it all warmed up. You guys go watch football or something."

Liam looked at Emily, who was staring back at him and hadn't said a word since she'd arrived. Her eyes were wide with worry and wanting to say something to him. Liam walked over and took her hand.

"Do you want to join me in the backyard of a few minutes?" he asked her. She nodded and followed him out the back door to the garden. They sat together on the garden bench. It was uncomfortable for Liam, but he couldn't stand any longer.

"What happened?" Emily demanded as soon as they were alone.

Liam paused. He wasn't sure how to explain this, and he didn't want to sound weak with her. "I guess I should just be honest," he said. "My dad's been beating the crap out of me for awhile now. Yesterday he went full-out crazy on me. Broke my ribs, bruised my kidneys, and well, you can see the black eye. Mr. Bailey found out and it was decided that I would stay here from now on."

Emily was quiet for a long time, then she slowly leaned over and kissed him softly.

"I'm so glad you're safe now," she whispered, holding back tears. "I was so worried about you, when I couldn't reach you and your phone was disconnected. I didn't know what to think, but this is so much worse that what I was imaging."

"I'll be OK now," Liam assured her. "I'll just need to heal. I'll be back on my feet soon enough. But can you please, just keep this between us. I really don't want anyone knowing my business."

"Of course, Liam!" Emily replied. She took his hand and rested her head on his shoulder. They sat there saying nothing until Grace knocked on the back door and waved them to come in for the meal.

The dinning table was set with a full Thanksgiving meal: turkey, stuffing, cranberry and a variety of side dishes covered the table. Liam took a seat beside Emily as Amy placed the last of the dishes onto the table.

"Well, dig in," she invited them to start. She gave Liam a small smile as she took her seat across from him.

"Amy, please thank your parents for this. This is amazing, and I had completely forgotten it was the holidays," Mark said sadly as he filled his plate.

"We thought as much," Amy said, giving Mark a smile. Liam's heart raced even though that smile wasn't directed at him. He hated that he noticed how great Amy looked in her sweatshirt and jeans.

Amy and Emily attempted small talk throughout dinner. Emily shared the new drills that the high school had been running the students through, just if an evacuation was called. Amy updated Mark on the emergency response plans for the fire department and hospitals that her parents had been telling her about.

"I guess I need to return to the land of the living soon." Mark sighed. He looked at Matt. "My boss has very awkwardly tried to ask me to come back to work. He knows I'm not up to it, but given the current situations, everyone is worried, and they want me to come back in."

"You're not seriously thinking of going back to work while Mom is still missing?" Matt said angrily.

"They need me to," Mark said apologetically. "But I was thinking that if I go into the city I can check out some of the leads that Lance has given us. But perhaps this is something better discussed after such a great meal."

Liam glanced at Matt to see if he would get the hint. Matt looked like he would object, so Liam gave him a quick kick under the table. Matt shot him an angry look and Liam gave a quick glance at the girls, hoping that Matt would understand that whatever his dad was planning wasn't something that should be discussed in front of Grace, Amy and Emily. Matt eventually clued in.

After supper, Mark excused himself and headed upstairs while the others went to clean up the dishes. Liam was feeling exhausted again and slipped into one of the kitchen chairs.

"Are you alright?" Emily asked, concerned.

"I think I need to go and lie down," Liam said. He was barely able to hold himself up anymore.

"You guys go hang out in the TV room. We got this," Amy offered. Matt was about to object, but she tossed him a towel to dry dishes.

Emily helped Liam to the sofa, where he lay down, exhausted. She sat on the edge of the sofa next to him.

"The last time I was lying on a sofa with you, we almost got in trouble." Liam grinned at her.

"Well, you aren't much use in this state, are you?" she said, gently running her hand across his chest. "I'm scared Liam," she said softly. "All this talk about war and evacuations. There are soldiers everywhere you go, as well as extra police. My parents are talking about leaving now, before anything happens."

"Where would you go?" he asked, taking her hand in his.

"My grandparents live up north. Far up north. They want to go there. They want to leave Monday after the holiday."

"Monday?" Liam said, shocked. "For real? They are that serious about it?"

"Yes, it's basically a done deal. Come with us?" she said desperately.

"I can't Emily," Liam said. "I'm still healing, and I can't leave Matt and Grace like this."

"I figured that. I don't want to go," she said sadly. Very gently she lay down next to him and placed her head on his shoulders. "Is this OK?" she asked.

"Yes," he said, pulling her a little closer to hold her. He could feel her quietly crying into his shoulder. "If you go, at least I'll know that you are safe," he whispered in her ear.

They lay together on the sofa until Amy came to say she needed to leave. They got up slowly and Liam walked Emily to the door.

"We are going to be packing up tomorrow," Emily said. "I don't think my parents will let me come see you again before we leave."

Liam took her in his arms again and kissed her softly. She let out a small sob and wiped her eyes.

"We'll stay in touch," he said to her. She nodded and followed Amy out the door.

Matt closed the door behind them. "It's not just Emily's family who are leaving," he said. "Amy told me there are a bunch of kids already gone from school. People are really scared, and a number of families are just packing up and leaving the neighbourhood."

Liam was already feeling exhausted, but now he felt drained from saying goodbye to Emily. Even though he wasn't sure exactly how he felt for her, he cared for her, and he was worried for her.

"I need to hit the hay," Liam said. Matt nodded, and Liam went upstairs.

Chapter Ten
Matt

Mark had been in contact with his boss over the weekend and reluctantly agreed to go back to work Tuesday morning. Mark had told Matt he would try and connect with some of the security in the building where Heather had worked. He wanted to understand who the key people were in that office and start his own investigation. Mark also agreed that school continued to be optional. Although about a quarter of the school's population had moved away, the school was still trying to maintain regular classes (some teachers had left as well), though attendance was not being enforced. Mark was told this when he called the school to advise them on Liam's absence and new living arrangements. Matt had no intention of returning to school, especially while Liam couldn't.

It was mid morning when Matt finally got out of bed. He found Liam downstairs, looking out the living room window.

"What are you looking at?" he asked as he entered the room.

"Kevin has circled the house twice now," Liam explained.

"What — are you serious?" Matt headed to the front door.

"Matt, stop. What the hell do you think you are going to do? Besides, he's not there now."

Matt paused and then returned to the living room and sat next to Liam to watch out the window.

"Are you sure it was him?" Matt asked.

"Fairly sure. He's still in that car you saw last week. I think he probably saw your dad leaving in his uniform and realized he's gone back to work, leaving us alone."

"What do you think he's waiting for?"

Liam shrugged, "An empty house, or a chance to grab you or Grace if you go out alone."

Matt recoiled thinking about Grace being harmed. He realized that he needed to be smarter about this and stop trying to run into danger. He wasn't concerned for his own safely, but he could allow nothing to happen to Grace.

"I also saw Jay circle the house a few times," Liam said. "I think this Kevin guy has predicted the police patrols. He's been able to avoid them. And they have been very routine; it's about every hour and a half. They must have a regular route they are driving and are only late at shift change or donut break."

"How do we get to him?" Matt said more to himself and Liam.

"Seriously? You want to go after a kidnapper? I say we call the police the next time he drives by."

"A lot of good they have been," Matt said angrily.

"We can call Jay?" Liam suggested.

"*No!*" Matt objected. "I know you like him because he kicked your dad's ass, but he still works with Carson, and the two of them have been useless on this case." Matt was trying hard not to direct his anger at Liam.

"OK bud, chill," Liam said, raising he hands in surrender. "I have an idea, but it's risky as hell."

"What's your idea?" Matt asked, still angry.

"Let me try to talk to him."

"Wow you are brilliant," Matt said sarcastically.

"Just shut up and listen," Liam said. "I have been sitting on your sofas for three days now. I can tell you exactly when the shift changes are and when a patrol will come within a fifteen-minute window. I think Kevin's figured this out too, like I said. The only cop smart enough not to make his patrol routine is Jay, but I think he was on night shift the last couple of days, including last night, so he's off now and another guy came around the last time."

Matt shook his head. "That still doesn't tell me how you want to talk to Kevin."

"OK smartass," Liam sighed. "I'll try to signal him that I want to meet up with him and talk."

"I should go talk to him," Matt corrected.

"No way. It could be that he's trying to kidnap you or Grace to get your mom to talk. We can't let him get either of you. And someone needs to stay in the house to take care of Grace. I'll do it and report back to you. If he refuses to meet, then we know he's after you. If he meets with me, then maybe we can negotiate."

"And if he grabs you? It's not like you can defend yourself right now," Matt tossed out.

"Why bother trying to grab me? It doesn't give him any advantage."

"OK how do we do this?" Matt said reluctantly.

They debated the details and eventually decided that Liam would wait on the porch and would signal Kevin when he passed. If Kevin wanted to talk, Liam would lead him up the street to one of the back alley's and try to get Kevin to meet there. If Liam was right and Kevin had figured out the patrols, he would also know that the biggest gap in the patrols would be late afternoon when it was shift change. Matt was nervous and didn't want his friend to put himself in danger for them, but he also agreed with the argument it would be too risky for him to go. They agreed that Liam would have his phone on and dialed to Matt. This way Matt could hear everything that was said and know if Liam got into trouble.

Eventually Grace came to the living room, complaining she was hungry. Liam happily helped made her lunch. Matt continued to stare out the window, and sure enough he saw a patrol driving by only a few minutes earlier than Liam had predicted, but definitely within the fifteen-minute window Liam had identified.

Liam

Liam positioned himself on the steps. It was late afternoon, about an hour before the shift change and likely two hours before the next patrol. He decided that when Kevin drove by he would signal to him to follow him. Hopefully his body language would be unthreatening enough for Kevin to follow. Liam was aware this was a stupid idea, but he knew that if he didn't do it Matt would continue to blindly run after the car and get himself kidnapped or killed. Liam had his headphones in and the line was open to Matt's phone, who was watching from inside the house.

"Anything yet?" Matt asked for the hundredth time.

"No bud, be cool. You're making me nervous," Liam said softly, trying to look casual. "You never know. Seeing me outside might deter him. Wait a sec." Liam looked up the street and noticed a car slowly turning down the street. He was certain it was Kevin. He slowly stood and made eye contact with the driver, then motioned him to follow. Liam saw that Kevin had seen the signal; he gave Liam a nod and slowed the car. Liam walked down the street toward the side alley.

"Here we go," he said nervously to Matt. He slipped the earphone out of his ear and let it fall under his shirt. The microphone was clipped to the inside of his collar, so Matt could still hear. Liam continued to the end of the street and then turned into the alley. Kevin pulled the car over and parked.

"Who are you?" Kevin asked, slowly getting out of the car. He was a short, skinny man, wearing a golf shirt with a blazer and jeans. His face was bruised like he had recently been in a fight.

Liam walked to the car but was careful to stay out of arms reach.

"Really? I think the question is what the hell did you do to Heather," Liam said.

Kevin shook his head and carefully pulled his blazer back, showing Liam a gun tucked into his belt. Liam took a few steps back and whispered *"Gun"* into the microphone so Matt would know.

"Look kid, no one needs to get hurt here," Kevin said, letting his blazer fall back into place. "You wanted to talk, let's talk."

"You're Kevin, right?" Liam confirmed. Kevin nodded. "Where's Heather?"

"I can't tell you that," Kevin said.

"Is she still alive?" Liam asked.

"For now," Kevin said cautiously. "OK kid, or should I just call you Liam? You don't think I'm not resourceful?" Kevin added when he noticed Liam's shocked face when he called him by name. "If you are a friend and are willing to help, you need to find something for me. There is a flash drive somewhere in that house. It might be the only thing that can save Heather."

"Why should I believe you?" Liam challenged.

"Because her interests and mine are aligned. Our employer knows that we are the only two people that truly understand what's on that flash drive. I was willing to play ball and try to make this all go away for them, but Heather wanted to go to the authorities. That's why the company is giving me a last chance to fix this and Heather's the one being held captive."

"It sounds like the flash drive being lost is the only thing keeping her alive," Liam observed.

"For now, but if the company has comfort that it's lost for good, then they will kill her."

"How do I know for sure she is still alive?" Liam asked.

"You don't," Kevin replied flatly.

"So hypothetically speaking." Liam would bluff; he knew it was risky. "If I knew where this flash drive was, I'm assuming you would want that printed report too?" Liam knew about the report from what Matt had told him. He figured this would give his bluff credibility and convince Kevin they may know where the report and drive were.

"You have the report and the flash drive?" Kevin challenged.

"Yes." Liam tried to sound convincing. "I might be able to get my hands on it."

Kevin approached Liam. Liam held his ground; he didn't want to show any hint of how terrified he was.

"Kid," Kevin said quietly, "if the company suspects that you have any understanding of what's in that report or on that flash drive, you, as well as the whole Bailey family, will be killed. If you care about them, you will bring both those items to me as soon as you can." Kevin handed him a card. "That's my cell number. You better work quickly. Like I said, if they think the information is lost, they will kill Heather as the last link to that information, but if you can find it we can cut a deal and make an exchange." Liam nodded in understanding.

"So why don't you just run?" Liam said. "Sounds like you're in danger just as much as Heather."

"There is nowhere to hide from these people!" Kevin said, a little panicked. "Kid, you have no clue what they can do." Kevin got back in his car. "Call me soon, or it will be too late," he said, leaning out the window. "I'll try to keep this meeting from them, but you don't have much time and if they find out about you —"

"Yeah you said I'm dead."

Kevin drove away down the alley and Liam walked back to the house. He took a few deep breaths to calm is nerves. He had never seen a gun for real, and the idea that Kevin could have just shot him terrified him. He was shaking as he walked back, but he tried to compose himself before he returned to the house. He didn't want Matt to know how much the encounter had frightened him. Just as he approached the end of the driveway, he saw an SUV heading towards him. As it got closer, he saw it was Jay in civilian clothing. He pulled the car up next to the sidewalk.

"Hi Liam," Jay said through the open window. "You're looking better."

"Hi," Liam responded, approaching the car. "Yeah, I'm on the mend."

"I heard Mark was back to work," Jay stated. "I made a few extra laps around this street today. I just wanted to make sure you all were safe." Jay looked at Liam carefully. "I didn't see you a few minutes ago when I circled, but Matt was watching intently out the window." Liam didn't respond, and Jay kept looking at him. "I suspect that your loyalty will be to your friend," Jay said softly. "But if you are doing anything that could interrupt a police investigation I need to warn you to stop. These are dangerous people."

"Police seem a little busy these days. You know with a possible nuclear war starting and all," Liam said a little more sarcastically than he meant to, he didn't want to be rude to Jay.

"True, but that doesn't mean you and Matt can put yourselves in danger." Jay pulled out a pen and a notepad, wrote something down and handed it to Liam. "This is my number. Call me, Liam, don't you guys think of doing anything. Call me for help."

Liam took the paper. "Why are you coming around anyways on your off time?"

"Because I know that everything Mark has told the police is the best and most likely lead we have. And even though there may still be a whole community we need to protect, it doesn't mean the Bailey's problems go away. Liam, we have the same goal here, to help them and bring Heather back. Let's work together and I can keep you guys safe."

Liam looked at the paper in his hand and nodded. He considered telling Jay everything right then, but he knew Matt was still listening and he didn't want to betray his friend.

"We aren't up to anything, but I'll keep your number on speed dial, just in case we find a cat in a tree or something," Liam said, being sarcastic again.

"The fire department gets the calls to help cats, smart ass," Jay called after Liam as he walked into the house.

Matt

Matt had his hand on the doorknob when he heard Liam whisper "Gun." It took all his self constraint to keep himself in the house as he listened to Liam and Kevin's conversation. He was furious and wanted to take down Kevin. Without a doubt, Kevin knew where his mother was, and he was helping the people who had her. He wouldn't go to the authorities to tell them the truth to help bring an end to this all. He was just trying to save his own skin. When Matt knew that Liam was on he way back, he returned to the sofa and watched out the window. He saw Liam approach Jay, and Matt continued to listen as they spoke.

Liam walked through the door and joined Matt in the living room.

"We need to find that flash drive," Matt said.

"Or make Kevin think we have," Liam replied. "If we can convince him we have it, maybe he will agree to a trade."

"And when he finds out we tricked them, they come and kill us?" Matt noted.

"We can get the police involved," Liam suggested.

"And when we get the police involved they come and kill us?" Matt repeated.

"OK, we need to find the flash drive. So, where the hell can it be?" Liam said, frustrated.

"My dad's been through this house a few times; he hasn't found anything," Matt said, shaking his head.

"Think outside the box: was there anything that your mom mentioned before they took her? Did she leave any hints or act weird about anything?" Liam questioned.

"She was a bit more paranoid than usual," Matt confessed. "But that was about a nuclear war starting." Matt stopped himself.

"A war she was worried her company was moving money for," Liam spoke Matt's thoughts.

"She knew things were going to get bad. She saw the money go; that's why she was being paranoid. We just laughed," Matt confirmed sadly.

"What was the plan?" Liam asked. "If things get bad what is your family's exit plan?"

"She told me to take a car, grab Grace and head to the cottage," Matt said slowly. "Oh shit, I might have an idea." Matt jumped up from the sofa and ran through the house. Liam followed him as he headed through the mud room door to the garage.

"There is supposed to be a box here somewhere, marked 'cottage stuff.' She told me I had to take it with us; it had a bunch of first aid stuff she wanted me to take." Matt looked around and found the box neatly tucked on one of the shelves. He pulled it down and opened it. He emptied the box, pulling out iodine pills, a first aid kit, the water tablets, a couple of Tylenol bottles, and bandages. Matt sat on the garage floor shaking his head.

"Damn it, I was sure it would be in here." He picked up one of the Tylenol bottles and threw against the wall. The cap of the bottle popped open on impact, and the pills went flying across the garage. The bottle bounced off the wall and went rolling across the floor, spinning. As it spun closer to Matt, he saw something black inside the bottle. He went over and picked up the bottle and looked. Taped inside was a flash drive, he looked at Liam, amazed.

"We found it!"

"The report must be in here somewhere too," Liam said looking through the box contents closer. He examined the gauze pads from the first aid kit and then ripped one open. Inside, instead of a pad, were three sheets of paper folded into a square. Liam carefully unfolded the papers. "It's the report," he said after reviewing it for a second.

Just then they heard a car pull into the driveway.

"It's my dad," Matt said urgently. "Not a word to him, right?"

"Yeah of course," Liam confirmed, helping Matt pack up the box again and return it to the shelf. He handed Matt the report, Matt refolded it and stuck it in his pocket along with the flash drive.

"Hi guys," Mark greeted the boys when they found him in the kitchen. Grace was sitting at the table, frowning.

"Hungry?" Matt asked her when he saw her. He realized that they had basically ditched her in front of the TV the whole day.

"Yes," she said grumpily.

"Still lots of leftovers," Mark suggested, looking in the fridge. They pulled out dishes and reheating food, eventually a fairly decent meal was set on the table.

"We should talk about what's going on out there," Mark said as they sat down to eat. "People are evacuating the city. I would think at least a third of the population has already headed north. The authorities are saying they know for certain

North Korea has missiles aimed at the U.S. and possibly Canada, but they don't know the exact targets."

"Do they have missiles that can reach this far east?" Matt questioned.

"I would doubt it, but I'm not going to bet my life or yours on it." Mark paused and looked at the kids. "I think you should leave. While it's still safe to do so."

"What about you?" Matt asked, panicked.

"I want to stick around to see if I can do anything more to find your mom," Mark explained.

"I don't want to leave," Matt said angrily.

"I need to know that you are safe," Mark said. "I'm going nuts worried that you guys are in danger. I need you to take care of Grace."

"Where would we go? The cottage?" Matt asked.

"Yes, at least for now. I know it's not ideal, but your mother did plan for this. She left months worth of food and water up there. Well more than what you will need. And you will be hundreds of kilometres away from any large city. Hopefully that area will remain untouched by this. Electricity will likely stay on, which means you will have heat and running water. And failing that we have the generator there."

"And I imagine Mom stockpiled gas for that too?" Matt muttered.

"Very likely," Mark agreed. "I'm not saying that I won't be coming, I'm just going to be a couple of days behind you. There are a couple of more things I want to confirm and then I will join you. Three days max, I promise." Mark looked at Grace to see if she was understanding. "Are you OK with this Grace? You going to the cottage with Liam and Matt for a little while?"

She looked from Matt to Liam. "Sure," she said carefully. "But how would we get there? Matt doesn't have a license."

"I'm thinking that's not much of an issue these days," Mark said. "He's a good driver. We will practice more tomorrow if that makes you feel better." Both Matt and Grace nodded. "You too Liam," Mark added. "You'll need to learn how to drive too."

"Sounds good," Liam agreed.

"OK then, it's settled." Mark concluded. "We will take tomorrow to get ready and then you guys leave Thursday. And I'll come after you, by Monday the latest." He looked at Grace to assure her.

After dinner, Matt and Liam offered to clean the dishes, this allowed them to talk in private.

"We need to get in contact with Kevin," Matt said urgently.

"Should I text him? Let him know I have what he wants?" Liam said in a hushed voice.

"Yes, I think we need to organize a trade," Matt considered. "But my dad will be around all day tomorrow."

"And he expects us to leave Thursday for the cottage," Liam finished.

Matt stopped with the dishes and looked at Liam. "Maybe this will work to our advantage," he said. "What if we get him to meet us there? That way my dad can't interfere."

"Are you sure we don't want your dad in on this?" Liam challenged.

"No, he's just going to get the police involved," Matt objected. "Besides you saw the guy, we can take him if we needed to."

"Except he's packing," Liam reminded Matt.

"Yeah, but he said his objective is to get the information back. He doesn't want anyone to get hurt."

"This is a man that helped get your mother kidnapped. You are going to trust him?" Liam protested.

"This is the best chance we have to getting my mom back!" Matt said angrily. "Are you going to help or not?"

"Of course I'm going to help." Liam sighed. "So, you want me to send him a text and tell him to meet us at the cottage."

"Yeah, send the message."

Liam pulled out his phone and the business card that Kevin had given him. He typed in the number and sent the text. *I have what you want. We want to exchange Heather for it. Meet at the family cottage we will be there by Thursday night.* A response came quickly, *Good work kid, send me the cottage location we will be there Friday morning.*

Liam showed Matt the response. Matt nodded. He took the phone and sent back the cottage address.

"We need to think this through. If he's tricking us, we need to find a way to keep Grace safe," Liam said.

"Yeah of course," Matt said. "I know a good hiding place she can stay. A few years ago, I built her a treehouse in the forest. Only she and I know about it. We can put her there until we have my mom back."

"And you," Liam said. Matt was about to protest. "Once I know for certain that Heather is safe, I'll call you. But this way if he is misleading us, he doesn't get what he wants."

"No, but you might be dead," Matt pointed out.

"Ideally not," Liam said sadly. "We'll work on that part."

That night Matt sent Amy a text to explain that they would leave. She said she would come by the next day to say goodbye. Her parents were asking her to leave as well and she had finally agreed.

Matt woke early that morning and found his father, Grace and Liam in the kitchen already planning the day. Since Liam had never driven before, Mark was giving him a quick tutorial before he got behind the wheel for the first time. Liam had made bacon and omelettes and handed Matt a plate when he walked in.

"Wow thanks, this looks good," Matt said as he took a seat. "At least I know we will be well fed when we are in exile."

"I guess I'll do the cooking and cleaning and you can do the manly hunting and gathering," Liam joked in a high pitch voice.

"Don't forget to pack your apron, sweetie," Matt teased, blowing Liam a kiss.

"OK guys!" Mark scolded, but also laughed.

Grace was giggling, "You guys are goofs," she said. "You sure you want to leave me with them Dad? I might be safer in a nuclear war."

"Oh no, Matt, did your sister just chirp us?" Liam exclaimed.

"Yeah, I don't think we can let that one go," Matt said, getting up and walking over to Grace. Following cue, Liam got up, as Matt pulled Grace from her seat Liam took hold of her feet and started tickling her toes. Grace screamed with laughter, "Daddy help!" she yelled between laughs.

Mark was still laughing. "OK guys, I think she's had enough," he chuckled.

Matt gently put Grace back in her chair. She was wheezing to catch her breath, but she had a big smile on her face.

"First things first, some driving lessons," Mark said. "Then we pack you guys up."

"Um Dad," Matt said shyly. "Amy's coming over later. She's leaving tomorrow too; we wanted to say goodbye."

"Of course, no problem." Mark nodded to Matt.

Liam's driving lesson was disastrous to start. Grace and Matt giggled in the back seat as Liam rolled very slowly through the empty parking lot Mark had selected for their lesson.

"Just remember to keep looking where you want the car to go," Mark explained. "If you keep looking at the steering wheel or sides, you will end up driving all over the road. Just relax; you'll get it."

After about another hour, Liam finally felt comfortable to try roads and bring it up to a normal speed limit. He was still tense, but he wasn't slamming the brakes every two minutes, sending Matt and Grace flying forward. Finally, Mark told Matt to get into the driver's seat.

"OK kiddo," Mark said. "Let's do a little on the roads, but I want you to try the highway again. You'll have lots of highway driving tomorrow."

Matt took a few side streets to the highway and then pulled onto the on ramp and merged onto the highway. It reminded him of the last time his mother had taken him driving. He thought about his mother and that he would be seeing her again soon. Of course, he hadn't said a word to Mark about it; he wanted nothing to interrupt the plan. It was already too imperfect, but he was feeling alive and happy for the first time in weeks. He checked his speed. He was following the traffic, but he was traveling well over the speed limit, and his father wasn't complaining.

"You're doing fine," Mark said. "Keep with the flow of the traffic. If it's going too fast for you, move to the right lane and go the speed you are comfortable with."

"I'm good, I'm not nervous at all," Matt said. He was feeling comfortable behind the wheel. "What if we get pulled over?" he asked.

"I have a feeling the police are a little too busy these days to be handing out speeding tickets. Just drive safe and I doubt anyone will question you," Mark said. "You seem good with this. You can take us home now."

When they got back to the house, Mark started to bark instructions for packing; take only what you need, warm clothing as the days and nights are getting colder, no Grace you don't need fifty teddy bears. Eventually everyone was limited to one duffle bag. Once Grace and Liam were submersed in their packing jobs, Mark called Matt to his room.

"I want you to take this," Mark said pulling a case from under his bed.

Matt walk around to the bed and looked inside the case as his father opened it.

"A gun?" Matt said, shocked. He never knew his father even owned a gun.

"It's just a precaution," Mark explained. "I'll be up there soon enough, but I would feel so much better if you take this with you."

"What are you worried about that you think we may need a gun?" Matt asked.

"I don't know, if war starts, and people start getting desperate, there's no telling what the world will look like. I need you to be able to protect yourself and your sister." Mark closed the case and locked it, then handed Matt the key to the case. "Keep it locked up; don't let your sister get near it. It is loaded right now, all you have to do is pull the trigger." He pulled another box up and placed it on the bed. "More bullets," he explained.

Matt stared at the keys in his hand. Taking the gun terrified him, but it was exactly the advantage they needed for when Liam met with Kevin again.

Mark sat on the bed and put his head in his hands.

"You OK Dad?" Matt asked, concerned.

"No, Matt I'm not. None of this is OK. I'm handing you my gun so that you can flee our house to avoid a possible nuclear war. I'm encouraging you to drive two hundred kilometres with your little sister, without having a driver's license. And I'm not going with you because I want to follow up on a lead to find my missing wife." Mark's voice cracked. "None of this is OK, and I am so sorry that you need to go through all this. I would never ask this of you, except that I believe things will start getting really bad here, very quickly."

"Dad it's OK," Matt said. "I promise, Grace and I will be fine. I might even say the same for Liam, as long as I don't let him drive." They both chuckled at that. "And besides, like you said you will be with us by Monday. Just keep your side of the promise." Matt looked as his dad. He wanted to tell him so badly that he didn't need to follow up on his lead — that their mom would be there at the cottage when he got there — but he held back. He didn't want to worry his dad.

"I will, Monday the latest, I promise." Mark gave his son a hug. "I'm going to leave early tomorrow to get into the city. You guys can sleep in a bit, but I want you on the road by ten, alright?"

"Yeah Dad, don't worry, I'm going to go as soon as we get up," Matt assured him again. "Besides, it's not like we can't call you anytime too. I'll make sure to text you as soon as we get there. And if you like every twenty minutes while we are driving?"

"No texting and driving." Mark smiled.

Matt headed to his room with the gun locked securely in it's case. He put the gun and additional ammunition in his duffle bag. There was a soft knock on his door and Liam entered.

"You packed?" Liam asked, sitting at the desk.

"Yeah, you?" Matt asked.

"Well, it's not like I had a lot of time to unpack and get settled in. What were you and your dad talking about?"

"He gave me his gun," Matt blurted out.

"Seriously?" Liam exclaimed. "That's a huge help!"

"I know, I was shocked, but I feel a lot better about Friday morning now," Matt said, staring at the case in his duffle bag.

"When's Amy coming over?" Liam asked.

"Soon. I don't think she was at school today."

"So, are you planning anything?" Liam pried.

"No, not really?" Matt said, confused.

Liam shook his head and stuck his hand out to Matt. "Here, take this," he said.

Matt took what Liam was offering him and realized it was a condom. He wasn't sure what to say. His first thought was to just throw it back at Liam, but when he looked at Liam, he wasn't joking.

"I'm assuming that you would know what to do with that?" Liam said seriously.

"Yes, well, I guess," Matt stuttered, looking at Liam embarrassed. Matt knew all about Liam's experiences the summer before while he was hanging out with his brother. Once the stories got around school, Liam confided in him, including telling him how much he regretted sleeping around with the girls. Liam was young and ignorant to the emotional repercussion his actions would cause. He vowed to Matt he would not repeat those same mistakes, and he learned to respect women. Matt was surprised at Liam's suggestion now.

"Look, I don't know what's between you and Amy. Maybe it's nothing right now," Liam said. "But I know she does care for you. And a goodbye like this could get emotional, and if things start leading in a certain direction, you may want to make sure you planned ahead."

"This is a really awkward conversation to be having with you," Matt admitted.

"Well if you like, I can call your dad in here, if that's less awkward," Liam joked. "I mean the man did just give you a gun, I'm sure he will support you firing off your—"

"Stop," Matt yelled as he pitched a ball of rolled socks at Liam's head. "How can you go from being so sentimental one second to totally disgusting the next."

"I know, it's a gift," Liam smirked.

"You and Emily never went in *that direction*, as you put it?" Matt asked.

"No," Liam answered honestly. "She wanted to, but I couldn't. I just didn't feel that way for her."

"Lucky for you there could be a nuclear war starting, otherwise you may have had to break up with her properly," Matt teased.

"Shut up," Liam laughed. "I liked her well enough. Maybe if we don't all die of radiation poisoning I'll give her a call again."

They heard the doorbell ring and Grace running down the stairs to answer it. A moment later both Grace and Amy were in Matt's room. Matt realized that he still had the condom in his hand. He subtly slipped it into his jean's pocket when he was sure that Amy wouldn't notice. Amy explained to them that her parents were basically on twenty-four hour shifts now, sleeping at the station or hospital. She had barely seen them in the last couple of days, and that was the main reason they wanted her to leave. They agreed to let Amy stay one extra day, to say goodbye to the Baileys and then she would pick up her grandmother in the morning and head north to her aunt's house.

"I don't want to go," Amy said. "I don't want to leave my parents, friends, even school. I mean, what if nothing happens and all this panic was for nothing?"

"I think I would rather be panicked, safe and wrong, than be here and get bombed," Matt said.

"Maybe you can come with us?" Grace said hopefully.

"Oh Gracie, I wish I could, but I have to take care of my grandma," Amy explained. "See, you guys are lucky because you get to hang out at your cottage. I have to go to my aunts, and I'll probably just have to go to school there and hang out with my aunt and her cats."

"You're going to go to school there?" Matt asked.

"Well, yeah, if I can. What else would I do? I don't want to sit around the house with a bunch of old people playing Canasta," Amy replied.

"So you'll make new friends, meet new people," Liam led her on. "Maybe meet some new guys?" Liam suggested.

"Hey Gracie," Matt interrupted Liam suddenly. "I bet Liam wants to see that high school music movie that you love so much," Matt suggested quickly. "You should watch it one last time before we go. In fact, I think you should show him all four!"

A big smile crossed Grace's face, "Oh Liam you have to come watch with me! He's right I won't get another chance for a long time!"

"How could you possibly say no to that face?" Matt said as Liam scowled at him.

"Sure Gracie, lets go watch," Liam said through clenched teeth. He flipped Matt the finger behind Grace's back as she pulled him out of the room enthusiastically.

"So, you have a problem with me meeting new people, particularly guys?" Amy asked once Liam and Grace were gone.

Matt laughed, "Maybe, but I also wanted them to leave so we could be alone."

"Really?" Amy questioned him. "It's been awhile since you've wanted to be alone with me. What's changed?"

Matt checked the hall to ensure his dad wasn't upstairs and then closed his door to his bedroom.

"I'm going to tell you something, but you have to promise not to tell anyone." Matt waited for her to agree.

"Sure, OK," Amy said, sitting down on the bed.

Matt sat on the desk across from her. "I'm going to get my mom back," he said quietly.

"What? How?" Amy exclaimed.

"Liam and I found something that her kidnappers want. We are going to exchange it for her. They are meeting us at the cottage Friday morning," Matt explained enthusiastically.

"Wait, so are the police going with you? Or your dad? I don't understand," Amy probed.

"No, Liam and I set this up. We can't involve the police. I just want to bring my mom home, and the kidnappers agreed they will do the exchange. They just care about getting their data back."

"Matt, this isn't making any sense. And how is this safe? They are probably just going to kill you!" Amy was almost yelling.

"Shh!" Matt tried to wave her quiet. "Please Amy, my dad can't know. This is the best—the only—chance we have to get my mom back. The police have done nothing up to this point; Liam and I already cut the deal. It's going to be fine."

Amy looked at him sadly, "You should tell your dad!" she scolded.

"No," Matt said. "He will just want to get the police involved and then we will lose any chance we have to making this deal."

"Do you really think this is the only way?" Amy asked, still furious.

"Yes, we already met with Kevin once. He's agreed to the meeting and the exchange. It's going to be fine," Matt assured her.

Amy shook her head and stared at Matt. Matt felt positive that his plan would work, he didn't understand why Amy couldn't just be happy for him.

Liam

Liam was suffering through Grace's tweeny movies, contemplating what he and Matt needed to do on Friday morning. He was playing out the possible scenarios in his mind. Unfortunately, most resulted in him ending up dead. He started again mapping out the events in his mind. It was almost like playing a chess game in his head, except instead of *checkmate*, it was *Liam's dead.* First, they would ensure Grace was safe. Matt would keep the flash drive and report. Matt would stay with Grace. Liam would go to meet Kevin. He would get Heather, then signal Matt to bring the flash drive and report. But what would stop Kevin from killing everyone once he had what he wanted? Liam changed the pieces. He would have the report and flash drive, Kevin would deliver Heather, Kevin would get what he wanted and kills Heather and Liam. The gun was key. Liam felt he should have the gun. It was the only insurance he had to get out of this alive. Kevin would also never suspect that a bunch of kids would have a gun. *Too bad neither of us actually know how to shoot,* Liam thought. Liam concluded that the best scenario with the least risk to everyone was that he would do it alone. Matt would keep Grace safe, Liam would make the exchange, he would have the gun for protection and he would hand over the report and flash drive in exchange for Heather. If anything went wrong, Matt could get Grace to safety.

Liam was frustrated. The plan sucked, but he wanted to help his friend. As he had told himself a hundred times already, if there was even the slightest chance this would bring home Heather, he owed it to the Baileys to help them. Mark had helped Liam at his greatest time of need, and Liam needed to return the favour. Liam thought about his own mother and how she had just left him. He wondered how different his life would have been if he had been born to parents like Mark and Heather—people who cared about their children and tried to make a good life for them.

When he compared how he had grown up, even during the time before his mother left, he was hard pressed to remember happy times. He remembered when he was very young, and his brothers were still living at home. His parents *seemed* happy then, but that could have been just his childish recollection of it. He could have been ignorant to what was happening around him. Mostly he remembered his mother crying, his parents fighting, his father passed out drunk. He wondered if his brothers knew how bad their father could get. They were older, maybe they had seen it and that's why they left when they could. In which case, they were just like their mother. They had abandoned him with a dangerous man and were only concerned for saving their own skin. But then, maybe they didn't know. Their father only got violent with him after their mother had left. He considered writing them an email. He had told no one from his family about what their father had done to him and that he had moved out.

He pulled out his phone, opened a new email and added in his brothers' contacts. He wasn't even sure if the contacts were current. It had been a couple of months since he had heard from either of them. Then he started to write.

Hey guys, I wanted to let you know that I moved out. Dad went ape on me he almost killed me. He beat me unconscious and left me bleeding on my bedroom floor. If you want the gruesome details, go ahead and ask (you sickos). Anyway, I moved out after that, and I'm staying with a friend. But now with the threat of war, we are evacuating to his cottage in a remote area east of the city. I wanted to let you know.... He paused. He wasn't sure what he wanted to let them know. That he forgave them? But they didn't know he had anything to forgive them for. That he would be alright? He couldn't say that, since he already knew that almost everything about Friday's meeting with Kevin would not be alright. He sighed and finished his email with, *I wanted to let you know what was up. Maybe I'll catch you later.*

He hit send on the message. There were no undelivered messages, so he assumed that the email would get to his brothers eventually. He sunk deeper into the sofa drifting to sleep when suddenly he was smacked on the head from behind.

"What the...." He looked behind him to find Amy standing there.

"You and me, in the garage, now!" she demanded, turning, not waiting for his response. Liam had about twenty seconds to run through his head the possible reasons that could have made Amy this mad, but he came up with nothing.

"What the hell Liam?" Amy said once they were in the garage, she was trying very had not to yell.

"What?" Liam asked, confused by her anger. This made her even more angry and she slapped his shoulder.

"You are seriously going to pretended everything is OK?" she demanded. "Matt told me about Friday!"

Liam didn't know how to respond. He agreed with Amy's concern, but he didn't want to betray his friend.

"Aren't you going to say anything?" She asked, almost yelling. "Tell me why I shouldn't go tell Mark right now what you are planning."

"Amy, just calm down," Liam tried to explain.

"*Calm down?*" Now she was yelling.

Liam threw his hands in the air, trying to shush her. "Please, just let me explain!" he said, trying to get her to be quieter.

"Fine, you have one minute before I go to Mark."

"I know it's a bad plan," Liam started.

"Then why are you letting him go through with it?" Amy interrupted.

"I'm not," Liam said quickly, and Amy looked him confused.

"I'm not going to let him do anything," Liam continued. "I'm going to do it."

"And how is that any better?" Amy said, only slightly calmer.

"Amy, I'm not going to let Matt or Grace get themselves into any danger. I promise. I'm going to keep them away from everything and take care of it myself."

"Why on earth would you put yourself in danger?"

"Because if there is any chance that we can get Heather back safely then we have to try. And if I don't help Matt, he *will* do it himself, alone. Likely these people are more interested in kidnapping a Bailey kid than me. I want to make sure that doesn't happen." Liam paused and looked at her to make sure she was understanding. "At least this way, I can control the situation to some extent and only I will be in danger, not him or Grace."

"Liam no," Amy whispered, stepping closer to him. "Why don't you just go to the police."

"They are a little preoccupied these days, in case you haven't noticed," Liam replied. "This case isn't close to being a priority right now. And Matt doesn't trust them not to mess this up."

Amy stared at him for a long time. She was visibly still trying to be mad at him, but he could see she knew her anger was misdirected.

"Why do you always have to play the hero," she said, sadly looking up at him. "Why do you think you have to put yourself in harm's way for others all the time?"

Liam was about to deny this, but he needed to get her buy in to stop her from going to Mark. It was Matt's mistake for telling her what they were up to; he almost wanted Amy to go to Mark, just to sabotage everything and involve the police. He personally had thought about texting Jay a hundred times already to let him know what was happening, but he also wanted to stay loyal to his friend.

"Matt has this great family that cares about each other," Liam said to her. "And it was ripped apart. It's not fair to them. My family ripped itself apart on purpose. I guess I just want to try to save something that is worth saving." Liam placed his hands gently on her shoulders. "You must have noticed that Matt's a different person today. He has hope; he's happy. He truly believes that this is the only way we can get his mother back. He will not listen to me or you or anyone on this. Believe me, I have tried, and the more I tried to tell him this was a bad idea, the more he pushed away. I know he will do this behind our backs if we don't support him. If we try to stop him, he will resent us and put himself in danger. As far as I can see, the only way I can keep him safe is to support him." Liam looked deep into her eyes. "And if Matt is right? If all this guy wants is this information back, and I can get Heather and myself out of there unharmed, well I think it's worth the risk. But one thing I know for certain is that if we don't try this, and something happens to Heather, Matt will blame himself, and possibly me, forever, and that's not something he will be able to come back from."

Amy surprised Liam by wrapping her arms around him and hugging him.

"Do you promise me you will keep Matt and Grace safe?" she said softly.

"Yes," he said, resting his cheek on the top of her head.

"Do you promise you will take care of yourself as well?" she said, her voice cracking as she held back tears.

"Yes," he lied as he hugged her a little tighter

He closed his eyes and held her for a minute as she rested her head on his chest. He noticed her hair smelled like vanilla and was soft and silky. Her body fit perfectly in his arms as he held them around her. His mind screamed at him to remember, once again, this was Matt's girlfriend.

"I'm going to go find Matt," Amy said after a moment as she dried her eyes. She turned to leave and then stopped. She came back, took Liam's hands in hers and gave him a soft kiss on the cheek.

"Thank you so much for taking care of him," she said and then left.

Liam stayed in the garage a little while longer. He thought about his promise to Amy and wanted to ensure that he could keep it. He kept playing the possible scenarios over in his mind. But there was no certain way to keep Matt and Grace safe. Then it came to him: the only way he could keep them safe was to change the plan and not tell Matt.

Matt

Amy had left Matt's room furious, but Matt was also angry with her. He wanted her support and couldn't understand why she wasn't happy for him. He was so close to getting his mom back and ending this all. When she stormed out, he waited to see if she would get in her car and leave, but from his bedroom window he could see her car parked on the street. She never left. He debated if he should go find her. But he was angry, and he also didn't want another argument. He lay down on his bed and stared at his ceiling, trying to clear his head. He wasn't sure how long he lay there, but eventually there was a soft knock at the door.

"Come in," he said.

Amy opened the door and entered. "Can I join you again?" she asked quietly.

"Sure," Matt shrugged, not getting up.

"I'm sorry," she said, standing next to the door just inside the room.

Matt sat up and looked at her. He wasn't expecting an apology, at least not that quickly.

"You are?" he questioned.

"Yeah, I spoke with Liam. Let's just say he put it in perspective for me," she said, looking down at her feet.

"So, you're not going to rat us out?" Matt asked, a little stunned.

"I promise I won't." She cautiously sat on the bed next to him. "I still think this is a really bad idea, but I understand, and you can trust me."

He took her hand in his. "Thank you," he said. Then he leaned forward and kissed her. She kissed him back immediately.

Suddenly a loud "Ah hum," came from the door. Matt looked over to see his dad standing at the door. Mark looked almost as embarrassed as Matt felt.

"I was just going to see what you all wanted for dinner," Mark said casually. "I'm happy to order pizza?"

"Thanks Dad. That sounds great," Matt agreed, but he would have agreed to liver and onions at that point just to get his dad to leave.

"Pizza it is. Amy I'm assuming you are staying for dinner?" Mark said.

"Thanks that would be nice. Both my parents are working all night."

"Alright, we are happy to have you then, and Matt, this door stays open."

"Of course," Matt agreed quickly.

Mark headed downstairs and Matt waited for him to be out of sight before he turned back to Amy. She was smiling at him.

"Sorry about that," he said shyly.

"That's OK, I like pizza," she teased. She gave him one more quick kiss. "Perhaps we should go find Grace and Liam before your dad gets too suspicious," she suggested.

They found Liam back on the sofa politely watching the movies with Grace. Matt sat in the armchair and pulled Amy down to sit next to him, except the chair was too small for two, so she was mostly sitting on his lap. He wrapped his arms around her and kissed her shoulder gently. She giggled and leaned closer to him. Matt noticed Liam didn't acknowledge them or even look in their direction. He wondered if Liam was mad at him now for some reason. He decided he would worry about that later. Right now, he just wanted to enjoy being happy with Amy.

"What's going on in this movie Grace?" Amy asked.

Grace jumped into a lengthy explanation of the various love triangles that were apparently unfolding dramatically in the movie, all in various songs no less. Amy listened intently to Grace.

A little while later the pizza arrived. Amy and Grace jumped up to help Mark in the kitchen. Matt stopped Liam before he could go too.

"Everything good?" he asked Liam.

"Yeah," Liam shrugged. "Just had to talk to Amy earlier. She was upset, but she seems fine now."

"Yeah, she's fine," Matt grinned. "Thanks for talking to her. I was worried she would just leave."

"I think she cares too much for you," Liam said, but his voice sounded tired and sad. "Just remember that." Liam walked past him to the kitchen.

They made small talk while they ate. It was an awkward dinner. Mark was a bit emotional but kept reassuring Grace he would see them again by Monday. When they were all done, they helped clean up, which was just tossing their paper plates into the garbage.

"Daddy, will you play a game with me? Please?" Grace asked once everything was cleaned up.

"Yeah of course sweetie," Mark replied.

"You too Liam please!" Grace begged.

"Um sure," Liam agreed a little reluctantly.

"Hey, Dad," Matt said quickly. "Amy and I are going to go for a walk, if that's OK"

"No problem, go ahead," Mark agreed.

They grabbed their jackets and Matt took Amy's hand as they headed outside. "It just feels like there are too many people in my house tonight," Matt said as they walked down the street. The sun had set, and the streetlights had already turned on. The cool, damp night air had settled.

They walked towards the path that took them out of the neighbourhood and to the lakefront. Most of the lake front was fenced off as a conservation area, but there was a large hole in the fence where kids always crept through. Once past the fence, there was a small beach and then forest. Amy led the way along the beach. No one else was around. The sound of the neighbourhood and roads were buffered by the forest. They continued to walk along the beach, Amy seemed to have a specific destination in mind. After a few minutes, they stopped, and Matt understood why Amy had brought him to that specific spot. In front of them was the lake, but they could see nothing in that direction except darkness. The only reason they knew the lake was there was from the sounds of the waves gently slapping on the beach a few feet away from them. From the spot where they stood, they could look along the beach and see the city lights far off in the distance. It looked like a small dome with tiny skyscrapers lighting up the shoreline forty kilometres away. Between them and the city they could also see the lights of the nuclear power plant softly glowing.

"Wow," Matt whispered. "From here everything looks so calm, and small. It's like we are the only ones left."

Amy smiled at him. "I know, it's hard to believe, looking at the city from here, that there are millions of people between us and those lights."

Matt sat on the beach and pulled Amy down to sit in front of him, so she could lean back against him. He wrapped his arms around her to keep her warm and they sat there quietly for a long time, just looking at the lights and listening to the water.

"I'm scared," Amy said finally. "For you yes, and I don't want to talk about that again. I'm just scared about everything. It's all changing so fast and I wish it didn't have too."

"I know," Matt said, gently running his fingers through her soft hair. "We haven't had any time together and now who knows when we will see each other again. I'm sorry that I pushed you away. I was an idiot."

"No, don't say that," Amy said. She ran her hand along his leg. "Nothing has been normal these last few weeks. You were just trying to survive."

"OK, so let's make a promise," Matt suggested, "that if everything goes to hell in the next little while, we promise that we will meet up one year after the war stops, when it's safe again."

"OK where?" Amy questioned. "If there is full-out war, what would be left?"

Matt considered this. He needed to think of something that couldn't be affected by a war.

"What about Niagara Falls?" he suggested.

"Sure, that would likely still be there," Amy thought. "But how would we know the date?"

"OK, when's your birthday?" Matt asked, he was actually surprised he didn't' know.

"January twenty ninth."

"If all hell breaks out and there is a full out war and there is no way to communicate, then we will meet on the first January twenty-ninth that comes after the war officially ends."

"OK sounds like a plan, I promise." Amy held up her pinky finger. Matt wrapped his finger around hers.

"Well that's a solid promise then. Can't break a pinky swear," he laughed.

"Nope, you will be cursed forever if you do," Amy said. She turned around to face him directly. "I don't want to leave tomorrow," she whispered.

"I know," Matt responded. He gently pulled her close and kissed her.

"I don't want to leave you," she said even more softly.

Matt kissed her again. This time she kissed him back passionately. Her hand rested gently on his knee and he was very aware of the warmth it was radiating. Matt pulled off his jacket and lay it in the sand and gently led Amy to lie down on it. He lay next to her, holding himself up on one elbow. She placed one hand on the back of his neck and pulled him close to kiss him again. Suddenly Matt felt lost. He had no idea what he should do next. He didn't know what Amy would expect; from the way she was kissing him she was taking control. She unbuttoned his shirt and ran her hand softly across his chest, tracing her fingers across his abdomen. He tried hard to relax his breathing, but his heart was racing. He decided to be brave and kissed her neck and then lower on her chest. Amy smiled and breathed in deep.

He kissed her again, and this time he decided to be braver and allowed his hands to venture. He ran his hand softly up her leg and hip, resting it just above her waist. He gently pulled her hips closer to his. Now the full warmth of her body was pressing against his. She eagerly received his kisses and her body moved closer to him with every breath they took. She ran her hands over his body, up and down his back, and then rested on his belt. Matt froze, not sure what to do next, but Amy slowly pulled her shirt over her own head and gave Matt a shy smile. Matt realized then that he still had the condom in his pocket. He silently thanked Liam for his foresight.

They lay on their jackets, holding each other. Neither wanted to admit that they needed to go home. The night had turned dark and the stars were bright absent a moon in the sky. The cold air had settled close to the ground and they started to shiver.

"We need to head back," Matt said, softly kissing her on the forehead.

"I don't want to," she whispered, though she was shaking in the cold.

Matt stood up and offered his hand to her to help her up. He then shook the sand out of their coats and placed hers on her shoulders. They held hands and slowly walked back to the house. When they reached her car, Matt took her into his arms and kissed her again. They held each other for awhile until Amy slowly pulled away.

"Call me tomorrow when you get to the cottage," she insisted.

"I will," he promised. She got into her car and drove up the deserted street. He watched until she turned off the street and was out of sight.

Matt walked into his house and found it quiet, except for the TV on in the family room where he found his dad watching the late evening news.

"Long walk," Mark commented as Matt walked in.

"Went down by the lake and talked." Matt hoped he sounded convincing. "What's going on in the news?"

"Basically, all hell is starting to break out," Mark said, keeping an eye on the TV. "North Korea has said that they will sink Japan into the ocean and turn America into dust. They have been firing missiles over Japan all day. Nothing has hit directly, but they are getting closer."

"How is the U.S. responding?" Matt asked taking a seat next to his father.

"Not much publicly," Mark frowned. "Their melon-head President is way over his head here. He just keeps adding fuel to the fire; it's almost like he wants a full-blown war on American soil. But the frightening thing is that Canada never joined the U.S. missile defence program, back in the nineties when it was being developed. The U.S. has no obligation to protect Canada should they start sending missiles our way."

Matt felt sick to his stomach. "So, we are basically sitting ducks?" he asked.

"Yes, so you can see why people are so nervous. Now of course it is in the U.S.'s interest to protect Canada, but if there is a coordinated attack on Canada and the U.S., I'm sure they will protect themselves first."

"And that's why everyone has started to move north, to remote areas?"

"Yes, about ninety percent of the population of Canada lives within one hundred fifty kilometres of the U.S. border. There is so much land north, so that's where people are going, but it's also frozen for half the year," Mark explained. "There have been riots in the bigger cities in Canada and U.S. as people start scrambling for supplies, there is price gouging going on and a lot more break ins as people just take what they want."

"Dad? If they start bombing Canada, what do we do?" Matt asked. He knew he sounded like a frightened child.

"Stay hidden in the remote areas until it's over. That's why it's key for you to go to the cottage now. The next two weeks will be the tell. North Korea's actions are acts of war, the UN and the U.S. need to respond strongly now. Either they will be able to stop North Korea or there will be full-out war."

"What do you think is likely?"

Mark shook his head sadly, "With these two lunatics running the countries, I'm going to bet that we are at war by next week. The UN hasn't been able to defuse this at all. That's why I want you guys out of here and safe."

Matt nodded. He was worried to say anything; the secrets where piling up.

"I put extra gas cans in your car, and like I said, your mom really stockpiled the cottage. I feel like a jerk for not helping her. Damn she was right about everything. I just hope she got enough to last awhile. She said there is at least three months worth; that was based on four of us. Ration things so it will last a lot longer." Matt nodded in understanding, and Mark continued. "I'm going to talk to one more person tomorrow in hopes of finding Heather. But I also ordered a few more items for protection. I'm able to get that Saturday, so I'm thinking I should be there Sunday now. Unless my lead on your mom works out. Then I'll let you know."

"Can't you tell me more about it?" Matt asked.

"Not right now kiddo. I don't want to get your hopes up," Mark said sadly. "But you know I have to try. I don't want to give up on her, but I also have a commitment to you kids. And I feel that Heather wouldn't forgive me if I didn't keep you safe. It's bad enough I'm sending you ahead without me."

The World
Chapter Eleven

The missiles first hit Anchorage, Alaska, then Seattle, San Francisco, Los Angeles, and finally Vancouver. The cities were hit in the early morning hours and had only an hour warning for evacuations, which were issued while most people still slept. The armies did their best to warn people, driving the streets, blasting horns and yelling instructions, but in the end, there was just devastation. Thousands of lives were lost, and those who survived were left in chaos.

In the east, most people had started their day as normal. They heard the news about the attacks as they were getting out of bed or having their morning coffee. At first there was a wave of shock, while people watched the news reports of the burning cities on the west coast. Then local alerts started, asking people to remain calm, gather necessities and get at least twenty kilometres away from major city and the nuclear power plants.

Instantly the cities in the east went into chaos. Streets were jammed with cars and people trying to evacuate. Train stations were overrun, and any trains leaving the city were packed to capacity.

Matt

Matt woke up to his phone ringing and Liam banging on his door at the same time.

"Matt, get up! We need to leave *now!*" Liam yelled, opening his door and then heading down the hall to Grace's room.

Matt reached for his phone. His father's number was showing as the incoming call. "Hello?"

The other end of the phone was just static and then the call dropped.

"Liam, what's going on?" Matt yelled as he jumped out of bed and pulled on jeans and a shirt.

"The west coast just got bombed. We need to leave now before everyone else decides the same thing," Liam was in Grace's room helping her take her bags downstairs.

Matt grabbed his luggage and followed them.

"My dad was trying to call me," he explained. "But the call dropped."

"Yeah same happened with me," Liam said. "I think the network is overloaded right now with calls and who knows what service disruption these bombings will have. I sent him a text to say we are leaving. Hopefully that will get through."

"Liam are we safe?" Grace asked, looking completely terrified.

"Yes," he said confidently. "Where the bombings happened, it's very far away. We just want to leave now because everyone else will want to also, and traffic will be really bad."

Grace nodded and seemed satisfied with that answer. Liam ran into the kitchen and grabbed a shopping bag and filled it with all the fruit and bread he could find. Then he grabbed whatever juice or water he saw and filled a second bag.

"Get the bags to the car. We need to go," Liam called to Matt. Matt, still half asleep, picked up Grace's bag and headed to the car. Grace followed him closely, still looking very afraid. She climbed into the back seat and buckled her seatbelt. Matt looked up and down his street and he noticed that many neighbours had the same idea. Many people were in their driveways filling their cars up with whatever they could. Some carried coolers, others had arms full of suitcases. Liam came out carrying the food bags and a few sleeping bags.

"Good thinking," Matt said, placing the items into the trunk. He headed back to lock the front door. Before he did, he took one last look at his home. He felt emotional; they had no intention to leave it so quickly and under these circumstances. He had barely had time to process what Liam had said was happening. He sadly locked the door and headed to the car.

"So, what the heck happened?" Matt asked as he got back in the car.

"I had the TV on as I was getting breakfast together," Liam explained, "and suddenly there were reports of missiles hitting various cities on the west coast. They hit Vancouver!"

"Oh my god." Matt gasped as he pulled the car out of the driveway. "We gotta get out of here." He pointed to the radio. "See if you can find a news channel," he said to Liam.

Liam searched for the news station turned the volume up as he found one.

"The military is advising everyone to remain calm. We have no direct threats on any of the cities in central North America or the east coast," the radio announcer was saying. "Right now, we can confirm that Anchorage, Seattle, San Francisco, Los Angeles, as well as Vancouver have been hit with a number of missiles that were launched from North Korea. The missiles hit at approximately five a.m. pacific time. Reports have confirmed that those cities have lost power, cell coverage has been disrupted and we have no communication. The military is responding, and we are standing by for the prime minister to make a statement."

"No threat to central and eastern north America?" Liam questioned.

"To hell with that," Matt replied. "I wonder if they said that to the people on the west coast."

Many people seemed to share Matt's opinion. The roads were unusually busy with families trying to leave. They merged onto the highway and traffic slowed immediately.

"This may take awhile," Matt said, frowning. "See if you can text Amy. I want to make sure she made it out."

Liam pulled out his phone and typed. "No service," he said after a second.

"Crap. Well, keep trying," Matt said.

Amy

Amy threw her suitcase into her car and quickly got behind the wheel. She had been slowly sipping her morning coffee when the news had reported about the attacks on the west coast cities. Her phone rang, and it was her father. He told her he believed central and eastern Canada could be attacked as well and she needed to leave immediately. The call was dropped just as he was telling her he loved her.

Amy pulled out of her driveway and tried to call Matt, but the phone just generated a busy signal and then dropped the call. The networks were overloaded; her parents had warned that could happen. She knew what she had to do: get to her grandma and then get to her aunt's. Simple. She turned onto the main street and traffic was already crazy. Everyone was in a panic. Those that had already left to go to work were rushing back home; those that were at home were now on the roads trying to get out of town and clear of the city.

Amy stopped at a red light and waited for it to turn green, once it did, she started through the intersection, and then suddenly there was a loud bang and she felt her car being thrown through the intersection. Someone had run the red light and hit her on the driver side, pushing her into the next lane and causing the car next to her to hit her again. Amy's head snapped sideways, and she felt her forehead hit the side window. Her belt locked, and she felt her chest getting crushed as the car spun around. The car eventually came to a stop on the curb on the opposite corner. Amy couldn't see; it was like a grey vale had been pulled over her eyes. Her ears were ringing, and she had no concept of where she was. She struggled hard to clear her eyes and head. She was faintly aware of someone knocking on her window and calling at her. She felt someone pull her door open, reach across her to undo her seatbelt and gently pull her out of the car. She felt herself being lifted into someone's arms and carried, then she was placed gently on the ground. Someone was talking to her, but she couldn't make out what was being said.

"I can't hear anything," Amy whispered, shaking her head, trying to clear the ringing sound from her ears. She felt someone placing a cloth on her forehead. "I can't see," she said to whoever her savior was. Slowly her head cleared, the ringing in her ears got quieter and she was able to focus a little again.

"Can you hear me now," a voice close asked her calmly.

"Yeah," she answered, still trying to focus on who was there.

"I'm sorry I moved you, but your car was smoking. I thought it might catch fire," the voice said. "I'm going to check you for other injuries, if that is OK."

"Yeah," Amy said again. The voice sounded slightly familiar.

"OK hold this." A hand gently guided her hand to the cloth being pressed to her head. "Tell me if it hurts anywhere when I touch you."

She felt hands gently press down her spine and up her neck, then along her arms and hands.

"Any pain?" he asked.

"No." She shook her head and focused on the person sitting with her on the grass. He gently turned her wrists and she kept shaking her head no to indicate there was no pain.

"You have a fairly deep cut to your forehead," he said. "I think you should get to the hospital.

"No," Amy said. "I have to get to my grandmother. I have to leave town." Amy now focused on the man in front of her. He looked familiar, but she wasn't sure who he was.

"Your name is Amy, right?" he asked.

"How did you know that?" she asked, confused.

"I'm Officer Jay Harris, we met at the Bailey's house the night Heather went missing."

"I remember now," Amy said. She focused on Jay. He wasn't in his uniform, so she hadn't recognized him; he was wearing jeans, a T-shirt and a ball cap. "You fingerprinted me."

"Yes, that's right. Seems your memory is OK." Jay smiled at her. Her eyes were having a hard time focusing on his face; she was still dazed. Over his shoulder she could see that traffic had continued and was working hard to get around her broken car. But no one else had stopped to help. There were no onlookers or rubberneckers; everyone was too busy trying to save themselves.

"I have to get to my grandmother," Amy repeated.

"Your car isn't taking you anywhere," Jay said. "The axel is broken. The phones are down, so I can't even call you a tow truck."

"Where's the car that hit me?" Amy asked confused.

"It was a truck, he left, along with the other car that hit you. Those vehicles could still move so they just took off."

"If I can get home I can get my dad's car, it's there. I can take that to get my grandma." Amy tried to stand but tripped almost immediately. Jay quickly helped to steady her.

"OK, stop!" he said holding her up. "Let's go to my car. I have a first aid kit there. I can take care of your head, and then we can figure this out." Jay gently guided her to his car, which he had parked on the street nearby. Amy noticed that it was a black mustang and wondered how a rookie cop could afford a car like that. He pulled a first aid kit out of the trunk and took the cloth, which she had been holding, off her forehead,.

"This is going to sting," he said as he opened a package and pulled a wipe out. He cleaned her cut, then he pressed a clean bandage to it.

"The bleeding has almost stopped," he explained, "but you probably need stitches."

"Is it really bad? I really need to go and get my grandma; she's expecting me and she's going to worry." Amy knew she was rambling again, but she was about to panic; she just wanted to leave town.

"You'll probably have a good scar, but it's just under your hair line so it won't be too noticeable." Jay gently pushed her hair from her forehead, away from the cut. "I have surgical tape in my kit. It would likely do the trick, but the scar will be a lot more noticeable."

"Let me see." Amy pulled her phone from her pocket and turned on the camera to front view. She examined her scar. It was about two centimetres long, over her left eye. It was on top of a big bruise that was swelling quickly. But Jay was right, it was close to her hair line and might not be that noticeable once it healed. "Use the tape," she instructed him.

Jay complied and carefully applied the medical tape, trying hard to close the cut as best he could to minimize the scarring.

"How far does your grandmother live?" he asked as he applied the tape.

"Not far, just a couple of streets over," Amy replied.

"I'll drive you over," Jay said. "I want to keep an eye on you; I think you have a concussion."

"Don't you have to go to work? With all that's going on," Amy asked.

"Yes, likely, I'll make sure you and your grandmother are on the road safely and then report for duty." Jay gave her a smile. "All done. I hope I didn't do too terrible of a job."

"Thank you," Amy said.

"I'll get your stuff out of the car," Jay said, closing the passenger door for her and walking back to her car. A moment later she heard him loading things in his trunk and closing it. Then he got into the seat next to her and passed her, her purse.

"Thank you," she said. "So, I'm just going to leave my car there?"

"I'll report it when I get to the station. I imagine we will have a few cars to clean up once everyone is out. But cell coverage is off and on at best right now. I can't even call it in. So where are we headed?" Amy told him the address and Jay started in that direction. She stayed quiet as he drove. Her head was aching and looking out the window of the moving car was making her nauseous. She wanted to hide these symptoms from Jay. She was certain he would make her go to the hospital if he suspected how bad she was feeling. He pulled up to the building where her grandmother's apartment was. Amy got out of the car and Jay followed quickly. She was going to tell him he didn't need to, but she doubted he would listen.

She hit the call button to her grandmother's apartment and there was no response.

"That's strange," Amy said. "She should be expecting me."

"Do you have a key?" Jay asked.

"Yeah." She searched her purse for the keys — she was still thinking slowly. Eventually she found them and unlocked the door. "Third floor," she said as they headed for the elevator.

As the elevator came to the ground floor, several people exited in a hurry, all carrying boxes and luggage. Jay and Amy rode the elevator to the third floor, and then Amy guided him to her grandmother's apparent. She knocked on the door, but again there was no answer. Amy pulled her keys out again and unlocked the door. The apartment was dark; the curtains were all closed. There was light coming from the TV turned on to the news channel reporting on the bombings.

"Grandma?" Amy called. There was no response. She gave Jay a puzzled look. She slowly walked towards the TV and came around to the front of the sofa. As she got closer, she could see feet at the one end of the sofa—someone was lying down on it. A horrible feeling hit the bottom of her stomach. She knew there was something terribly wrong.

"Grandma?" she called louder, but somehow, she knew her grandma wasn't just sleeping on the sofa. Jay's instinct must have kicked in as well; before she knew it, he was at her side.

"Amy, don't look," he said, but it was too late. As Amy approached the front of the sofa, she saw that her grandmother was lying there, lifelessly staring at the TV. There were several different prescription medication bottles scattered across the table, all empty—she had taken them all.

"Oh my god Jay, is she, is she...." Amy started to cry.

Jay bent over her grandma. He examined her only briefly to confirm what they already knew. "I'm so sorry Amy—yes, she is dead."

"No...No.... Oh my god *no!*" Amy sobbed and knelt next to her grandma. She took her grandmother's hand in hers; it was already cold to touch. All the warmth of life had drained from her. Amy was overcome with sadness. She loved her grandmother so much. She couldn't process she was gone and had done it to herself. After awhile, Jay took Amy in his arms and held her. She cried against his chest until she thought she couldn't cry any more. Jay just held her and comforted her.

"What am I going to do?" she finally managed to say.

"I'll take you wherever you need to go," he said. "I won't leave you until you are safe."

"I need to contact my mother," she said slowly. "I don't know what to do, I don't know if I should still leave?"

"Let's try to reach your mother then," Jay confirmed.

Amy pulled out her phone. "I think there's cell coverage again. I'm starting to get messages." She dialed a number but only got a busy signal. "Damn it!" she yelled.

Jay pulled his phone out and tried to make a call but had the same result. "But it looks like some of the messages are starting to get through," he said as he read through his texts.

"I'll text my mom then. I'll let her know I'm heading home and she needs to tell me what to do about my grandmother."

"Amy you need to leave — and now," Jay said urgently.

"What?" she asked, confused.

"I have a message here from work. There is a real threat now against the city and the nuclear power plant. They are going to start to evacuate the city and all the towns within ten kilometres of the power plant. I'll take you home, you take your dad's car get to your aunt's house, then I need to get to the station. I'll take care of things with your grandmother."

"Wait, I don't understand. What's the threat? Why wouldn't you leave too."

"The intelligence units believe that the power plant is a target for some kind of attack," Jay explained. "They are going to start the formal evacuation in an hour; they are trying to get as many emergency personnel in as they can to help with the evacuations. You need to leave now before the traffic gets worse."

"I can't just leave her here!" Amy protested, looking at her grandmother.

"I promise I will do what I can," Jay said, leading her to the door and down the hall, still reading his phone. "But you don't have a lot of time. I'm not even sure when this message was sent. I'm just getting all the messages that were backlogged in the system." Jay continued to read more messages.

"Shit," he swore loudly, very upset at what he had just read.

"What is it?" Amy asked, a little frightened by his reaction.

He looked at her and shook his head. "There is a message here from my sergeant," he said. "They found Heather Bailey's body."

Amy frozen in her spot; her legs stopped working and she was fairly sure she would faint. She blinked her eyes to stay focused and tried to process what he had just said. Heather was dead; that wasn't possible. Matt and Liam were going to save her tomorrow morning. They had it all set up. Matt had been so excited; he was sure his plan would bring her home.

"No," she whispered. "That can't be."

"I'm going to take you home and then head over to the Bailey's place before I go to the station," Jay said, leading her to the elevator.

"They aren't there," Amy said, almost yelling in panic. "I got a text from them. They already left. But Jay, they are doing something really stupid!"

"What do you mean Amy?" Jay stopped her in the hall, so she could explain.

"They are heading to the cottage to evacuate, but they have this plan. They are meeting this guy, apparently they have a flash drive with information and they think they can exchange it for Heather."

"What the hell!" Jay said angrily.

"I know, it's so stupid!" Amy cried.

"Where's Mark in all this?" Jay demanded.

"He doesn't know. He was going into the city today. He was doing his own investigation into something. Matt, Liam and Grace went by themselves, Mark was going to join them Monday."

Jay slammed his hand into the wall. "*Damnit*," he yelled. "I'm sorry," he said quickly, looking at Amy crying. "I'm sorry. I just can't believe that they would do this behind my back. When are they supposed to meet this guy?"

"Tomorrow sometime," Amy said quietly.

"If that guy shows up, he's going to kill them," Jay said flatly. "Do you know where their cottage is?"

"On the southeast end of Kasshbog Lake," Amy replied. "I have never been there, but I have seen pictures."

"OK, I'll take you home and I'll go after them," Jay said.

"I'm going with you!" Amy yelled.

"No," Jay replied forcefully. "There are already three kids in danger, I'm not going to do the same to you."

"I'm not a child; I'll be eighteen in January!" Amy protested.

Jay sighed and gave her a doubtful look. "OK, you're not a child but I'm not putting you in more danger."

"If you don't take me, I'll just follow you anyway," Amy threatened. She paused for a moment to allow this to sink in with Jay. She wasn't bluffing, and she wanted to make sure he knew. Then she said more calmly, "Please don't leave me by myself. My parents are both on the list for emergency services; they will be the last to leave."

Amy could see Jay struggling to decide. "Fine," he finally said. "You can come, but once we find the right place, I am leaving you someplace safe and far away from the danger." He hit the button for the elevators. "Just keep trying to text them. Maybe we can get a message through to them before the meeting."

"Won't you get in trouble or fired for leaving town?" Amy asked as they rode the elevator back down to the lobby.

"Probably. I'm not too concerned about that right now," Jay said. "The lake is north on highway forty-six, right?"

"Yeah I think that's what they said. Do you know it?"

"I've been fishing there, when I was a kid," Jay responded. "I can get us to the lake; you'll have to help find the cottage."

When they got back to his car, Jay opened the trunk. He had a black duffle bag in there, and Amy watched as he pulled his gun out, slipped it into his belt and pulled his shirt over it to hide it, then he pulled out his police badge and put it in his pocket. He noticed that she was watching him and walked over to her.

"Can't be too safe, right?" he said, speaking gently to her now. "I know you are probably in shock with everything that's just happened to you, but if you insist on coming with me, I need you to try and hold on just a little longer. We will mourn for your grandmother and Heather, I promise, but if we are going to save Matt, Grace and Liam, we need to stay focused."

Amy nodded slowly. Jay opened the car door for her and she got in.

"We have to make one stop, but it's on our way out of town," Jay said, putting the car in drive. Amy took one last look at her grandmother's apartment building. She tried to remember what Jay said; they would have time to morn later.

Jay navigated the traffic, probably breaking a dozen traffic laws, as they drove across town. They were heading to a south-end neighbourhood, where some of the most affluent families lived.

"Where are we going?" Amy asked.

"I just need to pick up a few things from my place," Jay explained as he pulled into a driveway. The house they were at was massive, one of the bigger ones on the street. Jay hit a remote on his dash and the garage door opened. The garage was big enough to park three cars at least, but there was only one other in there, an Audi SUV.

"You can come in," Jay said, getting out of the car.

Amy followed hesitantly. "This is your house?" she questioned as she followed him.

"Yeah." Jay shrugged as he unlocked the door leading into the house and quickly entered a code into a keypad to disarm the alarm. "We will likely have a long drive ahead of us," he said. "If you want, the powder room is just down that hall on the left. Meet me back here in three minutes."

They entered the house through a mudroom, though it was the largest and cleanest mudroom Amy had ever seen. As Jay disappeared up a stairway, she slowly walked down the hall; there were several rooms before she found the powder room. A beautiful home office was the first room she passed, then a home theatre room that housed a TV that had at least a hundred-inch screen. She saw a massive kitchen at the back of the house with state-of-the-art appliances and granite counters. She found the powder room, which was just as impressive as the rest of the house; in fact, it was bigger than her bedroom.

She met Jay back at the garage. He was loading her items, and additional luggage and sleeping bags, into the back of the SUV.

"So, you can afford all this on a cop's salary?" Amy said as Jay finished loading the car.

"No," Jay said with a laugh.

Amy got into the SUV and admired her new transportation. The SUV, like the mustang, was fully loaded: leather interior, sun roof, rear view cameras, individual climate seating and more.

"Nice car," Amy said suspiciously as Jay got into the driver's seat.

"It's a long story," Jay said with another laugh. "I have a feeling we will have a lot of time in the car together. Maybe I'll fill you in later. Let's try to get onto the highway first," he said as he reversed out of the driveway and headed down the street.

The streets were packed with cars, and once they reached the highway, it was a slow crawl. Cars were driving everywhere, including the shoulders of the highway. This just added to the confusion as more cars merged onto the highway. They were heading east away from the city, but the westbound lanes were just as packed.

"Why would people be heading into the city?" Amy stated, confused.

"Maybe they have family there they are trying to get out," Jay suggested. "The buses, trains and subways are probably overloaded. Or they could be heading west and then north. There are two bigger highways west of the city that head north—there are more small towns and cottages that way too."

Amy remained quiet as Jay continued to slowly move along with the traffic. She stared out at the cars around her. Most were packed with families, trunks and roof racks overflowing with whatever belongings they felt were important enough to grab in their last-minute scramble to preserve their lives. She wondered what people would take: photo albums? Maybe some important heirlooms? Food? Water? What would be most important to them if nothing else was left in a few days? She thought about the cities already bombed and wondered what type of chaos the survivors there were going through. She understood her grandmother's decision. Even though she didn't agree with it, she understood how someone would feel that desperate right now. She understood how her grandmother thought she was protecting Amy by doing what she did. She went on her terms and not be a burden to Amy. Her grandmother's sacrifice now allowed Amy to go with Jay, to save Matt, Grace and Liam. Amy's heart had broken when she'd found her grandmother dead, but worst of all, she felt guilty for being thankful to her for doing what she had done.

"You alright?" Jay asked. "You need to stop thinking about it." He was reading her mind.

"I know, I just can't. It's too much to process for one day, and I'm trying hard to make sense of it all."

"Don't," Jay said. "It's exactly what you said; it's too much to process. You won't be able to. Try not to think about it. You may go into shock, or PTSD. And no offence, but if we want to give Matt and Liam a chance, I need you to hold it together."

"Yeah, so you have said," Amy said angrily.

"OK, sorry, you're right. I don't need to be a dick about it." Jay gave her a sideways glance.

"You are being a dick," she agreed with a pout.

"Alright, tell me about yourself. What do your parents do that they are stuck in this mess?"

"My dad's a fireman and my mom's an ER nurse."

"Wow, good for them. But yes, they could be stuck there for awhile. As you saw, people were being pretty reckless."

"I don't want to think about them either. Can we change the subject?" Amy requested.

"OK." Jay thought for a minute. "Why don't you fill me in on what you know about the cottage, so we can find it easier."

"Sure." Amy paused, trying to recall all the pictures she had seen at the Bailey's home. "I know it's on the southeast end of the lake. They have a big dock in the water and there is a fair bit of land between the lake and the cottage. There is a lot of forest, and they own a few acres of land up there so there aren't any neighbours near them. From what Matt told me, there is a private road that takes them to their place; it's a couple of kilometres long from the sounds of it, and the cottage is at the end of that road."

"That's very helpful," Jay said. "If we are lucky enough to get cell coverage back, see if you can find it on Google Earth. I bet that would be easy to find knowing the general location and this description." The car was barely moving, so he turned to look directly at her. "Look, I mean it when I said I'm dropping you somewhere safe, OK?"

"OK," Amy agreed, reluctantly.

"Tell me everything you know about this stupid-ass plan of theirs," Jay requested.

"I don't know much of the specifics. Matt and I kind of had a fight about it. Liam's against this though. He told me that he was taking care of everything and that Matt and Grace would be staying somewhere safe. Liam was going to make the exchange."

"Seriously?" Jay questioned. "Why would he do it knowing it's dangerous?"

Amy sighed. Was it really only yesterday she was standing in the garage with Liam demanding he answer the exact same question? He had been adamant he would do it, to protect Matt. He had held her tightly in his arms and promised they would all be safe. He knew what he was doing would be dangerous; he had accepted that. Was he accepting that he could be killed?

"He knew Matt would do it without him," Amy explained sadly. "He had tried to talk sense into Matt, but he wouldn't listen, so Liam had to go along with it to make sure he could still control it and support Matt. Liam convinced Matt to let him do the exchange. Somehow, they figured this was the better plan. Liam is being realistic at least. He knows it's a long shot. But he said he owed it to Matt to at least try, and I think Liam feels he owes Mark something."

"I don't think that includes getting himself killed." Jay shook his head. "Keep trying to text him; tell him that we are on our way. Tell them to stay away from the cottage and I'll take care of it."

"Should I tell them about Heather?" Amy asked.

Jay considered this for awhile. "Send the messages to Liam. Tell him about Heather. They need to know, but it's better Matt hears it from his friend rather than a text. Tell them not to take things into their own hands; I'll be there to arrest the guy. They are not to put themselves in danger."

Amy typed on her phone as he spoke. She hit send on the message and the phone just showed the message as stuck.

"It's not going through," she said, shaking her phone in frustration.

"We have time," Jay said. "Just keep trying."

"So, what can you tell me about the investigation? How dangerous are these people?" Amy asked.

"Very," Jay stated. "The man they are supposed to meet, Kevin, I don't believe that he ever had any chance of returning Heather home safely. He worked with Heather but was from the New York office. As Matt and Liam discovered, she took a report and downloaded some data from their work. I believe that people from the company are holding him responsible for that, and if he doesn't get the information back to them, he will likely end up dead as well, along with anyone else who knows this information exists. I think they want Kevin to clean up his mess, so to speak. There is another man working with him—the guy's name is Jack. He's the one I'm really worried about. The cottage is a good remote location. Jack will be able to take back that flash drive and likely kill Liam and Matt to tie up loose ends."

"I don't understand," Amy said, shaking her head. "Why are they willing to kill over this missing flash drive?"

"I have my guesses, but I would rather not say," Jay explained. "I would hate to get you into danger too."

Amy stared out the window. She was trying to take Jay's advice and not think about it all. It was all too much to process. Her number-one priority was to get to Liam before his meeting. She checked her phone again but there was still no service. They had been on the road for a little while now, but they had barely gone ten kilometres. The good news was that they were outside of the evacuation radius for the nuclear power plant. However, at this speed, they wouldn't arrive at the cottage until Saturday night. Suddenly there was a rumbling noise, like thunder but louder and longer, coming from behind.

"Oh my god!" Jay said, looking in his rear-view mirror.

Amy turned around to see a cloud of smoke rising far in the distance.

"What is that Jay!" Amy cried in panic.

"I think it's coming from the city," he said urgently.

"But we must be over fifty kilometres away!"

Cars slowed and then stopped as people noticed the smoke rising behind them. Some got out of their cars to see better. Realizing that they would not be moving right away, Jay put the car in park and opened his door. Amy opened her door to get out as well. They didn't have a good view from the road, so Jay carefully climbed up on the roof of his car. He offered a hand to Amy as she climbed up beside him. From the top of the car they had a better view of the smoke far away on the horizon. Looking along the shoreline, they could see a dark black smoke cloud rising from the direction of the city. It was a clear blue day and there was no mistaking, the cloud was not a rain cloud; it was rising from the ground.

They stared at the scene for awhile saying nothing, both too shocked for words. Amy tried to see if she could make out the tiny skyscraper buildings that made up the city skyline, but the smoke was too thick; it seemed to engulf the whole city.

"Do you think that missiles hit the city?" Amy asked eventually.

"I don't know, but that's a lot of damage if we are able to see it from this far away," he said, jumping down and then helping her down. "We need to keep moving." He got back into the car. Luckily everyone else seemed to think the same, and traffic started moving again, slow but steady. Amy kept looking back. The cloud had spread towards them and seemed to continue to get thicker. The fire must have been spreading.

"How many people?" Amy tried to ask, the question getting stuck in her throat.

"I don't know," Jay said quietly. "Millions work in the downtown core; who knows how many people would have been there this time of day. And who knows how many were able to evacuate."

"Oh my god! Mark!" Amy felt herself starting to hyperventilate. She felt herself slipping away—she wanted to scream and cry, and it took every bit of willpower not to. The world had gone mad; everything had changed in a matter of hours, and she wasn't able to comprehend what was happening. She could feel her heart racing and her breathing quickening. It was like she was on the edge of a cliff and her mind was screaming at her to jump; nothing was making sense. Jay read her mind again, and he took her hand and held it tightly. She felt some comfort when she realized he was shaking too. He took in a deep breath, held it for a few seconds, and then released it.

"We have one objective," he said.

"Reaching Matt, Liam and Grace," Amy finished for him. He nodded and held her hand tighter.

Matt

Matt continued with the flow of traffic. It was a slow and chaotic journey out of town. They had been listening to the news stations the whole way, but the reports were just telling the same thing repeatedly, which was basically nothing. No one knew exactly what the damage was in the cities that were hit. A couple of hours into their drive a formal evacuation order was issued for the city and the communities east of the city, where the nuclear power plant was. Then not long after that, the radio suddenly stopped broadcasting. They were on the highway heading north. The elevation had increased, and they were on the top of a higher point on the road when they had the view of the lake behind them and could see the smoke rising from where the city was.

Matt glanced at Liam; Liam had seen it too. He turned in his seat to get a better view. Matt gave Liam a warning look, which meant to tell him not to talk about it in front of Grace. Liam nodded and kept glancing behind them. Matt grasped the steering wheel and tried to concentrate on the road, but his mind was racing. He was worried about his father and angry with himself. If anything had happened to Mark it would be Matt's fault. The only reason Mark had gone to the city that morning was to find information on Heather. But Matt had already arranged to save Heather, had he let his father in on his plan he would be with them safe and heading to the cottage.

"He's OK Matt, he's smart. He got out," Liam said quietly. "I'm sure we will hear from him as soon as the cell coverage is back up."

Matt just nodded.

"I'm hungry," Grace whined from the back seat.

"Here," Liam said, handing her an apple.

She took it and stared at him. The novelty of the road trip had worn off after the first hour of being stuck in traffic. Once they headed north, the trip sped up a little. Many cars continued east, but there were just as many trying to head to remote areas in the north. They were about one hundred kilometres away still from their location, about half way, and the trip so far has taken hours. At this rate it would be evening before they'd arrive.

"I'm bored," Grace complained.

"Not much I can do about that Grace!" Matt replied sharply.

Grace kicked his seat in response.

"Real mature," Matt mumbled.

"Here, take this," Liam handed her his phone. He had downloaded a few games the night before in anticipation of a long ride. He passed her the earphones. "See if you like any of these games," he said, showing her the new apps.

"Cool thanks," she slipped in the earphones and started playing.

"Thanks," Matt said when it was clear Grace couldn't hear them anymore.

"No prob." Liam shrugged. "You came in fairly late last night?"

"What, you my dad now too?" Matt frowned.

"Just saying," Liam smiled. "Anything you want to tell me."

"Hell no!" Matt laughed.

"Enough said then," Liam remarked, smirking.

"You're an ass," Matt said, shaking his head.

"Was hoping for some details to pass the time," Liam said. "That's all, but if you don't kiss and tell I'll respect that."

"It was a little more than just kissing." Matt blushed.

"Uh ha,"

"I guess I should thank you," Matt said shyly.

"Yeah, I was kind of waiting for that," Liam joked. "I'm glad things are going well for you guys," he said, suddenly serious.

"Well they were. Who knows when I will see her again," Matt said sadly. Matt was using last night's memory as a source of motivation to keep him going. The drive had been stressful and exhausting, then seeing the smoke rising from the city and still not being able to reach his dad, he was almost at his wits end. Things were getting overwhelming, so he would think about Amy. He wished he could go back in time to the night before and pause there, because this day was sucking so far, and tomorrow would bring a whole different set of stresses.

"Do you think Kevin will show tomorrow?" Matt contemplated. "Now with the bombing and all?"

"Yeah, I think so," Liam said hesitantly. "I mean, he probably still wants this information, right?"

"I guess we will find out. You sure you want to do this?" Matt asked.

"Yeah of course." Liam didn't hesitate. "I mean, we have it all worked out. You and Grace hide, I'll make the exchange at the cottage, and when it's all clear I'll come get you."

"I hope it ends up being that simple," Matt said.

"Don't worry, I can handle myself. And if anything goes wrong, I'll take Kevin out or just run for it."

"You'll have the gun," Matt confirmed. "And worst case lock yourself in the cottage."

"Right, lots of options," Liam agreed.

Matt knew the risks were high, and he really didn't want his friend in danger for his sake, but it was the only chance they had at seeing his mom again. He regretted that he had to rely on Liam so much, but Liam had insisted that he be the one to make the exchange. Liam had said that was the only way to keep Gracie safe, but also this would prevent them from taking one of Heather's kids as a bargaining chip. It made sense in Matt's mind.

They drove in silence for awhile. The traffic moved slowly, but at least it was moving. Millions of people had evacuated, but as they headed to various locations north, east or west, the traffic lightened a little. Grace had fallen asleep in the back seat listening to the music on Liam's phone. Matt wasn't sure how appropriate Liam's music was for Grace, but then times were a little different now. The sun set, but Matt knew that they were getting close.

"We are almost there," Matt told Liam, as he turned off the main road. They followed the road around the lake and eventually came to the private road that led to the cottage. The gate was locked, and Matt jumped out of the car to unlock it. His legs ached and cramped; it was the first time he had walked in hours. He almost fell when he stood up. The fresh air of the forest hit him, and he breathed deeply and for a moment just took in his surroundings. The noise of the summer was gone, along with the smell of multiple bonfires. It felt like they were the only ones there; none of the other cottages were occupied. He figured more people would arrive eventually, but at this point they seemed to be alone. Matt unlocked the gate and headed back to the car and drove them down the private road to their cottage. It was now completely dark and impossible to see anything beyond the limited lights of the car headlights. Eventually they saw the cottage in front of them. Matt parked the car and turned to wake Grace up.

"Wake up kiddo, we are here," he said, giving her a little shake.

"Finally," she yawned.

They headed to the cottage together and Matt unlocked the door. Liam tried to flip the lights on once they were inside.

"No power?" he asked.

"The main breaker is likely off on the power box. Give me a minute." Matt headed into the darkness and a moment later they heard some clicking and the lights turned on.

"Yea!" Grace cheered.

They explored the cottage and took inventory of what supplies they had.

"Hey Matt, can you come here for a minute?" Liam called from somewhere in the back of the cottage. Matt followed Liam's voice until he found him just inside the storage room.

"What's up?" Matt asked.

Liam stepped aside so Matt could see inside the storage room. The small room had multiple shelves, all packed with cans of food, water, powdered milk and medical supplies. But what was most interesting was what Liam was pointing to on the top shelf. Matt pulled down a long black case, and opened it, inside was a hunting rifle.

"This is new," Matt said, lifting the rifle carefully. "And it definitely gives us another advantage tomorrow."

"Yeah," Liam agreed.

"Can we please eat!" Grace yelled from the hall. Matt quickly put the rifle back on the shelf, then scanned the shelves. There were several canned pastas.

"We are on it," Matt said, picking out two cans.

The cottage was an older building but a fair size. There were three bedrooms and a loft. The main common area acted as the kitchen, dinning room and living area. It was cozy, but a very adequate place to evacuate to, especially with all the supplies Heather had left. Matt and Liam had spent a lot of time at the cottage as kids. He had regularly invited Liam up for the family weekends. They would spend hours in the forest, pretending to be chased, or chasing some invisible enemy. He did see the irony now.

Matt tossed a pot on the stove and dumped the pasta in and waited for it to heat up. He was exhausted; who knew sitting in a car doing nothing would take so much out of you? He sat down at the kitchen table and rested his head in his hands while he thought. They had a new advantage with the extra protection Heather had left them. He wondered how that could work. Liam took a seat across from him.

"Thinking about tomorrow?" Liam asked

"Yeah," Matt confessed. "We seem to be in a bit better situation, maybe we should rethink this?"

"What part?"

"Well, I don't think you need to be out there alone?" Matt said. "I can be backup in the woods or something, like an ambush."

"Or you now have a way to stay with Grace and protect yourselves if anything goes wrong," Liam argued. Matt started to protest but Liam interrupted. "OK I have an idea, you make sure Grace is in her hiding place. We will get her out nice and early. Then you can take the rifle and position yourself across the road, but make sure you have line of sight to Grace."

Matt considered this. He could position himself hidden in the forest, but close enough to Liam that if anything went wrong he would be there. Grace would be well hidden; no one would know where to find her. "Assuming he's on time, he's not coming to the house until ten," Matt contemplated. "So, if I hide Grace early, I'll have plenty of time to get to a good position. You just have to make sure you stay in front of the house where I can see you."

"What are we telling Grace to make sure she doesn't come out of her hiding place?" Liam questioned.

"Maybe the truth, or at least a modified version of the truth," Matt said. "Let me handle it." Matt got up to check on the dinner. Satisfied that the pasta was adequately warmed, he called for Grace to join them. Once she was seated and eating, Matt turned to Grace.

"Gracie, we have to tell you something, and it's pretty important." He paused to make sure she was paying attention.

"OK," she shrugged, shoving the pasta into her mouth.

"Tomorrow we are going to meet a man that might be able to help get Mom back."

Grace dropped her spoon into her bowl, "Really!" she said enthusiastically.

"Yes," Matt continued. "But I need you to do something for me. You know the treehouse we built?"

"Yeah of course."

"I need you to hide there tomorrow and stay there until I come back to get you."

"Why?" Grace asked suspiciously.

"Because," Matt considered the next words carefully. He didn't want to scare her, but he wanted to make sure that she wouldn't leave her place. "I'm almost certain that everything will be fine, but I want to make sure you are safe. Ever since this happened to Mom, I don't trust anyone."

Grace gave him a long stare, "How long do I have to stay in the treehouse?" She asked.

"Not long, maybe an hour," Matt promised. "You can take games or the iPad if you want."

"OK," she said with no further concern. "By the way," she said. "What happened to Liam cooking? No offense Matt, but this is gross." She gave them both a big grin.

"Wow Grace," Matt laughed. "We haven't been here an hour and you are already complaining. You know Dad can't stop me from tickling you."

Grace jumped up from her seat and squealed. "No don't!"

She ran from Matt, but the cottage wasn't big enough for her to get far. Matt got up and tackled her to the sofa, tickling her until she was out of breath. He stopped once she was gasping and then he just gave her a big hug.

"Do you really think Mom will be home soon?" she asked, hugging him back.

"Yeah, I think so," he said.

Amy

They had been driving for hours. Eventually small talk ended, and Amy tried hard to stay awake, but her eyes felt heavy and her head was still hurting from the accident. She hadn't noticed it before, but her chest and shoulder were aching now too. During the accident, the seatbelt had locked to hold her in place, but it had left a deep bruise across her shoulder. She fell asleep; she wasn't sure how long she had slept for, but when she woke, the sun was setting, and they had finally changed direction to head north. They were off the highway and were following a two-lane road, which was the main street for all the small towns they passed through.

"I'm sorry I fell asleep!" she said to Jay.

"No problem. I'm glad you got some rest," Jay replied. "You snore by the way."

"I do not!" Amy said, appalled.

"Of course not," Jay said sarcastically. "If you want to see how much you don't snore, just pull the video up on my phone."

"You didn't!"

Jay smiled. "No, I didn't film you sleeping. That would have been mean. But I have been thinking about that joke for two hours now."

"Why didn't you wake me? I'm sorry." Amy frowned. She felt guilty for falling asleep and leaving Jay to do all the driving.

"Don't worry about it. I'm just teasing you."

"Do you want me to drive for awhile?" Amy offered.

"Um no thanks. I have seen what happens when you drive," Jay replied quickly.

"That wasn't my fault!" she protested.

"That's true. It wasn't your fault," Jay agreed. "I was a couple of cars behind you when it happened. I saw that the truck ran the red light."

"OK, please make sure you tell my insurance that too." She gave him a smile. "Do you know how far we are?"

"Not sure. It's getting hard to tell now that's it's getting dark," Jay said, a bit frustrated. "I don't want to pass the turn and go too far. There's a gas station coming up. I'm going to see if we can ask for directions."

They pulled into the gas station. It was the only building to be seen. The gas station also acted as a small country store, selling some groceries, cigarettes, and bait. There was a sign on the window that said *DVD Rentals, $1.99.* Amy laughed, and Jay gave her a puzzled look.

"DVD Rentals? People still do that?" Amy questioned.

"Out here? That might be the only thing to do," Jay laughed.

They got out of the car and Amy followed Jay into the store. The man behind the counter had a rifle lying across the counter. He slowly moved one hand to it when Amy and Jay entered the store. Jay immediately stepped in front of Amy to protect her.

"We're all friends here," Jay said, pulling his police badge from his pocket and holding it up to show the store owner.

"You're a cop?" the man said suspiciously. He was older, probably in his late sixties, very skinny and his shoulders slumped low, which made him look older than he was.

"Yes, I'm a little outside of my jurisdiction, but yes I am a cop." Jay kept his hands in the air, so the man could see them and asked, "Are we cool here?"

"I'm just trying to protect the little I have left," the man said, still with one hand on his rifle. "Been robbed three times so far tonight. None of the computers are working. Power has been off and on. Can only take cash, but all them city people only had cards. They were desperate, and some took off without paying. One punched me."

"I have cash," Jay confirmed. He slowly reached for his wallet. "We need gas, some food, and some directions." Jay pulled some bills from his wallet and slowly approached the man and placed the money on the counter. The man nodded and placed his rifle under the counter.

"Amy, why don't you go pick out some food," Jay requested.

Amy started to walk through the store. There wasn't much left on the shelves to pick from. She doubted that Jay was a potato chips kind of guy; he looked much too fit to be eating junk food regularly, but those were the only options left. At the end she found some crackers, a couple of bags of chips, a can of tuna, dried fruit and sodas. She brought everything to the counter and Jay gave her a funny look.

"Not much left," she said quietly.

"Just been talking to Bill here," Jay said, referring to the store owner. "He says we are still about twenty kilometres away from the lake."

Just then the door to the store opened and two men entered. Bill reached for his rifle again and Amy noticed that Jay's hand moved slightly to where his gun was hidden under his shirt behind his back, but he didn't pull it out.

"It's cash only tonight," Bill called to them as they walked through the store. They ignored him and continued walking through the store, taking things off the shelf. Amy watched them. Both men were in their forties; they were stocky and dressed in hunting clothing. Amy noticed that Jay made a point of keeping himself between her and them. He started to gently push her towards the far end of the counter as they approached. He then tried to give Bill a warning look to let things be, but Bill was looking terrified. The rifle was now across the counter again.

Before Bill could react, one man walked up to the counter, grabbed the rifle with one hand and then pointed a gun at Bill's head. The other man pulled out his gun and pointed it at Jay.

"We'll take the cash," the man pointing the gun at Bill said.

"And maybe the pretty girl too," the other man said, grinning at Amy.

Before Amy knew what was happening, Jay swung at the man in front of him, hitting him right in the face, he dropped to the ground, but not before Jay grabbed his gun from his hands and quickly tossed it behind the counter. The man pointing the gun at Bill turned towards Jay, but Jay was ready; he knocked his arms up and grabbed at the gun just as a shot was fired. It hit the ceiling and startled everyone. Amy yelled and ducked, covering her head. Jay held onto the man's gun and they struggled together until Jay brought his knee up and hit the man in the stomach. This was enough to have him release the gun. Jay quickly turned the gun on the men, the second man stumbled back to his feet.

"Get the hell out of here!" Jay yelled, aiming the gun at them.

At first Amy thought they would try to challenge Jay again. They looked at him, then to Bill who had his rifle pointing at them now as well, then they slowly backed out of the store. Once they were out, Jay quickly headed to the door to watch them drive away. Once they were gone, he turned back to Amy and Bill. Amy was shaking, and Jay quickly went to her. He placed the gun on the counter and took her in his arms.

"You're OK," he confirmed. She couldn't speak, and she couldn't control her shaking. He continued to hold her close as he turned to Bill.

"You certainly have some balls boy," Bill said to Jay.

"I'm surprised you didn't take a shot at them with that rifle."

"It's not loaded," Bill said, embarrassed.

"The gun behind the counter likely is," Jay noted, referring to the gun he had just tossed there. Bill reached down to pick it up and looked at it longingly.

"Can I keep it?" he asked.

"Against my better judgement, I'm going to say yes," Jay replied. He pulled out his wallet and placed a bunch on cash on the counter.

"That's not necessary," Bill said, placing the items Amy had picked out into a paper bag.

"It's for your troubles," Jay said. He pulled out a few more bills and left them on the counter. "We'll need gas too."

Bill nodded as he passed the grocery bag to Jay. "Of course. Use pump one; I'll unlock it."

Jay picked up the second gun that was still on the counter, picked up the grocery bag and took Amy's hand. They headed to the car and Jay opened the door for Amy.

"You OK?" he asked gently.

She gave him a half smile. "Just don't think about it, right?"

He gave her hand another squeeze and then went to pump the gas. Jay watched the street carefully as he gassed up the car. Amy knew that he was watching to ensure that the men wouldn't be returning. She stared at Jay as he continued to observe the road. He had his back turned to her, but she saw him run his hand through his hair and leaned back against the car, exhausted.

The road was still lined with cars, but they were moving at a steady pace now. Looking south, there was an endless line of car lights down the two-lane highway. Everywhere else it was dark. Now that they were in the country, the lights of the surrounding towns were fewer and farther apart. When Jay finished pumping the gas, he didn't return to the car right away. Instead he stayed behind the car, leaning against the trunk. Amy got out of the car and walked over to him.

"Are *you* OK?" she asked carefully.

"Yeah," he sighed. "I'm just thinking that we just got a small glimpse into what society is headed to."

"What do you mean?" Amy asked, confused.

"If this turns into a full-out war, I would hope people would be helping each other, but there will always be people like that taking advantage and willing to hurt anyone who gets in their way." Jay was staring angrily at the cars passing on the road.

Amy slowly took his hands in hers, "I thought they had shot you," she whispered, tears running down her face. Her mind was working overtime re-running everything that had just happened. When the gun had gone off, she had been certain Jay had been hit. The sound had been so loud and terrifying.

"I know," he said as he pulled her close and held her. She forced herself to stop crying. She took comfort in his embrace and pulled strength from it. He was quickly becoming her safety net, his arms forming a protective shield that stopped the crazy reality of their situation from seeping through and completely engulfing her and pulling her into madness. She let him hold her for a moment longer and then gently pulled away.

"I'm OK," she smiled at him, hoping to convince him.

"If you say so," Jay said with a forced smile, not believing her. He led her back to the front of the car and opened the door for her again. She noticed that he had done this repeatedly since they had started their trip together. He had been brought up a gentleman at least.

He started them back along the road. Bill had told them it was about another twenty kilometres, but traffic was still slow. It took another hour before they found a sign that directed them to turn towards the lake. Jay followed the sign and suddenly found himself on a dirt road that twisted and turned. They followed it for a little while; several roads intersected with the road they were on. Then the road they were on came to a sudden dead end. Jay turned the car around and tried another road. They followed this for a little while but then hit another dead end.

"I'm going to get us very lost in here," Jay said after the third dead end. "In this dark I have no idea which direction we are heading anymore, and we haven't seen a lake yet. I'm not sure if we are getting closer or further away."

"What should we do?" Amy asked.

"I think maybe we should just hang tight until dawn when we can see again," Jay suggested. "The lake has to be near; once it's light we will be able to find it."

Jay turned the car around and followed one road they had just gone down. It was a dead-end road and he parked the car there. There were no cottages around them, from what they could see they were just parked in the middle of the forest.

"Follow me," he said, getting out of the car. He went around to the back of the car and folded down the back seats and then pushed everything up, clearing up a good part of the trunk. He handed Amy a sleeping bag and water bottle and continued to move things around. Amy opened the water and realized she hadn't eaten or drank anything for hours. Jay then grabbed the shopping bag from the store and climbed into the back of the car, motioning for Amy to do the same.

"Nothing like a middle of nowhere tail gating, with tuna, chips, crackers and dried fruit?" Jay laughed as he pulled the items out of the bag.

"I tried to get as many of the food groups as I could," she joked, taking a seat next to him and wrapping the sleeping bag around her. "It wasn't like there was a lot left. I doubt you could have done better."

Jay opened the bag of chips and offered it to her; she started to devour them.

"Oh my god, I'm so hungry," she said with a mouthful of chips.

Jay opened the tuna and used the crackers to spoon the tuna out of the can. He got a good heap onto one cracker and offered it to her. She took it and ate it eagerly as he helped himself to the next serving.

"Wow, that's really disgusting," he said, taking another bite. "But you're right, I'm starving. I can't believe that we are actually eating this crap."

Amy offered him the chips back. "Try these, they aren't as stale as the crackers, and only slightly less past expiration than the tuna."

"Excellent, nothing like a little food poisoning to get you up in the morning," Jay said, and Amy laughed.

"So," Amy said as she leaned back, stretching out. "You never did tell me about the house, the cars and this fabulous five-hundred-dollar dinner we are eating."

"You noticed that?" Jay said shyly, referring to the money he had left Bill. He had extremely over paid for the gas and snacks. Amy had noticed that Jay certainly wasn't short on cash.

"Don't avoid the question," she accused him.

"OK," Jay said, taking the last bite of his tuna cracker and chewing. "It's my family fortune," Jay started. "When I was younger, eight years old, my parents were killed. It was a car accident; they were coming home late one night from a date, and a drunk driver hit them. He had been speeding and drifted into their lane of traffic. He hit them head on. He never walked again, but they died on impact." He paused for a minute, struggling with the memory. "I moved in with my grandparents. My grandfather was an extremely successful businessman and made some smart investments. He built a fortune over his lifetime. He passed away a couple of years ago, and eventually my grandmother died too just last year. I was the only one left in the family to inherent everything." He waited to judge Amy's reaction. He seemed to be deciding if he should continue. "It's a lot of money," he said. "If managed properly, I don't need to work at all. I decided to become a cop to keep myself busy and humble and to direct my misplaced hope that I might actually be able to help people. But I certainly don't do it for the paycheques."

"Wow, that's so sad," Amy said.

Jay gave her a funny look. "You are the first one I have told my story to that thinks its sad."

"Really?" She questioned. "But you're all alone."

"Most people can't see past the money. Usually I'm considered *privileged*."

"Why would you pick such a dangerous career?" Amy questioned. "I mean, if you want to keep busy and help people, there must be plenty of alternatives."

"I do have a number of charities that my grandfather's estate supports, but I have people for that. I just sign the cheques. And truthfully, being a police officer wasn't that dangerous, at least not in our town, up until a few weeks ago. Besides, who knows what's going to happen next with this war; the money may mean nothing once all this is over."

"So, you're all alone? No brothers or sisters? Cousins?" Amy asked, and Jay shook his head no. "Not even a girlfriend?"

Jay shook his head no with a laugh.

"OK, sorry boyfriend?" Amy suggested.

"No, not either," Jay smiled. "I have had plenty of *girlfriends*. But nothing that's worked out for a long-term relationship."

Amy stared at Jay; she found it hard to imagine that someone like him would be so alone in life. Even without knowing about his wealth, Jay seemed to be a good guy. He was handsome, took care of himself, and had a job. Amy thought he would be a catch for any girl.

"You're wondering what's wrong with me," Jay confirmed her thoughts.

"I wasn't going to say it like that," Amy replied. "But you are getting very good at reading my mind."

"One of my few talents is that I can definitely read people. I may have some commitment issues though," he said, lying down. "I'm making my shrink very rich; I'm his dream case.

With everyone I have ever loved dying, I have a fear of getting too close to people now. I won't allow myself to fall in love. Ladies love trying to *save* me, so I have had plenty of...um," he paused and gave Amy a shy smile, "let's say dates." Amy rolled her eyes. She knew what he meant. "But none have been successful in making me want to commit to a long-term relationship. I'm working through it with my shrink at three hundred dollars an hour, so I may one day have a *healthy and productive relationship.*"

"And what about your instinct to put yourself in danger to protect others?" Amy proposed. "You should maybe add that to the list."

"Good one," Jay agreed. "I'll remember to add that to the agendas."

"Oh, and definitely don't forget about your need to compensate for the lack of relationships by buying expensive material items."

"Wow, you have me all figured out in a few hours. What the heck am I paying the shrink for?" Jay laughed.

Amy smiled and lay down next to him. The air was getting colder, and she pulled the sleeping bag up to her chin to stay warm. Her mind drifted and she thought about Matt and Liam. She was terrified for them and was worried that they wouldn't find them in time. She was also still in shock with what they had seen with the city. Even from the distance they had been at, the smoke rising from the city was an eerie sight. And then there was the encounter at the gas station store. Jay had taken out those two men in a matter of seconds, but their intentions were clear; they could have killed to get what they wanted. Finally, she thought of her grandmother, seeing her lying on the sofa lifeless. Without realizing it, she had started to cry, her breathing had quickened, and her heart raced.

Jay reached for her and pulled her close. "You're thinking about it again," he said.

"I can't help it," Amy cried.

"I know, I understand," he said. "Your mind is in shock, and until that shock wears off, every time these things sneak back into your thoughts you are going to have these emotions—basically panic attacks. But eventually things will calm down in your mind. It will be able to comprehend it, and you will be able to deal with it."

"How long will that take?" Amy asked quietly.

"It's different for everyone," Jay explained. "You are a strong person, so I think you will be able to manage this better than most people would."

Amy rested her head on his shoulder and let him hold her as they lay in the back of the SUV. Again, she found Jay being her protector, but that's all it was. She felt completely safe with Jay in a time when nothing made sense and she was terrified. Her heart still belonged to Matt, and as she fell asleep, it was her thoughts of him that allowed her to finally find some rest.

Chapter Twelve
Liam

Liam had barely slept. He had tossed and turned throughout the night, and eventually he had decided to just get out of bed. He made himself a coffee and then headed out to the front porch. He took a seat in one of the Muskoka chairs that was carefully positioned to provide a great view of the lake. It was about an hour before dawn, the birds were calling to each other intensely and the forest was filled with loud chirping. Liam considered what he was about to do. He had told Kevin to meet him at ten. A half hour earlier, Matt would be getting Grace into her hiding place. Liam had also told Kevin to meet down the road, not at the cottage like Matt was expecting. When Matt took Grace to her hiding place, Liam would have to run to get to the meeting spot in time and before Matt noticed that he wasn't around. He hoped that Matt wouldn't be too panicked in the confusion, but it would likely all be resolved before Matt realized plans had changed. If things went wrong, Liam would be on his own, but at least they would be far from Matt and Grace.

Matt had unpacked the gun last night when Grace had finally fallen asleep and had given it to Liam, and as Liam held the gun in his hand he felt nervous. The cold hard metal resting in his hand gave him a feeling of security, even though he knew it was a false sense of security. He had never fired a gun, and he had no idea if he could actually bring himself to point it at another human with the intention to kill him. He had wished his father dead so often, and he had even convinced himself he could kill him after what had happened last week. But now that he had a weapon that could accomplish that, he didn't think he had it in him to bring himself to kill someone. He wanted to believe that if Grace, Matt or Heather were threatened, then he could do whatever was needed to protect them, but he was terrified that would become a reality.

Out of habit, Liam pulled out his cell phone, but it was useless. The phone systems had shut down after the city had been bombed. Even before that, no calls or messages were getting through. They hadn't been able to reach Mark since that morning when Liam had talked to him briefly just after the west coast bombings, but the called had dropped a minute in.

The radio had cut out, they weren't able to pick up any radio stations from the city. They guessed that likely multiple cities were hit in central and eastern North America for the communication to have gone completely offline like that. Eventually some local stations from the small towns they were passing through started to broadcast again, but they had no communications with the cities and could only speculate about what had happened. Matt had kept the radio off except for when Grace slept, to ensure she didn't hear the news about the bombings.

The sky turned grey as the sun peeked over the horizon. It was rising from behind the forest, so the darkness lingered longer around the cottage. It was a cold morning, and frost had settled on the grass and plants. There was a silver shimmer on everything as the daylight hit it. Liam sat and watched as his surroundings lightened around him. As it got brighter, he also noticed the birds' songs became less and less. Once the sun was above the forest, the birds had stopped signing, except for a few calls back and forth. The forest became quiet, and the slightest noise echoed loudly. He would have to remember that, though it was hard to judge exactly where noises were coming from. A chipmunk making a late attempt to gather food for the winter was rustling in the bushes a few feet away, but the noise was loud enough that Liam had thought he was right under the porch he was sitting on.

Liam heard someone walking around in the cottage, and after a moment Matt came outside holding a cup of coffee. He took the seat next to Liam.

"Did you sleep?" Matt asked, hugging his coffee mug.

"Nope, you?" Liam admitted.

"Nope," Matt also confessed. "So…you still willing to do this?"

"Yes," Liam said, without hesitation. "We aren't changing anything now."

"OK," Matt said, looking out at the lake. "What if…."

"Stop," Liam interrupted. "We aren't changing anything at this point."

"But," Matt started again.

"Nothing," Liam insisted. "Look, we can't start second guessing ourselves. This will never be a perfect plan. We just have to trust our instincts and hope for the best."

Matt nodded and gave his coffee his attention again. The sun slowly reached over the trees and light up the lake; it would be another unseasonably warm day. A perfect autumn day to spend at the cottage, Liam though ironically.

"I should get Grace up," Matt said, draining his coffee and standing up. "Did you want any breakfast?"

"Naw, I'm good." He felt like he would vomit if he tried to eat. "I'm going to take a walk. I won't be long," Liam said as Matt headed back inside. Liam got up and started down the road. He had estimated it was about two kilometers back up to the gate. He jogged up the road and he figured if he was running it, he could be there in seven minutes. He walked up the road a little; he intended to intercept Kevin before the gate. Liam walked off the road though and looked inside the forest. He wanted to see what his options were if he needed to run. He did not want to lead Kevin back to Matt and Grace's direction, so he made himself familiar with the forest that continued along the road and away from the cottage. He and Matt used to play in this forest as kids. There was a time when they knew the area like the back of their hands, but it had been years since they had played like that. The forest terrain was rough, with many hills and valleys, large rock boulders and fallen trees, and it made for some good hiding places. If Liam was recalling correctly, there was a valley not far, that dropped steeply and had a small creek at the bottom, and then the forest went on for a few kilometers before there were any more cottages or roads.

He checked the time; it was already well past nine, so he headed back to the cottage. He found Grace and Matt finishing breakfast. He picked an apple off the table; he wasn't sure his stomach would handle anything else and headed to the bedroom he had *tried* to sleep in the night before. He sat on the bed for awhile, trying to recall the landscape he had just observed. After awhile, he pulled the gun case out from under his bed and opened it. He held the gun for a moment in his hands, then he slipped it into his jeans' waistline. He then picked up the envelope that contained the flash drive and printed report. He folded it in half and shoved it into his back pocket, then headed back to join Matt and Grace.

"We are just talking about Grace's hiding place," Matt explained as Liam joined them at the table. "Grace is going to take her iPad and headphones, so she can watch movies while she is hiding."

"Perfect," Liam agreed. He checked the time again. "You should get going soon," he said to them.

"Yeah Grace, go use the bathroom one last time," Matt instructed her.

A few minutes later, Matt and Grace were ready to leave. Grace had a bag with her iPad, some food and drinks and a few random toys. Matt was carrying the rifle, still in it's case.

"You ready?" Matt asked Liam.

"Yeah," Liam lied. His stomach was doing summersaults.

"See you soon then," Matt said as he led Grace out of the cottage.

Liam waited just long enough to see them disappear into the forest. Then he took off up the road at a full run.

Amy

Amy woke to find herself wrapped in two sleeping bags and the sun shining on the car, but Jay wasn't there. She quickly sat up and looked around. She couldn't see him, her heart raced as she climbed out the back of the car and she still couldn't see him.

"Jay?" she called quietly. She listened for a minute but heard nothing.

"Jay!" she yelled louder, but the only reply was a bird she had disturbed. She walked up the small dirt road they had parked on, but she saw no sign of him. Her head spun, and her heart felt like it was beating so hard it would burst from her chest.

"JAY!" she yelled as loud as she could. This time she heard noise behind her, and she turned to see Jay rushing back to her.

"What's wrong?" he asked with urgency.

"I couldn't find you!" she accused him but rushed to embrace him. "I thought you left me."

"I'm sorry, I was just trying to figure out where we are. I took a hike up the hill a bit," he said, holding her.

She let go after a moment. "I'm sorry," she said. "I totally over reacted. I don't know what's wrong with me."

"Nothings wrong with you," he smiled. "No need to apologize. Good news is I know where we are, come, I'll show you." Jay took her by the hand and led her up to the hill in the direction he had come from.

"Look," he said pointing once they had reached a clearing. "There is the lake."

"You sure it's the right one?" Amy asked.

"God, I hope so. Unfortunately, we are on the north side of the lake. But if what you said about the Bailey cottage is accurate, that would put their cottage across from us on the far end there, that could be their dock." Jay pointed again. Amy looked across the lake, it seemed so far away.

"How are we going to find our way there?" Amy asked. "It's already getting late in the morning?"

"I was thinking I could *borrow* a boat," Jay responded. "Right below us is a cottage. It doesn't look like anyone is home, there is a canoe tied to their dock. But there isn't a *we* in this Amy. I need you to stay here."

"No Jay! Please don't leave me!" Amy panicked again.

"Listen, I can't have you come with me," Jay explained. "You stay with the car. I promise I will come back for you once everyone else is safe. Listen, if I don't come back before dark, you leave first thing in the morning, take my car, and head to your aunt's. There is a pile of cash hidden under the back seat; use it to get yourself safe."

Amy started to protest again, but Jay cut her off. "There is no discussing this Amy. You need to stay here. Be strong, I know you can be. I need to go if I want to get across and have a hope of finding them before Kevin shows up."

Jay walked her back to the car and handed her the keys. She looked at them and held back her tears. She was terrified that he was leaving her alone in the middle of the forest but was even more terrified at the idea that Matt, Liam and Grace were in danger. She gave Jay one last hug. "You better be back soon," she said with a smile.

"I will, I promise. Thank you for understanding, I need to know that at least you are safe." He held her for a moment longer and then turned to go. She lost sight of him quickly as he headed into the forest. She got back into the car and started her long wait.

Matt

Matt led Grace through the forest to the treehouse he had built her a few years ago. It was their secret place; not even their parents had known about it. He had built it for her when she was five. At thirteen, Matt had thought having a little sister was lame, there was nothing she did that was even remotely interesting to him. She was a huge demand on their parents' time and he felt he wasn't getting his fair share of attention. One weekend at the cottage, a rare weekend when Liam couldn't join them, Heather had fallen ill with a violent stomach flu. They would have headed home, but Heather said she didn't want to suffer a two-hour drive when she couldn't even get out of the bathroom for more than five minutes. Mark had spent most of his time helping her, and he left Matt in charge of watching Grace. After movies, swimming, and fishing, Matt was out of ideas. He decided they would go exploring in the forest. That was when they found the tree. It was the perfect tree to build a treehouse in. It was a large older oak tree. The lower branches were almost as thick as a person. There was some leftover wood at the cottage from a renovation they had done earlier that year. Matt took the plywood and first constructed a floor. He and Grace played that whole weekend in the tree. Over time, they continued to build on their little treehouse. Matt built walls and eventually a roof. He suspected that Mark knew they were up to something, but the fact that they were spending time together stopped Mark from ever asking them about it.

As they arrived at the treehouse Friday morning, Matt was relieved to see it was still in good condition. Grace climbed up first and Matt put the rifle case at the base of the tree and followed her up. The treehouse was getting small for him now. He'd been about half his size when he'd built this for Grace. Now he struggled to fit through the door.

"OK," he said to Grace, setting her supply bag onto the floor. "You promise you will stay here?"

"Yeah sure," Grace replied.

"You need to promise that, no matter what, you will stay here until I come to get you, OK?" Matt confirmed.

"I said yeah," Grace said, confused.

"OK, I'm going back to check on Liam. It won't be long though." Matt turned to leave, and then came back and gave her a hug. She looked at him confused but gave him a hug back anyway. Then he climbed back down. Once he was back on the ground, he walked back quickly to the cottage. He checked his watch. It was almost ten; there was still time to get back to help Liam. As he approached the road, he found a spot that allowed him to have a line of sight to the treehouse and the cottage and the road. From his spot, he would be able to see any car approaching, but he also had a clear view of the front of the cottage where Liam intended to meet Kevin. He unpacked the rifle and got low to the ground. He knew that he had no idea how to fire the rifle, and he certainly wouldn't try unless he had to; he didn't want to risk hitting Liam. If needed, it would act as an object of intimidation.

Matt lay watching the road for some time. But Liam wasn't coming out of the cottage, and there was no sign of any cars coming down the road. Matt started to feel uneasy. Why had Liam not come out to wait yet? He waited a few more minutes and then decided he would check on Liam. He kept an eye on the road to make sure no one was coming and went around to the cottage's door.

"Liam?" he called into the cottage, but it was empty. Dread filled Matt; he had no idea what was happening. Where had Liam gone? Had Kevin shown up early? How could Matt have missed them? Matt rushed out of the cottage and saw someone walking up from the lake. He turned and pointed the rifle at the person.

"Don't move," Matt yelled, his finger on the trigger.

"Matt it's me!" a familiar voice called urgently. "It's me, Jay!"

Confused, Matt lowered his rifle. "Jay? What the hell?"

"Long story. Where's Liam?" Jay said, running up to the cottage

"I have no idea," Matt said.

Just then they heard the first gun shot.

Liam

Liam reached the top of the road in seven minutes, as he had predicted. He closed the gate and latched it. Then he slowly walked up the road, trying to catch his breath. The road he was now on was the only route from the main highway to the gate. Kevin would have to come down this way to get to the cottage. He kept walking, trying to get as much distance between himself and the cottage before Kevin arrived. Kevin was running late, but that worked to Liam's advantage; he kept walking up the road and away from the cottage, Matt and Grace. For the hundredth time, he checked for the gun he had tucked in the waistline of his jeans. Then his hand went to his pocket where the envelope was. He suddenly didn't feel comfortable holding onto this information. He pulled it out and looked around for a hiding place. He stepped off the road and lifted a large rock. He gently lay the envelope on the soft soil and returned the rock to it's place. He noted the area to remember exactly what tree his hiding place was under. Just as he marked the spot in his memory, he heard a car approaching. He kept walking up the road until he could see the car, which slowed when it saw him. He could see two people in it but could not see who they were. They stopped a fair distance away and Kevin got out from the driver's seat.

"Hi Liam," Kevin said as he approached.

"Is that Heather?" Liam demanded, motioning to the other person in the car.

"Where's the flash drive?" Kevin asked, ignoring Liam's question.

"Safe," Liam replied, he figured he could be vague too.

"Look kid, I'm not playing games anymore," Kevin said.

"Neither am I," Liam said, lifting his shirt and putting his hand on his gun.

"Shit kid, come on, are you trying to get yourself killed!" Kevin said, frustrated.

"Where's Heather?" Liam demanded again.

"She's dead," Kevin hissed at him. "And if you don't give me what I want, me and my friend in the car are going to do the same to you, and then the Bailey kids. This is your last chance. Where is the flash drive?"

"I hid it," Liam confessed quickly.

"What the hell is the hold up Kevin?" the second man said, getting out of the car.

"Kid says he hid it, Jack," Kevin yelled back.

Jack approached Kevin and Liam. In his hand he had a gun, which he casually held at his side. "Well then," Jack laughed. "I guess you have used up your usefulness." Jack pointed the gun at Kevin and pulled the trigger. Kevin dropped dead at Liam's feet, blood seeping from a hole in his forehead. Before Liam could realize what had happened, Jack swung the gun at Liam and hit him in the face with the butt. Liam fell with a cry, his hands going to his face. Blood was pouring from his broken nose. Jack grabbed Liam's gun from his waist and laughed, throwing it deep into the forest.

"OK kid, here's how it's going to work," Jack said, crouching down next to Liam. "Come on, focus on me—don't pass out." Jack held him by his shirt collar. Liam couldn't see anything in front of him. It was just black, and he was clinging to stay conscious. "Come on kid," Jack said again, this time slapping him across the face. The sting brought some of Liam's senses back. "OK listen carefully," Jack continued. "You can go get the flash drive for me, or I can kill you and your little friends back at the cottage. Either way I accomplish my goal."

Jack grabbed Liam by the hair and pulled him to his feet. Liam struggled to get away, but Jack shoved the gun against the side of his head. "Where is it!" he demanded.

"In the forest," Liam gasped quickly. He was sure Jack would pull the trigger right then. Instead, Jack shoved him forward.

"Where!" he said, still pointing the gun at him.

Liam walked across the road. "Just in the forest a little," he said, heading into the forest. He wiped his nose with his sleeve, the blood was running into his mouth. He had only a few seconds to decide his next move and make a plan to get out of this alive. Jack was right behind him, the gun shoved into his back. Liam started walking deeper into the forest and then came to a stop.

"I buried it under a rock," Liam explained.

"Then get it," Jack said impatiently.

Liam looked around subtly and found a fair-sized rock not far from them. He walked towards it and he noticed that he had led Jack to the top of the valley. Liam bent down slowly, with Jack still standing over him. He picked up the rock and swung it as hard as he could at Jack's head. The attack surprised Jack, and Liam was able to hit him on the side of his head. He then threw himself at Jack with enough force to knock them both off their feet. They fell backwards together and rolled down into the valley. Liam was struggling to grab the gun; it slipped from Jack's grip, but went flying from both their hands, as they continued to fall down the side of the valley. At one point, Liam felt his head smash something hard, probably a tree stump. Liam tried to throw a couple of punches at Jack, but they were falling down the side of the cliff too quickly, and Jack was holding him tightly. When they came to the bottom of the valley, Jack was quick to his feet and kicked Liam in the gut before he could get up. Liam rolled, winded, but got to his feet as well. Jack made a motion towards Liam but seemed to reconsider. He looked up the valley and Liam saw what he was looking at. The gun had fallen about thirty feet away, up the side of the cliff. Jack turned and ran for the gun. Liam only had a split second to decide. He ran too, but in the other direction. He ran as hard as he could and ducked into the cover of the trees just as he heard Jack yelling at him.

"*I'm going to kill you!*" Jack yelled, and then Liam heard a shot being fired.

The bullet hit a tree just past his shoulder, Liam quickly ducked and changed direction. He kept running, deeper into the forest. He wasn't sure if Jack was following him, but he needed to find a place to hide and think for a minute. He found a large bolder he quickly slid behind and stopped. He listened hard for any sign of Jack approaching, but he heard nothing. Liam tried to focus, a man had just been killed in front of him. And was it true? Was Heather really dead? Was all of this for nothing? Had they put themselves and Grace in danger for a stupid false hope? Liam was terrified. He had no idea how he would survive this. He needed to stop Jack before he found Matt and Grace, and the only thing he could think of was to fight back. Slowly he rose from his hiding spot and looked for Jack, but he couldn't see him anywhere. He started to quietly walk back in the direction he had just come, trying to stay hidden behind trees and shrubs. He kept a watch all around him, but somehow Jack had snuck up behind him. Liam turned just as Jack's fist hit him in the gut. He doubled over, gasping again.

"I have ten years in the military kid," Jack said. "Do you really think you can get away from me?" He grabbed Liam's arm and twisted it behind his back. Liam felt like his arm would snap. He couldn't struggle, or he would dislocate his shoulder. The pain was radiating through him. He cried out, but Jack just laughed at him and twisted his arm more.

"God kid, you pissed me off," he whispered into his ear. "I should just shoot you right now. But I'll make you one last deal. You tell me where the flash drive is, I'll still kill you, but I'll leave your friend and his little sister alone."

"Fuck you," Liam gasped through the pain.

Jack yelled in frustration. He threw Liam against a tree and turned him around. Then he punched him once in the gut and then in the face.

"Fine, have it your way, but I'm going to enjoy this," Jack said, hitting him again in the stomach. Liam held himself up against the tree. He was trying hard to stay on his feet. He noticed that Jack had put the gun in his belt. He was smirking as he hit Liam again. This time Liam lunged forward and threw a punch back at Jack. He connected with Jack's head, basically the same spot he had hit him with the rock. Jack cried out, but more in frustration than pain. Liam ran again, but Jack was on him immediately. He tackled Liam to the ground and pressed the gun into his forehead. Liam closed his eyes, time seemed to stop, an eternity could have passed, or maybe just a split second, then he heard the gunshot.

Matt

Matt looked at Jay. "We have to get to the road," he said and started to run.

"Matt stop," Jay yelled. He ran after him and grabbed him by the shoulder. "I'll take care of it. Where's Grace? You need to make sure she's safe."

"She's safe, she's hiding," Matt said heading back up the road.

"You have to go to her," Jay insisted.

"She's fine!" Matt yelled back. "I have to go find my dumbass friend. This wasn't the plan." Matt ran. This time Jay let him and just followed.

"What do you mean? He changed the plan?" Jay said as they ran.

"He left his spot," Matt explained. "We were supposed to meet at the cottage, but he must have changed the plan. That gunshot, that came from the road!"

They reached the gate. Matt unlatched it and continued up the road. Jay was close behind him, then they came to a sudden stop. Just up a head of them was a car, and a body lying on the road. They approached the body slowly and Matt recognized Kevin with relief.

"Did Liam do this?" Matt questioned.

"I doubt it," Jay responded. "If he did, then where is he?"

Just then they heard a second shot, this one coming from deep in the forest across the road from them.

"Over there," Matt said, running into the forest. Jay followed again. They reached the top of the valley and carefully slid down the deep slope. Jay stopped Matt at the bottom of the valley.

"Shh," he said. He stopped to listen for a moment. "This way!" Jay ran through the forest. Matt struggled to keep up. He wasn't sure what Jay thought he had heard, but Matt could see no other options. Suddenly Jay dropped and grabbed Matt, pulling him down next to him.

"What?" Matt whispered.

"There's a man up ahead; it's not Liam," Jay said quietly.

Jay slowly rose from their place and glanced across the forest, Matt risked doing the same. Then he saw what Jay had seen. Far ahead through the trees he could see a man walking in the forest. He was walking slowing and carefully, trying not to be heard. Then they saw Liam appear, and the man came up behind Liam. They watched as the man started to beat Liam.

"He's going to kill him," Matt said desperately.

"Yeah," Jay said, getting up and running towards them. Matt followed again, keeping his eyes on the scene they were approaching. The man was really kicking Liam's ass. Liam got one good punch in, but he was easily losing the fight.

"I don't have a shot," Jay said in frustration.

Suddenly the man had Liam pinned to the ground and pointed his gun at Liam's head. Matt froze. He was sure that Liam was done for. Then he heard a gun fire next to him. Jay had his gun in his hand, he had just fired a shot, but he kept running towards Liam. "Stay there," he yelled over his shoulder at Matt. Jay fired another shot. Matt noticed that he wasn't shooting at the man; he must have been worried about hitting Liam. The shots were hitting the trees just next to them. The man was startled by being shot at. He grabbed Liam and pulled him to his feet, holding Liam in front of him, pressing the gun to his head.

Matt continued moving forward, but he tried to stay hidden in the trees.

"Let the kid go," he heard Jay yell. Jay was pointing his gun at them, but the man had positioned Liam in front of him and Jay wouldn't risk hitting Liam with a shot.

"You think I'm stupid?" the man replied. "Why don't you put your gun down and I promise I won't kill the kid."

"Considering I know you've killed at least two people this week, Jack, I'm not about to believe you," Jay yelled back. Matt tried to understand what was happening. How did Jay know who that man was? And who were the people he had killed? Matt continued to get closer, being careful to stay behind the trees.

"You're that pain in the ass cop," Jack yelled back at Jay. "God, this must be my lucky day, I'm going to be able to get rid of all the thorns in my side." Jack laughed and wrapped an arm around Liam's neck. Liam choked as Jack squeezed harder.

"Let him go," Jay yelled again. "You and I can settle this."

Jack just continued to laugh.

"Come on you chicken shit, or do you only beat up on kids and women?" Jay taunted him. "Great soldier you must have been."

"Shut the hell up. You have no idea what it means to be a solider!" Jack yelled, still holding Liam tight.

"Then why don't you come and show me. I can't imagine that kid's much of a challenge for you. Or are you too washed up now Jack? Though I hear you couldn't handle the army either. Kicked out, weren't you? Dishonorable discharge?"

"I'm going to bury your punk ass next," Jack shouted getting frustrated with Jay.

Jay was gradually getting closer, with his gun pointed at them both, but there was no way he could shoot Jack, who was still using Liam as a shield, Jay wouldn't risk it. Jack kept his gun pointed at Liam's head as he continued to strangle him. Matt could see Jack getting annoyed with Jay, but Liam was also turning blue; he wasn't going to last much longer. Suddenly Liam slumped in Jack's arm. Jack couldn't support his weight and let Liam fall to the ground. Matt couldn't tell if Liam had passed out or if Jack had suffocated him to death.

"Oops," Jack laughed as Liam fell, but he quickly pointed the gun at Jay and fired. Jay was ready and dove to the ground and quickly rolled behind a tree. Matt ducked in his spot to avoid being seen.

"Well come on then," Jack yelled at Jay. "I have a couple of orphans to kill next."

Matt was trying to process what Jack was saying. Why would he call him and Grace orphans?

"Do they know their dad was crushed to death when the building collapsed? Made my job a lot easier," Jack laughed as he made his way towards Jay, making sure to keep his path obstructed by the forest.

Jay stood up, keeping his back pressed hard against the tree. Matt moved slowly towards them again. Jack fired again at Jay, hitting the tree he was behind, which made Jay duck again. Crouching, Jay looked out and fired two shots at Jack, but Jack had taken cover again, and only splintered wood scattered through the air.

"How's your kids these days?" Jay yelled suddenly. "They like living with their new daddy? And your wife, finally with a real man!"

The hit a nerve with Jack. Angrily, he stepped out from behind the trees.

"You're a dead man," he yelled and fired repeatedly at Jay, who had hit a nerve. Jay took cover again, but Matt heard him yell in pain; he had been hit. When Jack finally stopped shooting, running out of bullets, he ran at Jay. Jay was behind a tree holding his left arm. He had dropped his gun.

"Stings, don't it," Jack mocked Jay as he approached quickly. Once he got close enough, he took a swing at Jay, who stumbled but fought back. Blood was seeping through Jay's sweatshirt at his upper arm, and he was obviously in pain and could barely throw a punch. Jack came at him again and landed a hit to his gut. Then Jack threw all his weight at Jay and knocked him down. Matt saw Jack land a couple of punches on Jay.

"You piece of shit rookie, you think you can get *me?*" Jack said as he landed another punch.

Matt panicked. He started to move quickly towards the fight with the intention of saving Jay, but then Jay grabbed a large branch lying nearby and hit Jack in the side of the head. Jay quickly dove for the gun he had dropped and pointed it at Jack.

Jack sat up, the side of his head bleeding from a big gash. Once he saw the gun, he stayed sitting on the ground obediently, a smug smirk on his face.

"Come on Officer Harris, take the shot," Jack laughed. "Do you think this is going to end by killing me?"

"You're under arrest," Jay said, out of breath, staring Jack down. Matt was now at Jay's side. He slowly pointed his rifle at Jack and looked from Jay to Jack.

"Matt, go check on Liam," Jay said to him urgently.

"Aw so this is Matt Bailey," Jack said, suddenly noticing Matt.

"Shut up," Jay yelled at Jack. "Matt go see if Liam is OK," Jay said again.

"Where's my mom?" Matt asked softly to Jack, ignoring Jay.

"What, you haven't told him?" Jack asked Jay.

"Just shut up!" Jay said, kicking at Jack, who only laughed again in reply.

"Tell me what?" Matt demanded. He could hear his heart beating in his ears. He already knew what Jack was hinting at, but he wanted him to say it. He wanted that confirmation directly from his mother's killer.

"What do you want to know?" Jack mocked. "That we took her? That we beat her? That she begged to be able to come home to you and Grace? Is that what you want to hear?"

Matt felt an uncontrollable rage building inside him. He started to shake; he pictured his mom being tortured by this man.

"Matt, don't listen," Jay warned.

"I wish I could say she didn't suffer," Jack continued sarcastically. "Oh, but she did. It's amazing what a woman can endure when she's trying to protect her children. And you know, even beaten and bruised, she was still hot, in a motherly kind of way."

"Shut up," Jay punched Jack on the mouth. "Matt, get out of here. Let me deal with him," Jay said urgently, but Matt wouldn't leave. The rage was holding him in place, fixated on Jack.

Jack spit out a tooth. His mouth bloody, he continued, "I took a piece of that ass, a few times actually." Jack laughed again, then his tone got serious. "She begged me not to hurt you, and in her last breaths as I chocked the life out of her, she prayed for you and your sister."

Something snapped deep inside of Matt. He no longer could hear anything or see anything. It was like he was inside a tunnel and Jack was sitting at the end of it. The forest was gone, Jay was gone, nothing was around him, only Jack was straight ahead of him. He slowly pointed the rifle at Jack's head. He saw Jack give him one last smirk and then he pulled the trigger. The rifle recoiled, and Matt felt it slam into his shoulder as he stumbled backwards. His ears were ringing, blocking out all other sounds. He saw Jack's body slumped forward in front of him, then fall flat to the ground. He felt Jay grab him and pull the rifle from his hands. Jay was shaking him and yelling, but he couldn't make out what he was saying. He was staring at Jack, now lifeless and faceless, lying in a pool of blood a few feet away. He had killed the man who had murdered his mother.

"Jesus, Matt answer me!" Jay yelled again. The ringing had stopped, but his head felt like it was in a cloud. He didn't hear the question Jay had asked. Matt turned a blank stare at Jay, who shook his head in frustration. He didn't know what to say; he was slipping into a void like his mind was slowly getting buried in a mudslide. From the corner of his eye he saw movement and he remembered that Liam was lying not far away. He turned his gaze in Liam's direction and Jay noticed Liam as well. He roughly pulled Matt to where Liam was trying to get up.

Jay pushed Matt against a tree. "Don't move!" Jay ordered. Matt thought that was a funny thing to say to him. He had no where else to go. He had just killed his mother's murder, where else would he go? He watched as Jay helped Liam sit up. Matt wondered if he should be feeling relieved that his friend was OK. A moment ago, he had been concerned that Liam was dead. Now he felt nothing. How strange? He felt like he was forgetting something. There was something else he needed to do but he couldn't remember what. Liam couldn't talk; Jay was trying to tell him not to try. Liam made a funny barking sound like a seal. That made Matt laugh, and both Jay and Liam stared at him with great concern. Jay leaned in close and spoke with Liam for quite awhile, but Matt couldn't hear what they said, nor did he care. He noticed again that Jay's right arm was bleeding; his sweatshirt was now stained with blood. Jay pulled it off and ripped it apart and tied a long piece from it, tight around his wound. Then he tended to Liam again. Slowly Liam got up with Jay's help.

"Matt, we need to get back to the cottage," Jay said to him. "We need to find Grace."

Grace! That's what he had forgotten. Matt nodded his head. Yes, finding Grace was the right thing to do. They needed to get Gracie. They walked back up the valley and to the road. Liam was slow, needing support from Jay. It was frustrating Matt, but he said nothing. Jay was dragging too;

his rag bandage was already soaked through with blood. It felt like it took forever to get back to the cottage.

"There's a first aid kit in the storage," Liam chocked out in a whisper to Jay. Jay helped Liam into one of the Muskoka chairs and headed inside. Matt sat next to Liam and stared at him. Liam was covered in blood from his nosebleed. His throat was bruised and purple from being choked, and he had two black eyes. He looked even worse than when his father had beaten him. A few minutes later Jay came back out his arm bandaged. He had washed up too. He handed Liam a couple of bags of ice, which he placed on his face and ribs.

"Matt, we have to go find Grace," Jay said to him. Matt just nodded. Yes Grace; he already knew that's what he had to do, why was Jay talking to him like a child?

"Liam, buddy, can you get yourself cleaned up?" Jay asked. "You will scare the shit out of Grace looking like that."

Liam responded with a tired thumbs up, as he held the ice pack to his face.

Jay pulled Matt out of the chair, "Let's go find Grace," he said again.

"Yeah," Matt agreed and headed to the forest. Jay followed close behind. Matt was confused; he was still stuck in the void. He felt like the trees were moving around him and that he didn't need to walk at all. Everything was moving for him; he didn't have to put any effort in, his legs were moving, but he couldn't feel it. Jay stayed close to him and kept asking for directions. It was annoying him. He knew where Grace was; he didn't need Jay to help. He just kept walking and ignored Jay.

Finally, they came to the treehouse. Jay knocked on the door and called to Grace, saying he and Matt were there.

Grace poked her head through the window. When she saw him, she waved and climbed down.

"What are you doing here?" she said to Jay, then she gave Matt a big hug. He hugged her back, but he wasn't sure why they needed to hug.

"I came to help," Jay replied.

"You're hurt," Grace declared.

"Yes, I got hurt," Jay admitted. "Look Grace, Amy's here with me too. She was also hiding, but on the other side of the lake. I need to go get her. I'll bring her back to the cottage, would you like that?"

"Yes!" Grace said enthusiastically.

Matt hesitated for a minute. Had he heard Jay right? Amy had come with Jay?

"Amy's here?" Matt asked angrily.

"It's a long story Matt," Jay said. "Probably not one to discuss right now."

Matt glared at Jay, he was suspicious of him. Why would he be with Amy? He didn't like that idea. They walked back to the cottage and Grace retold the plot of the movie she had watched while she was waiting. She hadn't heard a thing while she was in her treehouse. When they returned to the cottage, they found Liam sitting on the porch again. He had done his best to clean up; he had showered and changed into a clean shirt. But there was no hiding his bruises.

Grace looked at Liam. "Why is he hurt too?" she demanded.

"Grace, listen to me," Jay said, leaning down to get eye level with her. "I will explain everything, but I need to go find Amy first. I promise I will be back soon. Can you take care of

Liam for me? He needs lots of cold water to drink and new icepacks. Can you get him that?"

"Yeah!" Grace said, heading inside.

"Don't say a word to her until I get back," Jay ordered Matt. Matt shrugged. He was getting angrier with Jay. Who put him in charge? And where had he left Amy? Matt should be the one going to get her. Why was Jay suddenly giving all the orders? He couldn't' even take the shot to kill Jack. He'd left Matt to do that.

"I need your car keys," Jay said to Matt.

"Inside on the table," Matt snarled back. Jay gave him a questioning look but went in to find the keys. Matt's thoughts weren't making sense to him. He didn't understand why he was angry with Jay. He didn't understand why his head felt like he was in a cloud and everything was moving like a slow-motion movie around him. He had killed his mother's murder. It had been the right thing to do, right?

Chapter Thirteen
Amy

Amy had waited in the car for hours. When the gunshots started, she locked herself in and hid on the floor of the front seat. She knew the shots were coming from the direction of the Bailey's cottage. She was terrified, but she would follow Jay's instructions. If he didn't come back, she would not leave until the morning. No one knew she was there. No one would be looking for her. She also knew that she could do nothing to help. The longer it took for Jay to return, the more she was certain that they were all was dead. She sat crying on the floor, holding her knees to her chest. Then she heard a car pull up behind her. She glanced into the rear-view mirror and saw Jay getting out of the vehicle. Amy opened the door and ran to him. She was about to give him a hug, but he held up his hand to stop her. He walked towards her but once he got to the car he sat down on the ground, leaning against it. He was covered in dirt, his hands were muddy, he had a black eye and his arm was wrapped in a bandage soaked with blood.

"Oh my god you're hurt!" Amy cried. "What happened? Is everyone else OK?"

"Everyone is safe," Jay said. "But I need your help. I got shot, and the bullet is still in my arm. I need you to take it out."

"What?" Amy said, shocked.

"I can't do it on my own, Amy. I need your help." Jay pointed to the back of his car. "Get the first aid kit."

Amy complied and quickly pulled the first aid kit from the car and returned to him.

"OK, find the tweezers and the disinfectant." He pulled the old bandage off. Amy opened the first aid kit and pulled out the items he had requested. She poured some of the disinfectant onto the wound and then gave him a doubtful look.

"Think of it as payback for the lousy job I did on your forehead," he joked, giving her a smile.

"This is going to hurt you, isn't it?" she asked.

"Yes, but a bullet in my arm hurts more." He gave her another weak smile. "Did you ever have that Operation game as a kid?"

"Yeah, but I was really bad at it," Amy admitted. She pushed his T-shirt sleeve out of the way and inspected the wound. The bullet seemed to be deep; she couldn't see it at all, so she would have to find it by feel. She took a deep breath in and slowly inserted the tweezers into the wound. Jay grunted through clenched teeth.

"I'm sorry, I'm sorry, I'm sorry!" Amy repeated over and over as she dug into his arm. She couldn't reach the bullet and had to press deeper with the tweezers. Jay slammed his other hand to the ground, biting his lip, desperately holding back from crying out. Blood was oozing from the wound as she dug deeper still into the flesh in his arm. Then she felt the tweezers hit something small and hard. Finally, she had the bullet and pulled it out quickly as Jay let out a curse. He leaned back against the car with his eyes closed, breathing hard as she pressed a clean gauze bandage against the wound, trying to stop the bleeding.

"I might throw up," she said as she poured more disinfectant on the wound.

"Me too," he replied quietly with another weak smile. He was breathing heavy, still holding his eyes closed.

Amy did her best to clean and dry the area. She used the medical tape to close the wound and then wrapped another bandage around it. For good measure, she wrapped a tensor bandage around it. Jay had kept his eyes closed the whole time and tried to slow his breathing.

"I'm done," Amy said hesitantly.

"Thank you," Jay said. He was pale and looked weak.

"Can you tell me what happened?" she inquired.

She sat next to him, leaning against the car as he told her the whole story. He told her how Liam had changed the plan. He told her about he and Matt following Jack and Liam into the forest and how Liam was beaten and almost strangled to death. He also told her about Matt confronting his mother's killer and how he had shot him while he was unarmed and in Jay's custody. Then Jay explained that as he was returning to her, he had stopped to bury the bodies. He had dragged Kevin into the valley and dug a shallow grave for both.

Amy's eyes filled with tears. "Oh my god Jay, this is too much. You're hurt, Liam's hurt, and Matt! Will he be alright? How do we help Matt?"

"I'm not sure," Jay said sadly. "He needs to pull himself back from this. We can just be there and support him."

"Have you ever killed someone?" Amy asked.

"No," Jay sighed. "I had the chance. Jack had run out of ammunition, I had gotten into his head and made him lose his focus. I had him; he was right there in front of me. But I couldn't do it. I was just going to arrest him. My instinct was to preserve life, not take it, even for someone as foul as Jack. I realized, a half second before Matt did it, what he was going to do."

"Who was that man?"

"He used to be in the military in the U.S., and then became a mercenary. Someone at the bank must have hired him to clean up this mess for them. Eventually I was able to identify him from the surveillance video from the train station the day they took Heather. He was a real psychopath; he had a few arrests on his record for assault, including some domestic violence allegations. Eventually his wife left him, taking the kids and got re-married. I was trying to track Jack down. I was getting close, but then I got pulled from the case and was told to focus on community evacuations. Jack knew I was getting close too; I think that may have pushed him to kill Heather."

She took his hand and squeezed it. "It's not your fault," she said.

"And I didn't protect Matt," Jay continued. "I should have ended Jack. I should have known Matt was going to take the shot. I should have been able to read him better." Jay paused for awhile and turned to Amy, looking deep into her eyes. "I hear that when you take a life, it takes something from you, regardless of the circumstances. Matt did it out of anger, not self defense. He won't be the same. It was Jack's last sick joke—he egged Matt on, on purpose. He wanted to see how far he could push Matt. I can't imagine where Matt's head is at right now, but I know it's not in a good place. Amy, the things he said to Matt, about what he did to Heather, I can't even repeat them."

Tears burned in Amy's eyes again.

"I'm going to need your help with them," he said. "Liam's had the crap beaten out of him, again, and choked to an inch of his life. Matt's going to be suffering from significant PTSD because he just killed his mother's murderer, and Grace has no idea yet that her mother's dead. God help me if she finds out what Matt did. And that's not considering any of the insanity that has happened in the rest of the world these last couple of days." He squeezed her hand. "Can you be strong again, just a little longer, for them?"

"Of course," she said. "But can we take just a minute before we go back to them? Can we just sit here for a moment and pretend that none of this just happened or is happening, just for a moment?" Tears were streaming down her cheeks.

Jay wrapped his uninjured arm around her shoulders and pulled her close. She rested her head on his chest. Even with him hurt and weak, as he held her, she felt safe and protected.

"Yes please," he said softly. He leaned back and closed his eyes again.

Amy let Jay rest until the sun started to set, then they drove back to the cottage together. When they entered the cottage, they found it dark and quiet. Grace was asleep on the sofa; she was resting in Liam's arms, and he was also asleep. Amy was shocked when she saw Liam. He had been beaten badly: he had two black eyes and dark bruising around his neck. What frightened Amy the most was when she saw Matt. He was sitting in a chair in the corner of the room, staring at Liam and Grace with a heartless gaze.

"Matt?" Amy knelt in front of him. He slowly turned to look at her. The expression on his face was suspicious.

"What are you doing here?" he asked. There was thick resentment in his voice.

"You were in danger," Amy replied. "I wanted to help, so I came with Jay."

Matt's gaze went from Amy to Jay and then back to Amy. He shook his head slowly.

"No," he said softly. "Turns out we didn't need any help. You see, I killed him. I killed my mother's murderer." A slight smirk crossed Matt's lips and his expression changed. For a slight moment, Amy was sure he seemed proud of himself. She was frozen with fear. The look in his eyes was ruthless and hateful and led to an emptiness that felt cold. Amy held her breath, it felt like something had changed in Matt—something depraved. Then the smirk vanished, and Matt leaned forward and hugged her. He held her and cried in her arms. She held him tight until he calmed down.

"It's over," she whispered. "Grace is safe—you're safe—that's all that matters."

"Yeah," he said as he pulled away from her, wiping his tears. He looked at her again, and this time she only saw the pain in his eyes. Amy felt guilty; she must have been mistaken. She told herself it had just been the shadows of the dark room playing tricks.

"My mom," Matt started, but he couldn't finish his sentence.

"I know," Amy replied.

"My dad's missing," he continued, holding back fresh tears. "It's just me and Grace now."

"Shh, you don't know for certain," Amy tried to assure him. "I'm here, I'll help you."

"I'm not going anywhere either," Liam said in a harsh whisper, approaching Amy and Matt. "Whatever is happening out there right now, your mom knew. She prepared this place. Thanks to her, we'll be fine here, and we are staying with you. We'll ride it out together."

"Promise?" Matt asked. "Promise you'll stay with me."

"Yes," Amy said softly, kissing him. "I promise you won't have to do this alone."

Coming Soon

Seized
By N. S. Scholl

Part Two of the Ardenti Terra Series

Read previews at
nsscholl.com

Made in the USA
Middletown, DE
31 December 2018